SOMERS V. SOMERS

Recent Titles by Julie Ellis from Severn House

THE HAMPTON SAGA

THE HAMPTON HERITAGE
THE HAMPTON WOMEN
THE HAMPTON PASSION

ANOTHER EDEN
BEST FRIENDS
DARK LEGACY
THE GENEVA RENDEZVOUS
THE HOUSE ON THE LAKE
A NEW DAY DAWNING
ONE DAY AT A TIME
ON THE OUTSIDE LOOKING IN
SECOND TIME AROUND
SILENT RAGE
SINGLE MOTHER
SMALL TOWN DREAMS
SOMERS V. SOMERS
A TURN IN THE ROAD
A TOWN NAMED PARADISE
VILLA FONTAINE
WHEN THE SUMMER PEOPLE HAVE GONE
WHEN TOMORROW COMES

SOMERS V. SOMERS

Julie Ellis

This first world edition published in Great Britain 2008 by
SEVERN HOUSE PUBLISHERS LTD of
9–15 High Street, Sutton, Surrey SM1 1DF.
This first world edition published in the USA 2008 by
SEVERN HOUSE PUBLISHERS INC of
595 Madison Avenue, New York, N.Y. 10022.

British Library Cataloguing in Publication Data

Ellis, Julie, 1933-
  Somers v Somers
  1. Legislators - United States - Fiction 2. Legislators'
  spouses - United States - Fiction 3. Divorce - Fiction
  4. Political fiction
  I. Title
  813.5'4[F]

ISBN-13: 978-0-7278-6592-2   (cased)

All Severn House titles are printed on acid-free paper.

Typeset by Palimpsest Book Production Ltd.,
Grangemouth, Stirlingshire, Scotland.
Printed and bound in Great Britain by
MPG Books Ltd., Bodmin, Cornwall.

One

In the Somers' attractive – and heavily mortgaged – colonial, thirty-four-year-old Diane Somers sprawled in slumber across her king-sized bed – shoulder-length dark hair forming a halo about her face. She winced as her alarm clock shrieked its initial warning. Mediterranean-blue eyes closed, she reached out to silence the monster, as she stifled a yawn.

Her first thought was to call Paul to report on last evening's fund-raising dinner. No, she rejected. He was probably still asleep in their Washington D.C. condo.

Images of last evening's fund-raising dinner ticker-taped across her mind, elicited a satisfied smile. The results had been great – especially after the fund-raiser dinner – when the six heavy hitters had joined her for drinks at Linwood's newest hot spot.

She reminded herself that Paul had gone through the recent Congressional Primary in a clear field. Everybody in the party had felt sure that – as an incumbent – he was their best candidate. No potential candidate cared to run against him.

Still, she forced herself to acknowledge, their campaign funds were painfully low compared to the Republican bankroll. They'd have to be creative to hold on to Paul's seat in the House. His win in a Republican state had put the opposition on guard. They were out to take back that seat.

Still, it was only late July, 2006, she comforted herself. They could catch up between now and November, with luck on their side. And much hard campaigning.

She reached to switch off the snooze button, groped for a second pillow to prop herself into a semi-sitting position. In her usual waking-up routine, she focused now on her schedule for the day. As usual, forty-eight-hour efforts to squeeze into a fifteen-hour work day. Paul's major contribution was to put in an appearance in the House of Representatives.

Everybody knew the Republicans were desperate to defeat Paul in the coming election. They were pissed that their red state had sent a Democrat to Congress – and might do it again. When Paul was elected he broke decades of precedent.

Her eyes settled on the wall calendar above her chest of drawers. She froze in shock. Today was their tenth wedding anniversary! She hadn't bought Paul a present. How could she handle it at this late date? Perhaps she could ask Jill to shop something on her lunch hour. No deal, she rejected. Like Joan and herself, Jill would be eating lunch at her desk.

But Paul had probably forgotten, too. They were political animals – no time for anything else. In bed they talked about constituents to be wooed, polls, fund-raising. How to cover Paul's latest slip-up. Involuntarily she remembered earlier years – when passion had overruled politics – dismissed this with a frown. After ten years it was normal for the early zing to evaporate from a marriage.

She grunted in protest when the phone on the night table broke into the early morning quiet, then was suddenly alarmed. *Paul? What gaffe has he pulled off now?*

'All right, all right—' She reached for the phone. 'Hello—'

'Hey, we did great last night!' Joan Rubin – who'd become part of the law firm of Somers, Somers & Rubin right out of law school – was one-half of the hard-hitting team that managed Paul's political career. She and Diane shared the title of co-campaign manager. 'What happened when you headed off with the Big Six? I was sure it wasn't for a sex-au-sept romp.'

'We hit pay dirt.' Diane felt a surge of satisfaction. 'I'll give you the full breakdown in about –' she glanced at the clock on her night table – 'in about forty minutes.' They were careful what they discussed over the phone – wary of wire-taps. Stories of Watergate etched on their minds all these years later. 'Let me shower, dress, and get down to headquarters. Remember, I have a plane to catch at two twenty.' Paul needed her in Washington. Congress was still in session.

'I'll have coffee and a bagel waiting,' Joan promised.

Diane cut her shower short this morning – though this was where she did much constructive thinking – rushed to dress. It would be another of those 'somewhere in the 90s' days, she reminded herself – and nowhere was it hotter in late July than in Washington D.C.

She reached into her segment of the oversized closet, pulled down her Oscar de la Renta pantsuit – her sole designer outfit, which she'd worn to last night's fund-raiser. Elaine's voice – her close friend since preschool – filtered across her mind.

'When are you going to pay some attention to your wardrobe? You can't buy everything mail order!'

But she had no time for extensive shopping – and the clothes budget was limited. It was easy to pick up the phone and order a generic wardrobe. Classic stuff, she told herself defensively.

Grimacing in rejection, she hung the pantsuit – which she adored – back in the closet. In truth, the sizzling temperature called for something cooler. Besides, she reminded herself, today she must wear an uncluttered 'flight outfit'.

Wear drawstring slacks – metal-free – and a T-shirt and 'airport friendly' loafers that she could step out of with no sweat – and guaranteed by the manufacturer to have been made without steel shanks. No metal jewelry. No under-wire bra. Nothing that would set off that ugly alarm.

In minutes she was dressed for her flight. Beige drawstring slacks, matching T-shirt and loafers. No jewelry except her wedding band. Even Elaine – who made a fashion statement to shop at the supermarket – admitted this airport dressing-down was essential. Practiced by almost all frequent fliers.

She left the usual envelope with cash for Carmen, their cleaning woman. Flinching as she considered their weekly household expenses, both in Linwood and Washington. The first of the month was fast approaching. With hefty mortgage payments due on the house and on the condo. She worried that they'd refinanced their mortgage on the house to have money for a down payment on the condo in Georgetown – an area favored by Congressional members and their aides.

Paul was convinced they must have a condo in a luxury building, with ten-foot ceilings, terrace, an outdoor pool, tennis court, and fitness center – at a 'good' address. They'd been approved by the condo board of directors only because Paul's father had pulled strings.

Paul's pronouncement about their need for smart living accommodation ticker-taped across her mind: *'So we're from one of the smallest states in the country – and I'm one of the youngest Representatives in the House. I'm Congressman Paul Somers. I have to look the part.'*

She'd refrained from mentioning that far more prestigious male members of Congress shared modest apartments in unfashionable sectors while their wives remained back home in comfortable houses. But this wife was important to his career. True, they'd been about to be kicked out of their Dupont Circle sublet, leased on a month-to-month basis. They had to find a place to live – and fast. She couldn't visualize them shacking up in a city shelter.

She remembered what a real-estate broker had said – mistaking their political affiliation: *'Democrats rent – Republicans buy.'* But they were buying. The broker – a 'woman of a certain age' – must have remembered Paul's father, a Republican Congressman in his time.

She packed her oversized valise-on-wheels in haste. This commuting between Linwood and D.C. was a bitch, she admitted. It wasn't like social life commuting between a Park Avenue condo and a house in the Hamptons. It was like holding down two full-time jobs – which a lot of people were doing in the present economy. She had to make Paul understand that he must show his face regularly in his home district. People expected it. Too often she had to fill in, explain his absence. *'Paul's working so hard in Congress to get this new legislation through.'* Let them not realize his soaring absentee record.

When she complained on occasion at Paul's defections, Joan reminded her – in caustic tones – that he expected her to cover for him. She wasn't just Congressman Paul Somers' co-campaign manager. She was his voice. The brain behind the B-movie leading-man face.

She would be gone by the time Carmen arrived – but Carmen had a key. If she misplaced her key, Carmen knew to go to Elaine's townhouse to borrow the one Elaine held for such emergencies. OK, she summed up briskly. Everything was under control here. The car service would be out front in five minutes. She'd be off to the races.

Her driver this morning was one she knew from past trips. He greeted her with a warm smile. 'It's gonna be a hot one again,' he warned her.

'It'll be worse in Washington,' she surmised. 'How did we ever exist without air-conditioning?'

'Some of us still do,' he reminded her with dark humor. 'Thank God, my wife's been working since the kids are in school. Without her paychecks, we'd have no air-conditioning. No second car.'

'I remember reading somewhere—' Diane searched her mind for a moment. 'Somewhere,' she reiterated, 'that Eleanor Roosevelt said fifty plus years ago that American families needed two pay envelopes to survive.'

'Amen. How's the Congressman doing out there in Washington?'

'He's putting up the good fight.' *As long as I keep him in line.* 'He'll be back home in a week or two.' Maybe. Congress would go out of session early next month, but he was making noises about staying on in Washington. Why? 'It'll be prime time for campaigning.' But pushing Paul on the campaign trail was a major effort. He yearned to be re-elected on the basis of TV commercials.

'Wow!' The driver shook his head. 'It seems he just got elected.'

'These days members of Congress – all elected officials – start campaigning a month after being sworn in.' Diane managed a chuckle. Paul had just squeaked through. They'd known they had to start gearing up early for the next election. 'It's part of the times.'

Traffic was growing heavy. The driver focused on getting through the morning maze. Diane considered the date again. What was the tenth-wedding-anniversary deal? But she'd have no time to shop.

Their marriage had given way, she told herself with ruthless candor, to Paul's political career. *Their* career. All their efforts were in that direction. Instead of foreplay she and Paul discussed the points he was to emphasize in his next speech. It wasn't that he was in need of Viagra. It was just that sex had been replaced by politics.

They'd go out somewhere special for dinner tonight, she plotted. All at once wallowing in sentimentality. Remembering the early years. No talk of politics, she vowed. Ten years was kind of a landmark. Special.

She'd phone and make reservations at the Melrose. It was

one of the top restaurants in the area – and Paul loved dining
in fancy places. Prices were steep – but this was a special
occasion. And the Melrose provided a romantic atmosphere.

She was wistful that the first year's passion had disappeared
– but after ten years that was natural, she told herself again.
Not according to Elaine, she conceded. Elaine had been
married and divorced twice – very profitably. She was in
training for the third. Passion, she declared, did not die on
the vine under the right circumstances.

'*Di, look at my mother and dad. They've been married
thirty-eight years – and they've still got the hots for each
other. Maybe slightly muted – but they light up the sky at
regular intervals.*'

She and Paul were married their last year in law school.
When his apartment-mate – male – threw him out for a feminine replacement, he'd sought refuge in her studio apartment.
He'd casually suggested he sleep on her sofa. She slept on
her sofa. It was a convertible.

She'd sent him to the YMCA. He was an unhappy camper.
Three weeks later he proposed. They eloped when both sets
of parents uttered reproachful rejections. Why couldn't they
wait until they were out of law school? Because, Diane was
realistic, Paul needed a place to live immediately – and she
had no desire to announce to the world that they were sleeping
together without benefit of a marriage license.

Paul had been so handsome – still was damn good-looking
at thirty-five. He worked out at the gym on a regular basis.
Terrified of losing his hair – because his grandfather on his
mother's side had been bald, he was prey to every television
commercial that promised to save every hair on his head.

She'd been amazed – and wildly flattered – that he'd been
in obvious pursuit of her from their first encounter in a
classroom. He could have married any of a dozen more
attractive, glamorous women. She'd suspected his mother
had someone special in mind. Conservative Republican and
heir to a fortune, she gathered from casual remarks from
Paul on the subject.

Paul's family had been horrified when she'd switched his
thinking into more liberal areas. '*A Somers a Democrat?*' his
mother had screeched. '*When your father served four terms
as a Republican Congressman?*' A conservative Republican.

Of course, her own parents had been horrified when at eighteen she had become a registered Democrat.

In their first year at law school she and Paul had fallen into the habit of studying together. Sure, he wasn't the best of students – he just managed to get through law school, with much tutoring from her. But even then he was working on what he called his 'man of the people aura.' Convinced he had a great future in politics. And she switched his thinking to her own.

'My old man served six terms in Congress. Why can't I do as well?' became his mantra.

His father hadn't served six terms, Diane recalled – but then Paul was given to hyperbole. In college he was already on the campaign trail, won the presidency of their third-year law-school class – with Joan and her as his campaign managers. It surprised her that not just women liked him – men, too. He was movie-star handsome without being charismatic. Men didn't feel threatened, she interpreted. At thirty-five he was losing some of those movie-star good looks. He was concentrating on being 'just a regular guy – concerned about his fellow men.' And women, Diane reminded him at intervals.

'Look around,' Paul had said just a few weeks ago in a rare astute moment. 'The "man of the people aura" worked for Ron – it worked for George II.' *For a while.* Any talk about Ron on TV made her rush to mute the remote. Ditto for George II.

Paul had sounded terse, uptight when they'd talked last night – before the fund-raiser. He was playing the social scene in Washington, complained about Congress still being in session.

'We ought to be out at the Hamptons and relaxing. We've had a dozen invitations.'

She'd heard nothing about invitations. His parents had an oceanfront showplace in Southampton, but they'd never been invited. They'd be a bad mix with his parents' conservative Republican friends. And when he was pissed at being in Washington in this heat, why was Paul so dead set on staying on next month, too? The town would be deserted.

Everybody knew the summer was campaign time. Paul should have been at that fund-raiser last night. He could have flown in for the evening, taken an early flight back this morning. He should be back home campaigning next month.

Twice she'd announced his presence at a town meeting – both times she'd had to fill in for him.

Was Paul allowing this Congressman bit to go to his head? Too confident about winning re-election? He'd won his current seat by a handful of votes. A recount, no less. Was he forgetting that? He loved the role – but not the obligations that came with it.

Re-election would not be a snap, she warned herself yet again. They had a tough battle ahead. Didn't Paul realize that? So everybody said an incumbent was a shoo-in. Not so.

Two

Diane arrived in the early morning silence of campaign headquarters before anyone was on duty except for Joan. Their paid staff – headed by Jill – was small but enthusiastic. The volunteers were marvelous, she thought with gratitude.

Their volunteers were mostly young, but some were senior citizens. All disturbed by the route the present administration seemed determined to follow. And there were a few anxious wives and mothers of men serving in Iraq. National Guardsmen and Reserves who'd never anticipated being shipped off to fight a war halfway around the world.

Joan was on the phone. From her expression as she listened, Diane gathered she was talking with her mother.

'Mom, no—' Joan was grim. 'I don't want to go with you and Dad to the Goldsteins' anniversary party. I don't care that their single son – the one who writes grants in the Mayor's office – will be there.' She pantomimed her frustration as Diane approached with a sympathetic grin, covered the receiver with one hand as she listened.

'She can't adjust to an unmarried daughter who's thirty-four years old,' Diane murmured. 'Tell her to read the society pages of the Sunday *New York Times* – see all the women who don't marry until they're in their middle or late thirties – or older. It's fashionable now.'

Joan sighed. 'It's not that I'm turning down Mr. Right. He just hasn't surfaced.' She returned to the phone. 'Mom, I have to go – my other phone is ringing off the hook—'

'I know—' Diane's smile was sympathetic. 'She called early "before the office gets busy."'

'She's at her usual bit. The synagogue just started a singles group. She can't figure out why I'm not running to join. But what happened last night? Come on, dish out the dirt. I'll bring you coffee and a bagel.' Their usual routine during those frequent periods when Diane was in town.

'Coffee and bagel first, then I dish.'

The two women sat down in the cubicle that was Joan's office. With the tantalizing aroma of freshly brewed coffee as background and onion bagel in hand, Diane reported in detail on the late-evening meeting with the six most powerful Democrats in their district.

'They're behind us all the way,' Diane summed up. Refraining from mentioning that they had been candid in their belief that she was the brains behind the handsome young Congressman.

As always, the party leaders found it fascinating that Diane and Paul both came from solid Republican families. Diane's parents had lived in upper-middle-class comfort until their untimely deaths in a highway accident several years ago. Paul's parents were super-rich and powerful. His father – like several other retired Congressmen – had become a top Washington lobbyist.

'OK. We've got figures to go over before you cut out again.' Joan allowed herself a heavy sigh. 'Let's be realistic. We're not getting the major corporation contributions the way we'd like.'

'Wait a minute,' Diane scolded. 'What about that juicy check from—'

'Some substantial contributions, yes,' Joan broke in. 'The ones who're covering their asses – sending checks to both Democrats and Republicans. As the *Wall Street Journal* reports from time to time. But the Democratic contributions are on the short side,' she summed up.

'So we have to fight harder.' Diane refused to be pessimistic. 'Last night was a dream. Not all high-income people are concerned only about how to make themselves even richer. Some have hearts.'

'The theme song of most is still, "When do we have lower taxes?"' Joan muttered in distaste. 'The country runs up this incredible deficit – but the poor little rich families need to have their taxes cut. And they write these huge checks for the Republican Party.'

'We're bringing in the small contributors in droves.' Diane was defensive. The Internet, bless it, was a huge help in reaching people – both a labor-saving and postage-saving effort. 'They're disenchanted, scared for tomorrow.' But Diane interpreted the glint in Joan's eyes, geared herself to face what was coming. Joan was working her way up to discuss Paul's reception of late among their constituents. Not what they'd like.

'Every time Paul opens his mouth, the foot goes in.' Joan was blunt. 'You can't always be there to cover for him. We both know he's no great thinker. But this latest craziness – about hiring new speechwriters who are "more sophisticated?" Yucky. The way you work on the speeches that Curt and Adam bring in is great. People lap them up. What's with him?'

'I'll talk to Paul about that,' Diane hedged. She'd tried three times – was rebuffed each time. Something was happening to him. She was conscious of a new cockiness, an unfamiliar arrogance. 'He's uneasy about stepping on toes,' she said weakly. *That's a stupid excuse.*

'He was elected by a painfully slim margin,' Joan pointed out. Her eyes eloquent. 'The other Congressman from this state did far better—'

'A Republican.' Diane nodded. They were a small state population-wise, with a history of voting Republican. But 2004 had been a rough year in their district. They'd seized on the discontent, pushed Paul through to victory. Re-election could be harder. *No, don't think like that.* 'Remember,' she said, reaching for optimism, 'in the last Congressional election ninety-nine per cent of incumbents were re-elected.'

'OK.' Joan reached for her clipboard. 'Let's get down to work.'

Diane glanced up from the clutter on her desk to check the wall clock – hoping her watch was fast. It wasn't. She'd have to cut out soon. These days she spent as much time getting on the plane as in actual flight time to Washington. She reached for a phone, called the car service, ordered a car to pick her up in twenty minutes.

Joan appeared in the doorway of her cubicle. 'Di, there's this guy from the *Linwood Enquirer*,' she said with simmering impatience. 'He insists he has to talk to you. He won't talk to me. He's just back from Washington, says he needs to confirm an urgent rumor.'

Diane was instantly alert. It was important to keep a good relationship going with the local press. And the *Enquirer* was on their side. 'What kind of rumor?'

'He won't tell me.' Joan was exasperated. 'Shall I dump him?'

'Mrs. Somers,' a male voice intruded, 'I don't want to run this story without confirmation from you—' A tall, lean, good-looking man somewhere in his thirties – wearing jeans, a sports shirt, and a baseball cap – pushed his way into the cubicle. 'It's a bombshell.' His eyes were eloquent

'You've got five minutes.' Diane was terse, indicated to Joan that she'd handle this. What insane rumor must she squelch now? She had a vague recall of seeing him at a recent press conference. Sandy-haired, intense brown eyes. He'd asked intelligent questions. 'All right, what do you want me to confirm?'

'I'm Larry Grant, a freelance journalist. At the moment I have the *Linwood Enquirer* standing by for a front-page story. I'm just back from chasing around Washington hallways. The rumor hasn't made the full circle yet, but Congressman Somers was seen at a late-night dinner in a restaurant about thirty miles beyond Georgetown – with five high-level Republicans. Is it true that Congressman Somers is about to change parties? Is he prepared to deny this?'

Diane gaped in shock. 'Of course he'll deny it! Someone's making a ghastly mistake! I spoke to my husband last evening – he spent the entire evening at our apartment in Georgetown. Not at dinner with five high-level Republicans!'

'That's all I want to know,' Grant said quietly. 'I never run a story that I can't confirm.' *Did he get burnt on another 'bombshell?' There've been a flock of bad incidents of late. Two reporters at the* New York Times. *The Dan Rather flap.*

'Di—' Joan broke in. She had been eavesdropping. 'Your car will be here in a couple of minutes – and we have to go over your schedule before you take off.'

'Thanks for your time.' Grant was casual. 'The story's dead.'

'God, the creepy stories they dream up,' Joan hissed as Grant strode out of hearing. 'But he's cute.'

'All right, what have you got scheduled for me?' Diane reached for her purse, pulled out her small loose-leaf note-book.

Diane approved several speaking dates Joan had set up for her, OK'd two for Paul. Remembered his belligerent attitude about speaking to small groups. He didn't get the message that small groups provided votes, too. And small numbers added up to large ones. The phone rang twice, stopped. The signal her car was at the door.

Sitting in the car heading for the airport, she reviewed the brief encounter with Larry Grant. Outraged at such a rumor. Oddly, though, she'd believed him when he said the story was dead. That he wouldn't run it without her confirmation. He was probably an ambitious reporter reaching for the Big Break – but with a conscience.

But did some other journalist mistake somebody for Paul? That could have happened. Will some other newspaper run the story on their front page tomorrow morning? Some newspaper editor with more brass than brains.

Three

Larry Grant walked out into the hot noonday sun and to his car. His sister's car – on indefinite loan to him. He knew she harbored hopes that he'd settle here in Linwood, felt guilty about that. Not likely he could fit into a small town like this. He remembered her firm order when she'd visited him several weeks ago at the Bethesda hospital:

'When you're released, you'll come and stay with Jimmy and me for a while – until you get your act together. We'll set up a studio apartment in the lower level of the house – you'll be comfortable there. Give the kids a chance to get to know their uncle. You've always been popping in and out of their lives.'

Those weeks in the hospital had been rough – but the doctors had saved his leg. Already he could walk without a noticeable limp. But when he'd been discharged three weeks ago, he'd felt without direction. It seemed the right thing to do – to come here and stay for a while with Andrea and Jimmy and the kids. Until he got his act together.

Bill Taylor at the *Enquirer* threw him a couple of freelance assignments – probably because of his service in Iraq. Because he hated idleness he'd gone to that press conference Diane Somers held last week. She was one bright lady, he thought with a flicker of approval.

She wasn't lying to him – about her husband not planning to jump the fence, he judged. Yet the possibility nagged at him. Could it be that she didn't know? Was Paul Somers that kind of a hound? Bill disliked him – that came across loud and clear.

OK, go to Bill. Tell him Diane Somers denied what could be a blockbuster story. A major scoop for a small-town newspaper. Face it, he acknowledged – the *Enquirer* wasn't the typical small-town newspaper. It dug deep into national and international news. But it wouldn't run the story without substantial confirmation.

He wasn't ready to back down just yet, he admitted to himself. Sure, the lighting was soft in that expense-account restaurant – but the guy sitting there with those Republican big shots was either Paul Somers or a clone of him. *How do I nail down this story?*

He was there with Andrea and Jimmy and the kids to celebrate the couple's fifteenth wedding anniversary. Pricey for them, Andrea had objected – but he'd insisted. His eyes tender as he recalled Claire and Joey's excitement at going to a fancy restaurant – in the evening. Until now their special treat had been breakfast at a nearby IHOP. Sweet kids.

He swung into the parking area behind the *Enquirer*'s modest two-story building, left the car and headed for Bill Taylor's office.

'Hi—' Bill's longtime secretary, Carol, greeted him with a warm smile. She was privy to everything – she knew he was after a story from Diane Somers. 'Any luck?'

'Not so far,' he conceded, 'but I'm not giving up yet.'

'Go on in—' She gestured towards the open door to Bill's office. 'He's just cussed out everybody in the composing room – he's in a gentle mood.'

Bill Taylor greeted him with a hopeful gaze. 'She confirmed the story?'

'Outraged,' Larry reported. 'If anything's happening, Diane Somers doesn't know about it.'

'We can't run the story without confirmation.' Bill was grim. 'You consider it dead?' His eyes quizzical.

'No. Give me another three days. OK?'

'Done.' Bill grunted in distaste. 'If it's true, I don't get it – Somers sneaked into the House in the last election. Sure, I want to see a Democrat representing our district – but there's something so phony about that bastard.'

'You see it, and I see it – but some hopeful Democrats fall for that air of "Hey, guys, I'm on your side." I heard his wife at a press conference last week. I believe her. She's got that late-sixties passion about her.'

Bill snickered. 'What do you know about the late-sixties passion?' he challenged. 'You weren't even born then.'

'My dad fought in Vietnam – thinking he was going there

to save the world. He came home and fought against the war – like John Kerry. My sister and I grew up hearing about those years.'

'I was too young for the Vietnam scene,' Bill admitted. 'My big problem was convincing my parents to let me go to sleep-away camp with my best buddy.'

Larry's face tightened in recall. 'My mother and dad taught school for thirty years. When they retired, they became involved in fighting AIDS in Africa. They were killed when their truck was ambushed by some radical group. I guess some of that rubbed off on me.'

'So where do you go now with this would-be blockbuster?' Bill demanded. 'It's a whale of a story – if it's true.' A hungry glint in his eyes.

'I could fly back to Washington—' Larry considered. *But that's running up an expense account – Bill won't buy that.*

'Everybody's leaving Washington until after Labor Day,' Bill pointed out. 'A waste of time. You could be just running in circles on this. Maybe it wasn't Paul Somers you saw with those Republican big wheels.'

'You've given me another three days to try to run this down.' *Damn, I can't believe that wasn't Paul Somers.* 'Let's see what I can come up with—'

'Any time you bring the story in – with confirmation that's acceptable,' Bill emphasized, 'we'll run it. With your byline.'

'My gut tells me I'm not wrong. That was Paul Somers I saw in that restaurant. Hobnobbing with five high-placed, ultra-conservative Republicans.'

Larry left Bill Taylor's office with a dogged determination to follow his suspicions about Paul Somers' imminent switch in political party.

How the hell had a bright woman like Diane Somers – a woman clearly passionate about seeing the country move in another direction – become involved with a creep like Paul Somers?

Four

Diane's cab swung into the impressive circular driveway surrounded by exquisite landscaping, pulled up before the understated entrance to her posh Georgetown apartment building. She emerged from the cab, waited for the driver to bring out her valise. George, the daytime doorman, rushed to take it from him. As with all their service people, George was fond of her – the heavy tips, she acknowledged. She suspected he disliked Paul – apt to be tight in his tipping. Also – without thinking, she alibied from habit – Paul could sometimes be abrupt to underlings. She'd tried to make him understand. Underlings voted.

'You came home to another scorcher,' the doorman sympathized. *Does he think I've been lying on the beach at the Hamptons?* 'Be glad you weren't here the past five days.'

He talked with distaste about the weather while he accompanied her to the bank of elevators. 'It looks like the weather forecasters get it right one time in ten.'

She waved a friendly hand towards the concierge. She'd arranged for help for his five-year-old severely autistic daughter. Poor little kid. Poor parents. She felt sick each time she remembered how many American families had no health insurance, yet didn't qualify for Medicaid. They lived in constant terror of illness invading their lives.

High-level party members were convinced Paul rode to victory in the last election because of his work in the state legislature for health care for state children. Of course, it had taken her a while to make him understand the urgency of this. And to make him push for it.

We're the greatest country in the world, but it's foreign countries – Canada, Australia, Japan – that provide health care for their people. Not us. That's incredible.

As the elevator slid to a stop at the sixth floor, she remembered this was the day off for their part-time housekeeper. Good. She needed to grab an hour's nap before she was caught up in the rat race again.

Make a dinner reservation right away. The Melrose was very popular, apt to be booked solid. Please let there be a last-minute cancellation. If not, she'd try Palena or Cafe 15, both with a romantic atmosphere.

In the apartment she headed first for the living-room phone to make dinner reservations. She sighed with relief when she was told that Melrose had an 8 p.m. cancellation. Now she went into the bedroom, unpacked, hung away her clothes. Fighting yawns. She'd expected to nap on the flight from Linwood. She hadn't. She'd been too wired.

Paul resented that this was the least-favored line of apartments in their building – with no view of the Potomac. He resented that she rejected his insistence that they buy a two-bedroom condo. The maintenance on a one-bedroom was steep. '*Hell, I should have an office here, too.*' Not that he spent much time in his official Congressional office.

She'd set up a corner of the spacious bedroom for their computer and accessories. No sweat, she'd told him. When Paul was running for the city council, she'd worked in a corner of their galley kitchen.

She sighed in repetitious frustration. Paul had never learned the art of compromise. The only son among five children, he'd been spoiled from infancy. Somehow, it seemed that things always worked out right for him. Thus far.

He'd made it through a good college because his father made a huge contribution to the endowment fund. She'd tutored him through law school. But he needed to contribute more than his 'boyish charm' and his 'man of the people' aura to win re-election. Couldn't he realize what they were facing?

These last six months he'd showed signs of rebellion against their personal rule book. They'd agreed right from the beginning that they had to follow rigorous rules to push him ahead in his political career. Now he ignored them. Was he over-confident – or scared of losing?

His father had been a four-term member of the House – though on the other side of the aisle. Paul was determined to show his father he could do better. He had his eyes on the

White House. She'd kept her doubts about this destination to herself – but if he toed the line, performed decently, he might move into the Senate in a few years.

Surrendering to the need for sleep, Diane kicked off her loafers, stretched out on the bed. In moments she was off into troubled dreams, awoke two hours later with a start. A car alarm was shrieking close by. Damn noisy pest. Improvements in life came with price tags.

Now she realized she was hungry. Not even coffee had been served on their flight. The airline pinching pennies? A stewardess admitted she'd brought along her own snack.

All this cost-cutting, which led companies to outsourcing. She flinched in recall. Three weeks ago – at a meeting she'd set up in a small town largely populated with low-income factory workers – Paul had applauded the low prices provided by outsourcing. He forgot about all the lost jobs. That had been a bad night.

Diane went into the kitchen, foraged in the refrigerator for sandwich makings. A sparse selection – in her absence Paul ate out. Now she pulled out a package of sliced turkey, whole-wheat bread, put up a kettle of water. She'd settle for tea with her sandwich. Joan's obsession for fresh-ground coffee beans had killed her own taste for instant.

While she ate the turkey sandwich with the relish of the hungry, she recalled the outrageous rumor that the reporter – Larry Grant, was that his name? – had thrown at her. So many rumors floating around the halls of Washington, but this was unbelievable. Larry Grant was right – it would have been a bombshell.

She finished her sandwich and tea, went out to the kitchen and poured water for a second cup of tea, reached for a fresh teabag. Herbal tea this time. Let it steep five minutes to get the full flavor, Joan always insisted.

She enjoyed this solitary time in the apartment – the car alarm now quiet. A small parcel of peace. She'd wear something fancy for dinner tonight. Make it a festive occasion. Probably Paul wouldn't realize the date until she ordered a bottle of champagne.

Her mind jumped off on a familiar track while she waited for her tea. Their publicity woman was doing a fine job – providing Paul with much exposure, which he relished. But please God, let him not create more gaffes. Let him remember his need to be scripted.

She was stretched out on the sofa and sipping at her blueberry tea when she heard a key in the lock. She tensed in instant alarm. This was early for Paul. *What happened to bring him home this early?*

She put aside her tea, switched into her alert mode, and rose to greet him. Was he sneaking out of a session again when a vote might be imminent? She'd warned him half a dozen times about that. At intervals the media picked up these slip-ups.

Paul walked from the foyer into the living room. She tried to read his expression. Always bland.

'You're early,' she greeted him. *Why is he home at this hour?*

'I made a point of it today,' he began. *He remembers our anniversary!* 'I figured it was time you and I had a serious talk.' He walked to the sofa, sat down. *He's in his pompous mood now. Who insulted him?*

'All right.' She sat in the club chair at right angles to him. Their usual 'let's have a talk' mode. Most often because he felt her positions were 'too liberal.' Usually after a meeting with his mother.

He bounced up from the sofa like a jack-in-the-box, began to pace. 'This is long past due—'

'What's long past due?' She was wary, remembering his recent flights into fantasyland.

'Let's be realistic – the Republicans have all the money. I was elected to this term by a handful of votes.' *Not to mention a recount was required.* 'Our campaign's short on money – with election less than four months away. Face it – we don't have a chance to win.' A martyred sigh now. 'Di, the time has come. I've thought about this long and hard.' His eyes grew messianic. The way she wanted him to look when he was wooing voters. 'I'm changing parties.' *He's what?* 'I'll never be re-elected as a Democrat. Campaign funds are all going to the Republicans. I have to fight for my future.' He was pompous again. 'As a Republican I have a strong chance of re-election—'

She stared at him in stunned silence for a moment. 'You're out of your mind!'

'It's way past due – I've listened to you too long,' he railed. 'You've made me your puppet.' *Who's been talking to him?*

He never figured that out on his own. 'I'm on the wrong side of thirty-five now, staring at forty! I have to make the move now – or I'm finished.'

'What do you think changing parties is going to do for you?' she challenged, reining in rage. *Who's got to him? What's this all about?* 'You expect to be their candidate in this election?' she scoffed. 'Have you forgotten? They have a candidate. He's out there campaigning like the election was next week!'

'The Republican candidate from our district will retire,' he said in triumph. With a certainty that smacked of insanity, Diane's mind told her.

'Why would he do that?' she asked sweetly. 'You've got a hit out on him?'

'It's all legitimate.' Paul exuded smugness. 'It's all being arranged.'

'How will it be arranged?' she challenged. Her head reeling. That reporter – Larry Grant – heard right! 'They've guaranteed you this?' Meaning the powers-that-be in their district. 'Why?' *Is his father involved in this?*

'It's in the bag. They see me as a winner.' He seemed drunk with this assumption. 'The big wheels are ready to back me all the way. And you know – they can mow down the Democrats like a category-five hurricane.'

'I think you've lost it—'

'I know what's happening.' His face exuded conviction. 'This goes straight up to the administration. They're twisting arms. The current candidate will withdraw.'

'He just won their Primary last month!' June was primary month in their district. Paul had faced no opposition in their own Primary.

'He'll withdraw,' Paul repeated. 'No question about that. Like I said, the administration is behind me. In two weeks I'll send in a letter of resignation to—'

'You had dinner last evening with five top-level Republicans – at some restaurant thirty miles out of Georgetown,' she broke in, struggling for comprehension. 'And they told you this?'

He gaped in astonishment. 'How do you know I had dinner with them?' His voice deepened in outrage. 'You've had me followed by a private eye!'

'I wouldn't bother,' she dismissed this. 'Somebody at head-quarters saw you,' she fabricated. 'I didn't believe him. I said it must have been someone who looked a lot like you. Maybe you have a twin brother you never told us about,' she flipped.

'We don't want it to get around for a couple of weeks,' he emphasized. 'You can't say a word to anyone.'

Oh, really? They're going to put a lock on my mouth?

'They have to let this other guy know he's being replaced,' he continued. His eyes were suddenly opaque. 'I don't suppose you'll consider changing parties.' It was a statement, not a question.

'Never!' Fire in her eyes, she rose to her feet. But Paul was right – up till now he had been her puppet. She maneuvered him, tried to cover his missteps, pushed him ahead. That was what he'd wanted from their days in law school. 'What you're doing is traitorous,' she declared scornfully.

Paul ignored this. 'Another term as a Representative – then they'll push me into the Senate.' He was exultant. 'They've got great plans for me.'

'They'll throw you out on your ass!' she hissed. This was unreal.

'Our marriage has been dead for a long time,' he said, forcing an indulgent smile. *Where's he headed?* 'Still, it might be wise to hold up divorce. The party wants that kept under wraps until after the election.' *He's discussed our divorcing with the party?*

'No!' She stared at him in disbelief. Strangers knew he wanted out of their marriage before she did? It was like walking naked on a public street. She fought for composure. 'No, Paul—'

'What do you mean – no?' Belligerence tainting his voice.

'We'll be divorced immediately.' *I can't wait to have him out of my life!* Now she remembered Elaine's second divorce. 'But it'll be very quiet. Nobody will know.' *Unless I make the announcement.*

'How do you know that?' He was suspicious.

'We'll do what Elaine did – but it has to be a divorce accepted by both sides,' she pinpointed. 'We'll be divorced in the U.S. Territory of Guam – and it'll be recognized in every state in the country.'

'I don't get it. Elaine told you this?' He respected Elaine.

She'd acquired serious income-tax problems via her two divorces. She'd even threatened to turn Republican. *'Look what it'll save me in taxes!'*

'Everything will be handled by the attorney – no residency, no court appearances required of us,' she explained with deceptive sweetness. 'Special legislation allows this for non-residents of Guam. And it'll go through in less than five weeks.' *Over my dead body he keeps this insanity secret!*

'How do you know all this?' But Paul was wavering.

'Because Elaine got her last divorce that way,' she reiterated. *He's been planning this for weeks. No wonder he dodged attending last night's fund-raiser.* 'It works,' she emphasized, 'as long as both parties agree to the settlement.'

'Oh, that's simple.' His smile was smug. 'I'll keep the condo here. You'll keep the house back home.' *With its newly inflated mortgage.* 'You've always loved that house.' He was smirking now, sure he had a deal. 'Once the divorce papers come through – stating the settlement – I'll transfer ownership of the house to you. You'll transfer ownership of the condo to me.'

'All right,' she agreed. *Play it cool – don't let him know I'm reeling from all this.* 'You'll keep this apartment—' He figured she was out of the Washington scene now. He was in for a major surprise. 'I'll have the house. We'll split whatever's left in the joint checking account.' *A piddling amount.* 'I'll write out a check to me for half of what's there. OK?' Her eyes dared him to reject this.

'OK—' But he seemed insecure in this. 'You'll keep the Dodge Stratus at the house.' *Nine years old and constantly in the shop.* 'I'll keep the Lincoln Town Car.' *Less than a year old – but he'll have to keep up the payments.*

'Agreed—' Ten years resolved in a couple of minutes. She ought to be upset that they were ending a ten-year marriage. She was more upset at what havoc Paul was creating for the party. Dizzying to contemplate. They must call for a Special Primary, elect a new candidate.

'I have your word that you won't use our credit cards from this day forward?' Paul was in his pompous mode again.

She held up her hand as though swearing in a court of law. 'Scout's honor.'

'When the divorce papers come through, we'll arrange for

the official change in ownership of the house and the condo,'
he repeated. *Somebody warned him that to do this earlier
would spill the beans before they were ready.* 'But in the mean-
time, the house is yours, the condo is mine. The credit cards
will be—'

'I'll arrange for my own credit cards,' she broke in, fighting
exasperation. *He's been coached in this whole deal!*

'We have no certificates of deposit—' He searched his mind.
'You'll apply for your own health insurance, be off my
Congressional pension plan—' *Is the wife ever on it? And it's
only in effect if the Congressman – or Congresswoman –
serves a minimum of five years. We don't mean to let that
happen.* 'We'll—'

'We agree to the divorce – we'll sign all necessary papers,'
she interrupted with a gesture of impatience. Damn, he could
be long-winded! But it was mind-boggling to visualize herself
as a divorced woman. For over ten years Paul had been part
of her life. His career had been her career.

Paul cleared his throat, seemed searching for words.
'Nobody will realize we're separating, getting divorced.' *Can
he believe that?* 'A lot of Congressional wives stay out of the
Washington scene.' *But not this one.* 'We'll handle it.' He
cleared his throat in that way that said he was trying to deal
with a difficult situation. 'I'll spend the night at a hotel, give
you time to pack up and—' He gestured vaguely.

'I'll be out of here by noon tomorrow. You can come home,'
she drawled. *I can't wait to get out. I'll be on a plane by
noon.* 'And I'll arrange to have your things at the house shipped
to you at my earliest convenience—' *He blinked at that. What
will be my 'earliest convenience?'*

'What about the divorce lawyer?' His eyes mirrored a blend
of relief and suspicion. *He doesn't trust me. For once he's
thinking smart.*

'I'll get his name from Elaine. He'll be in contact with
you,' she assured him. 'Oh, he'll bill you,' she added. 'To
make you feel better, you'll be divorcing me. Irreconcilable
differences.' He wouldn't realize – until somebody clued
him in – that divorcing a wife of ten years would cost him
votes.

He seemed to debate this a moment. 'OK, let the lawyer
bill me.' A martyred expression on his face. Now he hesitated,

uncomfortable. 'I'll pick up a few things now and head for a hotel for the night.'

'Right,' she approved, and he sauntered away with an air of relief.

Diane stood motionless, gazed into space without seeing. Paul was bolting the party. Bolting their marriage. Small loss in the marriage, she conceded. *But what do I do with my life now? Paul's career was my life. Where will I stand with the party?*

Her life and Paul's had been wrapped around his political career. Every move they'd made had been plotted with the thought of advancing his career. With his election to the House she'd felt a new security. Now she felt adrift – without a life-preserver.

Struggling to clear her head, she walked to the telephone, picked up, punched in the Melrose number.

'Hello, the Melrose. Good evening.'

'Hello. I'm sorry – I must cancel a reservation for two at eight p.m. The name is Somers. Congressman Somers and his wife,' she added from habit.

For ten years that was my identity – Paul's wife. Where do I go from here? What will be my role in the party? My career was managing Paul's career. Where do I go now?

Five

Paul tossed his overnight bag into the backseat of the sleek black Lincoln Town Car, then slid behind the wheel. He would have preferred a red Jaguar. Diane – and his mother – had declared that ostentatious for a public servant.

He was whistling as he drove out of the apartment-complex garage. It had been testy there with Diane for a few minutes, he admitted to himself. He'd been real uptight. But life was on an upswing now.

He checked the clock on the car's dashboard. He'd be at Ronnie's house in Arlington in time for dinner – as planned. Arlington, of course – not in a Maryland suburb. He remembered Ronnie's father commenting on this:

'Democrats live in the Maryland suburbs. Arlington is the home of the Right. Naturally, I bought in Arlington.'

His smile triumphant, Paul reached for his cell phone, punched in Ronnie's number.

'Yes?' Ronnie's sultry voice – that matched the rest of her – came to him.

'Hi—' He visualized her, sprawled on the huge gray velvet sofa – those unbelievable legs crossed high, masses of auburn hair falling below her shoulder. Already, he felt that stirring low within him that she knew how to bring to volcanic pitch.

'Where are you?' A faint reproach in her voice.

'It's OK. I'm on my way. Make dinner reservations,' he drawled.

'How did the Big Encounter go?' she purred. 'Two gladiators facing each other in a roaring amphitheater?'

'I handled it right,' he boasted. 'Your dad would have been proud of me.' Rowena Collins' father was Addison Collins, a five-term Congressman and now a major lobbyist. It was Collins who was taking over his career, bringing in the big wheels to back him up. Collins would make enormous contributions to his campaign, expect the same from his inner circle.

'I can't wait to hear the details. We'll make it a late dinner.' Her voice was a sensuous promise.

'Late,' he agreed. Already envisioning them making love in her sprawling, much-glassed bedroom. Drapes discreetly drawn.

'Drive carefully,' she ordered. 'I'll be waiting for you—'

He was relieved that he was missing the heated rush-hour traffic. He hated the bumper-to-bumper deal – at seventy miles an hour. Diane was so damned afraid of his picking up speeding tickets. So damn careful about everything. But she'd never guessed about Addison Collins – and Ronnie.

He'd be back in line with the old man now. Addison had it all set up. They'd arrange a great reconciliation scene of father and son – much media coverage. Addison knew the old man from their days together in Congress.

As so often happened with ex-Congressmen, his father, too, had become an important lobbyist. Now he – the son – realized he'd been stupid to wander off the reservation. His father would welcome him back, support him in his race for re-election. The media would play it up big, he gloated.

He knew just what Addison Collins expected of him. In time he and Ronnie would be married – though not until after the election. He'd be Addison Collins' 'man in Congress.' Another term in the House, and Addison would push him up into the Senate. In time Addison Collins saw himself as the father of the First Lady. Addison would be able to pull all the strings he needed to make that happen.

Addison had bought this terrific contemporary in Arlington for Ronnie as an investment. These days real estate was considered the prime investment – prices could only go up. At least, in the cities where everybody wanted to live – like Washington and New York and San Francisco.

Ronnie's house – with its swimming pool and tennis court – was also a business investment. She entertained Addison's political friends when the need arose. It was Addison who had brought him together with Ronnie just seven weeks ago – at some splashy party for a foreign diplomat. Diane had been back at the Linwood campaign headquarters. Two nights later he was in Ronnie's bed.

In record time he was swinging into the driveway of Ronnie's contemporary, set on a beautifully landscaped three acres. Lighted up like a Christmas tree, he chortled – as always. As if to say, 'Here's where the action is.' But her bedroom was dark. There'd be action there soon, he promised himself.

Again, he was conscious of the stirring low within him. Once – long ago – he'd felt this way about Diane. When he was young and innocent. And she'd been useful, he conceded in a magnanimous moment. But he didn't need her any longer.

Ronnie was at the door to meet him – posing provocatively in a bright red bikini.

'I had a swim,' she murmured and thrust her seductive body against his. 'To cool off.'

'Not too cool,' he drawled. 'Not when I'm so hot.'

'No problem,' she whispered in his ear while his hand pulled away the sliver of bikini top.

'Oh wow,' he muttered. 'Let's get away from all these lights.'

Not until much later – when they sat over a steak dinner in a five-star restaurant favored by the super-rich and powerful in Arlington – did Ronnie question him about the encounter with Diane.

'She didn't give you a hard time?' Ronnie lifted one eyebrow in astonishment. 'I was afraid she'd put you through the wringer.'

'She knew I'd made up my mind. She's smart, Ronnie—' For an instant doubt about the future tugged at him.

Ronnie chuckled. 'Darling, you can buy brains. Dad says you must concentrate on spreading that "man of the people" charm around. Let Dad and his crew carry on the rest of the way. Guess where Dad is tonight?' she taunted with sly humor.

'Where?' Paul demanded.

'In a meeting with your old man. I know – he doesn't want the party switch to come out until after Congress goes on summer vacation. But there's a lot of work to be done. He's arranging for the blockbuster announcement of your switching parties to be followed by the Big Reconciliation. The son realizes the father is on the right side of the fence. Congressman Paul Somers has seen the light!'

'Nobody will know until after the election,' he confided,

'but I'll be divorcing Diane right away. There's this bit about the territory of Guam – it's U.S. territory. I dug around and found out about their terrific divorce laws,' he boasted. 'I can divorce Diane down there through a lawyer – no residency, no court appearance. And it's recognized in every state in this country,' he ended with a flourish.

'Diane will go along with this?' Ronnie was dubious.

'She was crushed,' he conceded, 'but she agreed to the divorce.' The inference being, he told himself, that she was still mad about him.

'I could never understand how you married such a frump,' Ronnie admitted. 'Oh, she's not a horror – not bad-looking. But the clothes she wears.' Ronnie shuddered. 'The way she wears her hair – it does nothing for her. And hasn't she ever heard about cosmetics? She lives in a time warp.'

'It's over—' He gestured in triumph. 'But your father warned that we shouldn't be seen together in public right now. Always make sure other people are with us and—' He stopped dead. Here they were in public – alone.

'Tonight doesn't count.' Ronnie read his mind. 'We're celebrating. Besides, with the lights so low here, who'd recognize us?'

Who in the other camp had seen him with Addison Collins and the four party big wheels? Who told Diane? Addison said they had to keep his changing parties quiet for at least two weeks – while he and his buddies were setting the stage for the Big Announcement.

Who the hell from my old campaign headquarters saw me? Addison will be so pissed if word about the party switch leaks out before he wants that to happen!

Six

Diane knew sleep would be elusive tonight. She'd swigged down an oversized mug of an herbal tea supposed to induce slumber. She'd tried almost an hour of meditation. But at 2 a.m. she was still thrashing about in bed – as wide awake as at high noon.

This was all so unreal. How could she not have foreseen what was coming? Damn, she'd been too involved in keeping Paul in line to see what was happening in front of her nose! He'd moved in so short a time span from the city council to the state legislature to Congress. And already he was talking about a run for the Senate? *What has he been smoking?*

Paul expected her to settle down with Joan in some small, low-earning law practice and disappear into the woodwork. Out of his life for ever. For over ten years he'd been her voice. He'd spouted her causes, followed her line of thinking.

I've lost my voice – my way of saying, 'This is what we must do to make a better world.' She felt like Pygmalion, betrayed.

Sure, she'd always been aware of Paul's mental limitations. But how could he be so stupid as to think she'd sit back and accept what he'd decreed without a single move? *I don't think so!*

She pondered now over her role in the party. She was in a weird position. She'd masterminded their candidate – and he was bolting. So what was her future? Where did she go from here? This would affect Joan, too, she realized all at once. The three of them had been a team.

She and Joan must fight to stay active in the party. Fight like hell. The district's Democratic committee knew Paul was her and Joan's creation – from the time he ran for councilman until today. Correction, she jeered at herself. Until he'd been sworn in as Congressman Somers. That's when the other party

– probably manipulated by the ex-Congressman Somers, Paul's father – decided he could be molded into a winner. For them.

At last she fell into troubled sleep, awoke at minutes past 6 a.m. – as usual. Instantly her mind was flooded with all that faced her today. She was moving out of the condo into another world. And she must tell the district's campaign leaders that they'd lost their candidate.

All at once alarm charged through her. The newspapers! Would there be front-page headlines about Congressman Somers and his switch in parties? Without her forewarning the party? That would be disastrous. So he talked about a two-week wait before the news broke. Could she believe him? No way!

She kicked off the sheet, ran in nightie and bare feet to the apartment door. A quick glance showed only an elegant, empty hall. She reached down to pick up the usual morning news-papers that lay at her feet. What did the *Washington Post*, the *Washington Times*, and the other papers carry on their front pages?

Her eyes swept the headlines as she carried the newspapers into the living room. She drew a deep breath of relief, exhaled. Nothing about Paul. Not yet. She sat on the sofa and flipped through the inner pages. But Paul's defection would hit the front pages, she derided her further search. It wouldn't be hidden in the inner pages.

Nobody had seen Paul at that restaurant with five top-level Republicans, she decided now. Except whoever passed the word along to Larry Grant. Or was it Grant himself who saw Paul but figured – after her denial – that he'd been mistaken? No mistake. Paul hadn't denied it.

Nobody knew Paul was jumping the fence except the handful of conservative Republicans who were masterminding the switch, she concluded. Why was he switching? Was he so scared of not being re-elected?

Larry Grant had been wary of pursuing the story without corroboration. The press was being overly cautious of late, she thought with a burst of impatience. That prize-winning *Times* reporter – Judith Miller – sat in jail for eighty-five days for not revealing her source for an article she hadn't even written. That wasn't good for the country. The press was so important a source of information – it should dig and tell.

In the current climate Paul was sure they could control the
announcement of his jumping parties until what they considered was the 'right time.' Sure, too, that she'd be silent at
his request. She allowed herself a devious smile. *How can he
be so stupid? He wants the story kept under wraps for two
weeks? I'm not sure about that.*

She glanced at the wall clock. Joan would be awake – she
was obsessive about getting up early to check on what was
happening in the local newspapers, on TV and radio newscasts. Buzz Joan right now – before she left for her commute
to campaign headquarters.

She reached for the phone. Her mind in high gear. Punched
in Joan's home phone number.

'Hello—' Joan sounded wary. Very early morning calls
almost always meant trouble.

'That business about Paul,' Diane began, choosing her words
with care. 'It's all true.'

'The lousy bastard!' Joan gasped. 'You'll give me the
whole story later.' Meaning, 'Be careful what you say on the
phone.'

'Right.' They had a gigantic problem on their hands. The
party was without a candidate – with their current Congressman
in office declaring he'd been on the wrong side. 'Joan, check
the local newspapers—'

'Hold on.' Joan's voice was raspy with tension.

Diane waited. She heard the TV switched on, the muffled
voice of an early morning news report. A door opened, then
slammed shut.

'Nothing,' Joan reported a moment later. 'Not a word. Not
in the *Enquirer*. Nothing in yesterday's *Evening News*. It'd be
headlined, of course.' She was checking the TV news as they
talked, Diane realized.

'I'll be on a noon flight out of Dulles,' Diane told her. With
the current security-check delays it would be a tight squeeze
time-wise, but she'd make it. 'Call Larry—' Joan would understand she meant Larry Grant. A man with ethics, she conceded.
She'd answered his question – he'd respected her reply. But
don't cheat the guy out of his Big Story. 'Tell him to be at
my office at five p.m.'

'Will do,' Joan said. *Joan's sharp – she's getting the
message.*

'Tell him it's urgent.' Larry Grant would understand something hot was on the griddle. He could still hit tomorrow morning's headlines. With his own byline.

'I'll be at campaign headquarters in forty minutes,' Joan promised.

'I'll be a little later than that,' Diane admitted. 'But it's going to be a long day. We've got a lot of work to do.' *Am I assuming too much? Are Joan and I out of the picture now?*

'I'll round up members of the district's committee, arrange for an emergency meeting tonight. About eight p.m.?'

'Set it at my house.' *Joan figures we're still part of the campaign. How will the committee feel?* 'Call the deli – arrange for them to send over cold cuts for the meeting.' The meeting could run very late.

They talked another few minutes, then Diane settled into the morning's activities. She'd pack all her clothes in their set of especially monogrammed Vuitton luggage – an ultra-expensive deal that replaced the signature initials with those of the purchaser. She'd suspected that Paul's mother had arranged for this – as though to say he demanded the best.

She guessed that – despite being estranged from his parents because of his political-party switch – Paul saw his mother at intervals. She was known to make secret campaign contributions. His mother had never been happy that Paul had married her. Who would she trot out as a replacement?

Out of the super-expensive Vuitton set, only the weekender Paul had taken with him to his hotel room last night would remain his property. She must arrange with the concierge to ship her luggage via FedEx. That way she'd waste no time at the airport in a long check-in line.

The morning proceeded on schedule. With a fervor born of fury, she emptied out drawers, pulled clothes from closets. The apartment wore the appearance of just-looted premises. She dressed with an eye to simplifying her trek through airport inspection. The usual deal. Beige drawstring slacks and matching top, beige loafers, no jewelry. Her wedding ring conspicuously planted on Paul's chest of drawers.

At 9.10 a.m. she was climbing into a car sent over by their usual car service. She carried only her customary Gucci attaché case and her Prada shoulder bag – her sole concessions to fashion. Her mind was supercharged. A whole new world awaited her. But at the moment she felt like a rudderless ship.

She struggled to conceal her impatience at the slowness in boarding her flight, even while she recognized the necessity of this. She sighed with relief when, at last, she was in her window seat in economy class. She had been paying her own traveling expenses – that called for tight budgeting now. She fastened her seat belt. The plane began its slow ascent.

Now her mind focused on her life for the past ten years. On her marriage. Be honest, she dared herself. For the first year it had been a real marriage. But that movie-star face wasn't sufficient to hold her in thrall. She'd pretended it was a storybook marriage – knowing the media would play it up big.

She'd poured herself into promoting Paul's career. Their career. Her concepts of what was right for their constituents. Sometimes Paul joshed about her being a throwback to the sixties. The *good* sixties, when young people had fought for civil rights, for peace, against violence.

Paul didn't realize it – a lot of people didn't – but there was a rebirth of the good '60s coming into being. And not just among the young. Generation X, baby boomers, seniors – many were shaken by the road the nation was taking. They didn't welcome the prospect of a two-tier society – the super-rich and the poor. They had respect for humanity. They were prepared to fight for a better world for everybody.

The party must find a replacement candidate fast. They couldn't afford to waste a day. But now she stopped short – again troubled about her own place in the campaign. *I'm not the voice behind our candidate any longer. What will be my place in the campaign from this point on?*

She and Joan would make a place for themselves, she vowed. Joan hadn't thought for a moment that they were on the outside now. They still knew how to manage a campaign. The emergency meeting was at her house tonight. The district committee knew she was a fighter. They knew she had been the voice of Paul Somers – city-council member, state legislator, Congressman from their district.

Paul's jumping the fence won't send me into oblivion. I won't let that happen! I want to contribute!

Yet as the plane prepared to land, she felt herself moving

into uncharted territory. She'd lost her puppet. She'd plotted every move in his career. She'd even supervised his wardrobe. It must say that Paul Somers had arrived. Harris-tweed jackets, Burberry topcoat, Sulka or Countess Mara ties, shoes from Johnson & Murphy. She'd created the whole image. Only the Georgetown condo had been his choice.

First thing tomorrow she'd call Elaine, brief her on what was happening. Ask her for the name of the attorney who handled her last divorce. The Guam Territory deal. Have him contact Paul, put their divorce in work. In five weeks she'd be a free woman. Not a bad scene, she told herself defiantly.

Off the plane she waited in line for a taxi. In record time she was walking into campaign headquarters. The cheerful greetings of staff and volunteers told her that Joan had not spread the word of Paul's defection.

But once she'd talked with Larry Grant, they must call everybody together, brief them on what was happening. Let them know before they read the headlines in tomorrow morning's *Enquirer*. Because she meant for the news to be there.

In most divorces, she reflected, the wife got the short end of the stick. It was the divorced wife who saw a huge drop in lifestyle. *That isn't going to happen with this ex-wife.*

Seven

Joan spied Diane, murmured something to the pair of volunteers with whom she'd been conferring, and rushed to greet Diane. Her face was casual, revealing nothing. But her eyes were solicitous.

'How're you doing?'

'I'm OK,' Diane said defiantly. *Am I?* 'Tell Jill to take over.' From the glint of alarm in Jill's eyes, she knew Joan had brought her up to date. 'Let's go next door for coffee.' Where they could talk in private. People could pop in and out of her cubicle and Joan's at any moment.

'Right.' Joan flashed a comforting smile, strode to talk with Jill, her savvy assistant.

Diane waved to a cluster of volunteers who were smiling in her direction. Damn, they were smitten by Paul – and the words she put into his mouth. But they wouldn't be so smitten when they discovered he'd dumped his loyal, hardworking wife of ten years. They'd rally behind her – and her candidate. She could still be an effective member of the campaign.

Joan returned to her side. 'Let's go—'

In the pleasant restaurant next door they settled themselves in a rear booth. Few people there at this off-hour. Later, there would be a line waiting to be seated.

'My mother's on a new kick.' Joan shook her head in frustration. 'She read somewhere that many people in their twenties and thirties are returning to the old homestead because of the staggering rents in a lot of cities today. She thinks my new rent increase should bring me back home.' She shuddered at the prospect. 'Wait till she hears about Paul. She'll never vote again.'

'You said the last election was the first time she voted,' Diane reminded, her eyes searching for their waitress. Once they ordered, they could talk.

'The only time.' Joan nodded. 'Somebody told her way back when that if she voted, she stood a strong chance of being called for jury duty. A fate worse than death. But she loved you – and she thought Paul was cute.'

Alice – their fifty-ish waitress who relished arguing politics with them from time to time – approached to take their orders.

'You're runnin' away from the salt mines awful early,' she commented.

'Just a quick break,' Joan explained.

'What do you need for resuscitation?' Alice knew the long hours they kept, joshed about their needing a union.

They ordered fruit salad to accompany their coffee. This gave them a reason to linger. Alice left them. Joan leaned forward, her eyes anxious.

'Talk,' she ordered Diane – brusque in her anxiety.

In succinct terms Diane repeated Paul's declaration to leave what he considered a sinking ship.

'Which leaves the party in a rough situation,' she wound up. 'We just squeaked through in the last election,' she reminded. 'We need a strong replacement candidate – and that won't be easy to find.' *In so little time!*

'We'll have to call for a Special Primary—' Joan winced at the prospect of this. 'We'll be lucky if we can schedule it in a couple of weeks. But right now every day counts.'

'It's urgent to settle on a candidate fast.' Diane's mind was charging ahead. The news that Paul was switching parties would give him tremendous exposure. Exposure added up to votes.

'We'll see a mad rush for Xanax,' Joan predicted. 'But let's tackle the first problem. How fast can we set up the Special Primary?'

'That's the district committee's job. You've called an emergency meeting for tonight?'

'Like you said. At eight p.m. sharp – at your house,' Joan confirmed. 'When I called, I didn't tell them what this is all about – but they realize it must be something cataclysmic. I figured you'd break the news to everybody at one time. Deli arrives at nine p.m. sharp – we don't want anybody to starve.' She sighed. 'How can I lose fifteen pounds eating gorgeous hot pastrami and potato salad?'

'Two ways to lose weight.' Diane's usual retort to Joan's frequent wailing about excess poundage. 'Exercise and restraint. Walk away from the fridge.' She ignored Joan's reproachful stare. 'But this is a hell of a situation,' she acknowledged. 'Paul was the incumbent – our best bet. He was facing no opposition in the party.' *Incumbents have a history of winning.* 'And he's fought hard for the district,' she added, all at once defensive.

'Bullshit,' Joan dismissed this. 'We fought hard for the district.' *Joan doesn't feel we're about to lose our place in the party. That's good.* 'But Paul's walking out this way – at almost the last minute – can throw our whole election process into a tailspin.'

'If we let it.' But Diane's face was troubled. 'It won't help our fund-raising.' Already a critical situation. 'We must find a way to turn this whole ugly mess around to our advantage.' Somewhere was the angle to do this – but it kept eluding her.

'Paul doesn't expect you to leave the party, too?' Joan asked in sudden alarm.

'He's not that stupid.' She took a deep breath. 'But where does that leave us? What role can we have when Paul's walked out?'

'Are you kidding?' Joan clucked in reproach. 'We're both major assets. Important wheels in the Democratic district. You're as well known as Paul. Everybody hovers around you for inspiration. You lead us!'

'Let's hope the others feel that way.' Diane's eyes were somber. 'Oh, and there's more—' Her smile sardonic. 'Paul wants a divorce.'

Joan's mouth dropped wide. 'I don't believe it!'

'He said it in plain English. No real loss to me—' But, somehow, humbling. As though she'd failed somewhere along the line.

'Why does he want a divorce? Because he's changing parties? Hey, look at James Carville and Mary Matalin – one Democrat, one Republican. They're staying together.' Joan considered this. 'But they're two smart people.'

'Nobody will ever accuse Paul of being smart. Many things they may say – in a magnanimous, blinded state – but never smart. But you're talking as though you want me to stay with him,' Diane accused. 'You know you've never liked him. Not even in law school. You tolerated him – because he was our candidate and won elections.'

'I stayed because of you. I trailed along because you're so smart – and because I love you. And no, I'm not a lesbian,' Joan added with a reminiscent chuckle because Paul had once harbored such suspicions, despite her on-and-off relationships with a string of men she labeled as 'sex-starved and irresponsible – terrified of making a commitment.' 'And I'm glad you're breaking up with the creep.'

'Paul said he's tired of being my puppet. I know – he didn't think that up himself,' Diane added quickly. 'Somebody threw it at him. He's the one filing for the divorce – at my suggestion.' A glint of complacency in her eyes. 'He doesn't realize that'll cost him women's votes.'

Joan was still shaken. 'What about you?' she demanded. 'I hope you come out of this divorce with a winning lottery ticket.'

'Only if his parents both die suddenly and leave him their heir – before the divorce comes through. You know the community property law in this state. Anyhow, I get the house—' She saw Joan grimace. Joan knew about the recently inflated mortgage. 'Paul keeps the condo and the Lincoln Town Car—'

'And you keep the nine-year-old Dodge?' Joan was indignant. 'What about alimony?'

'What year are you living in?' Diane clucked in reproach. 'Today alimony is ancient history for almost every woman alive. Unless she's married to Donald Trump.'

'Not your type.' Joan shook her head. Her eyes were worried. 'And you're an unpaid volunteer for the party. At least I'm on salary. Your status will have to change,' she insisted and shuddered. 'That makes two of us on a tight budget.'

'I'll survive.' Diane's smile was defiant. 'Let's focus on the Big Problem. Where the hell do we find a new candidate – within the next couple of weeks – who'll stand a chance of winning?'

'With the right handling anybody has a chance against Paul.' Joan was blunt. 'Without us to pull his strings.'

'He's got heavy money behind him,' Diane began, 'and for some reason – which I haven't figured out yet – they figure they can make him a winner. They must be counting on his "man of the people" image mowing down the average voter. They know what that did for Ronnie and Bush II.' She paused as Alice sauntered over with their fruit salad and coffee.

'Your coffee refills will be decaffeinated,' Alice warned them. 'You two gotta learn to eat healthy. You got a political campaign to run.'

When they were alone again, Joan pounced on the prospect of Paul's winning on the opposition's ticket.

'Why do they want Paul?' Joan probed again. 'Setting aside his image – as created by us.'

'I suspect Paul's father may have something to do with it,' Diane admitted after a moment. 'He wants to see the Somers becoming another dynasty, like the Kennedys and the Bushes. And he knows Paul can be manipulated.'

'Must be manipulated,' Joan said drily. 'So they figure they can mold him. Make him a replica of Ronnie and George II.' She shuddered. 'This is not a happy moment for us.'

'It won't be a happy moment for the opposition tomorrow morning.' Diane's eyes held a glint of laughter. 'Not after the *Enquirer* breaks the news. And it'll be picked up so fast by the Washington newspapers – and by the TV and radio news desks.'

'Eat up,' Joan ordered. 'You're seeing Larry Grant in about fifteen minutes.'

'We'll have to break the news to the staff – after my chat with Larry Grant.' Diane was somber now. 'And we must get on the phone with the volunteers.' She groaned in anticipation. 'That's going to be a long haul.'

'What about e-mail?' Joan suggested.

'Are you kidding? How do we know when they'll check their e-mail? We call. We can't let them read about it in tomorrow morning's *Enquirer*.'

We'll be on the phone with the volunteers – not just in Linwood but throughout the whole district – until late in the evening. Perhaps we can enlist the volunteers to help with the notification.

How many will we lose with this insanity?

Eight

Diane and Joan hurried back to campaign headquarters. It was almost 5 p.m. The daytime staff – except for Jill, who shared their fifteen-hour days – was preparing to leave. The daytime volunteers were taking off to hit their kitchens, Diane guessed – grateful for their presence. The evening volunteers would start arriving around 7 p.m. – after early dinners.

Diane welcomed the quiet that took over now. A brief lull before the vigorous activity of the evening volunteers. She needed her head clear for the meeting with Larry Grant. She gathered he'd told the *Enquirer* he was on the track of a blockbuster story – but without any hint of what it was.

He'd have his blockbuster, she thought in soaring satisfaction. He'd give it to the *Enquirer* in time to hit tomorrow morning's headlines. His editor wouldn't be disappointed. The Washington papers would pick up fast. Television and radio newscasts would grab at it.

At two minutes past 5 p.m. Larry sauntered into campaign headquarters. The way he carried himself told Diane he knew something big was about to happen.

Joan met him with an enigmatic smile. 'Diane's expecting you. She's in what passes for her office—' She pointed to the cubicle at the back, where Diane stood waiting for him.

'Thanks.' Even at this distance Diane was conscious of his charismatic smile. *Does he figure this story will catapult him into the big time?*

'You're punctual,' Diane approved. 'That's important these days.'

'Two minutes late,' he demurred. 'Traffic's heavy already.' His eyes were bright with curiosity.

'Come in – sit down.' Diane sat in the chair behind her desk. Larry lowered himself into a chair facing her. His eyes seeming to search her mind. 'When I told you that the rumor about Paul's switching parties was all wrong, I believed that. I've learned differently.' She was struggling for calm. 'It's true – Paul Somers is skipping the party. I just learned this some hours ago. In November he'll be a candidate for the opposition.'

Larry whistled softly. 'What about the current candidate? The one the party expected to be on the ballot?'

'He's being dumped.' Diane's gesture was eloquent.

'That's going to take a lot of explaining.' His eyes told Diane his mind was on a fast track.

'They'll fabricate some story about ill health in the family,' Diane surmised. 'If he has a shred of good luck, they'll contrive to have him appointed to some government job. I hope he's told he's no longer the candidate before he reads about it in the *Enquirer*.'

'Somers is going back to the old corral,' Larry interpreted. 'Back to where the big campaign money is – and where his father can be useful. Can't you visualize the Big Reconciliation scene between the two of them?' *He's sharp – I figured he was.* 'Just as well he'll be off the ticket.' Larry Grant was blunt. 'The people in this district deserve better. Begging your pardon,' he added with a wry smile. 'Anyhow, everybody knowledgeable about politics knows you ran his ship.'

'The party's trying to keep his jumping the fence quiet for a couple of weeks. That's naive.' Her smile was eloquent. 'Oh, there's more.' She took a deep breath, exhaled. 'He's divorcing me.'

'He's more stupid than I thought.' For an instant Larry's eyes were disarmingly appraising. *Thank you.* 'He'll be out there without his life-preserver.' *OK, he was talking from a political viewpoint. He realizes I ran the show.*

'It was more a political arrangement than a marriage in these last few years.' *Why am I telling him this?* 'I wanted to see good things happen in this country. In my own small way I thought I could help.' She forced a chuckle. 'I know – I'm being naive.'

'No,' he rejected. 'As time goes by, more and more of us want to help – to make a contribution. We're unnerved by the direction the country's taking.'

'Those in power are pushing us into a two-tier society,' she said with sudden intensity. 'It's scary.'

'The "haves" and "have-nots,"' Larry completed her thought. The atmosphere suddenly electric. *He thinks like me.* 'We saw what happened in the wake of Katrina last year. A lot of people – all age groups – were shaken. They realized we have to fight to keep this country a true democracy. We won't be silenced. We'll fight for what's right for the average person. That's what makes this country work.'

'I suspect you're a fast writer—' Diane struggled to brush aside the emotional moments that had erupted. 'I expect you'll have a headlined story in tomorrow morning's *Enquirer*?'

'If the paper has questions, you'll back me up?' His eyes held hers. Both conscious of a new bond between them.

'I'll back you up.' She paused a moment, exploring an earlier suspicion. 'You weren't following rumors in the halls of Washington,' she guessed. 'You saw Paul with the opposition.'

'Yes. But I couldn't afford to write the story without your corroboration. The *Enquirer* wouldn't run it.' He shrugged. 'I knew I wouldn't get the truth from Paul Somers. Not until he and the opposition considered it the "right time."'

'Are you based in Washington or here in Linwood?' She was trying to get a handle on Larry Grant. Not easy to do.

'My sister and her husband – Andrea and Jimmy Martin – live here in Linwood. They've been here fourteen years.' He seemed oddly uncomfortable. *Does he think I'm prying?* 'They set up a studio apartment for me in the basement of their house. I kind of commute between here and Washington. When in Washington I bunk with an old college buddy. I – I was in the Walter Reed Army Medical Center in Washington for a couple of months.'

'You were in Iraq?' *Why am I astonished? Over a hundred fifty thousand Americans are over there.*

'I was there for nineteen months – until our convoy was hit. For a while they were afraid I'd lose a leg. The doctors were stubborn. They saved it.' A glint of triumph in his smile now.

'It must have been rough—'

'It wasn't a summer at the Hamptons.' His smile reminiscent, rueful. 'Sure, some American military bases provided air-conditioned trailers equipped with all the amenities. Television, refrigerators, microwave ovens. Decent chow, a gym, Internet café. But for most of us life was rough.'

'We've read about the intolerable heat, the blinding sand-storms,' Diane sympathized.

'We'd be choking on dust, wrapped up in body armor – often family supplied,' he said with an ironic smile, 'because we didn't know when we'd be attacked. The temperature soaring to triple digits. There were times we couldn't shower for weeks, slept any place we could find. But I asked for it.' He shrugged. 'I enlisted. I figured I would get a better insight into what's happening in the Middle East in uniform than by reporting as a journalist.'

'You wanted to write about it from the inside—' She nodded in approval. 'Digging down to the nitty-gritty truth.' Larry was a man of action – someone she could respect.

'Not just for the newspapers,' he admitted. 'A book – one of these days. This isn't like other wars. All those National Guardsman fighting in Iraq never expected to serve beyond a limited period. They're losing jobs back home despite all the great talk. Their families fighting to survive financially. And look at the ages of the casualties – some National Guardsmen, some regular army. Mostly nineteen to twenty-five.' He closed his eyes for an instant in anguish. 'Too young to die.'

'So many in their teens,' Diane whispered. Remembering the names and ages she saw nightly on public TV. 'They should be back home in college. Not coming home in body bags.'

'A lot of them enlisted with the hope of getting their college education when they were discharged – because without a college degree they saw no jobs, no hope for the future.'

'Write the book,' she said urgently. *If he had some political background, he'd make a tremendous candidate. He exudes strength of character, charm. He'd be great on the campaign trail. On television.*

'Right now I'm just making notes.' He was somber. 'I'm still too close to do more than that.'

'But you have a writing background,' she assumed. 'Newspaper articles—'

'I've moved around a lot—' *He regrets talking so freely.* 'I spent a year in the Peace Corps. Sold a few articles from that experience. Went into public relations for a while – got bored with that. Handled some Middle East reporting assignments for minor magazines – did some TV reporting from over there. Then I enlisted.'

'Working up to a book—' She remembered the Iraq veteran who ran for the House in a special election in Ohio last year. But he'd been a town-councilman and was a lawyer – that was political background. No chance she could promote Larry Grant as their new candidate – even though he was an Iraq veteran.

'You've got a tough road ahead.' Larry swept her back to the moment. 'Losing an incumbent is never good.'

'We'll come up with somebody fast. And we'll put up a real fight for him.' Diane exuded determination. 'Or her—'

Larry rose to his feet. His eyes quizzical as they rested on Diane. 'I'd better get this show on the road if I'm to hit tomorrow morning's *Enquirer*.'

'If your editor wants confirmation, tell him to give me a ring. I'm always here till around eleven p.m.' She paused. 'Correction – tonight I'll be here until about 7.45 – then I'll be at this number – ' she reached for a notepad, scribbled her home number – 'until God knows when. We're having an emergency meeting of the district's Democratic committee this evening.'

He nodded in comprehension. 'That figures—'

'I'll probably return to the office after the meeting. Your editor will be able to reach me at one number or another.'

'Great.' He seemed to be in some inner debate. 'What if I can set up a TV interview on our local station for tomorrow morning? As a follow-up to the *Enquirer* story?' *This guy doesn't waste time.* 'Will you be available?' His eyes were challenging.

She hesitated for only a moment. *Why not?* 'I'll be available. Provided you're handling the interview,' she added in sudden caution. Not some wise-guy Republican – a wannabe Tucker Carlson or Ann Coulter. 'You said you've done TV reporting—'

He grinned. 'I wouldn't have it any other way.'

'I'll be at one of the numbers I gave you. Call me if you've set up an interview. We'll need to talk. I wouldn't want to go into it cold.'

'I'll call you, one way or the other.' A glint of anticipation in his eyes, he rose to his feet. 'But I suspect the TV wheels will grab at it. I'll buzz you the moment I have definite word.'

'Good. I'll accept calls at our emergency meeting.'

Here was payback for her rotten almost-ex-husband. Did that make her appear a vindictive bitch? No, it was smart politics. Preparing the way for their replacement candidate. Great exposure for their campaign. Maybe – just maybe, she toyed with the thought – their new candidate would be a woman. In a corner of her mind she searched for prospects.

Joan sailed into the cubicle moments after Larry Grant left.

'So?' she demanded. 'The bombshell strikes tomorrow morning?'

'Larry's running with the story.' She stared into space. He was a complicated guy. He just might be useful in the coming election. He said he was freelancing. How were they to use him? 'Oh, another bulletin. He's trying to set up a rush interview with me – on local TV. Tomorrow – after the *Enquirer* hits the streets. As the woman the Congressman is about to divorce.'

'Call the beauty salon!' Joan ordered, her face alight with anticipation. 'You have to have your hair done. Maybe some highlights—'

'No time,' Diane dismissed this. 'Our meeting at my house,' she reminded. 'The television audience will see me – warts and all. But I'll be the rejected wife,' she murmured with candid pleasure. 'That'll land Paul in the doghouse for a lot of women voters.'

At 7.40 p.m. – when most of the evening volunteers were working away at assigned tasks – Jill summoned them all to attention.

'We've arrived at a shocking moment in the Congressional campaign from our district,' she told them with contrived calm. 'What Diane is about to tell you now must be kept secret until the announcement becomes public knowledge.' Jill allowed herself a faint smile. 'You'll understand when you've heard Diane.'

Diane emerged from her cubicle, walked to a central spot in the volunteers' sprawling area.

'We won't permit what's about to happen to interfere with our campaign efforts,' she assured them. 'We can't allow that to happen,' she emphasized in the sudden quiet. 'But Paul Somers, our candidate for Congress, is withdrawing—' She paused at the sounds of shock this elicited. 'He's leaving us to replace the current Republican candidate – which is being arranged.' Her voice loaded with implications not lost on her audience.

'You're not leaving?' a senior-citizen volunteer cried out.

'I'm not leaving.' Diane lifted her head in defiance. 'But I'm leaving Paul. Or rather, he's divorcing me.'

Now questions were hurled at her from indignant women among the volunteers. The male volunteers appeared cowed. She replied in succinct terms to every question.

'Does this mean we don't have a chance of electing a Democrat from our district?' a young volunteer – her husband fighting in Iraq – demanded in outrage.

'No!' Diane shot back. 'We're going to fight harder than ever for our candidate!' *Is this going to cost us our volunteers? That would be devastating!* 'It's urgent that Democrats take back the House,' she declared passionately. She glanced about at the sea of faces before her. No, they weren't going to lose volunteers. These were dedicated human beings, fighting to see the country headed in the right direction. They were still fighting together. 'We're holding an emergency meeting of the district's Democratic committee tonight. A Special Primary will be scheduled quickly. We'll have a candidate – and we'll fight for him. Or her. We'll see victory on November the seventh, 2006!'

'Where will we find a candidate capable of winning – when our man in Congress took a powder?' an older man – veteran of other campaigns – challenged Diane. 'It'll be a bitch—'

'We will find him,' Diane vowed. 'Or her. And with us all fighting behind him, we'll put him over the top.' She took a deep breath, gearing herself for what must be said. 'Paul Somers was never the ideal candidate. We fought like hell to make him appear that. We can beat him.' Her eyes swept about the volunteers. 'We will beat him.'

Nine

In the cluttered office of Bill Taylor – the publisher and editor-in-chief of the *Enquirer* – Larry Grant leaned back in his chair while Taylor read his just-written article about the pull-out of Paul Somers as their district's Democratic candidate for Congress in the 2006 elections. Taylor had held space open on the front page in the event he decided to go along with this, Larry reminded himself. A sign of healthy interest.

Taylor dropped the computer printout on his desk, swerved back and forth in his swivel chair.

'It's great—' But his tone was somber. 'You're sure you got the facts straight? You know how every newspaper and magazine editor is sweating these days—'

'I got it right from the horse's mouth,' Larry began and chuckled. 'Straight from the candidate's wife and alter ego,' he corrected. 'Buzz her,' he urged. He checked his watch. Minutes before 10 p.m. 'She's at one of these two numbers—' He reached into a pocket, pulled out a scrap of paper. 'She'll be happy to confirm.'

Taylor still seemed ambivalent. *He's hungry to run it. It'll be a real scoop.* Now Taylor reached for the phone. 'Isabel, get me this number. I want to speak with Diane Somers.' He held the receiver away from his ear, turned to Larry. 'We've run some stuff from her,' he recalled. 'I heard her once at a town meeting. Smart woman. Good-looking.'

'The way I hear it in Washington, she runs the show. He's the face, she's the brains.' Excitement welled in Larry. This would be a sharp move for him professionally. Help in finding a publisher, once he'd written the book.

'This district needs somebody who'll make waves in the House,' Taylor began and paused, phone at his ear now. 'Yeah?'

'Ms. Somers isn't at this number,' Larry could hear Isabel explain.

'Then try this one,' Taylor barked and gave her the second number.

'She's still at that top-level meeting,' Larry surmised. 'They have to get a Special Primary in motion. At this late date.' He grimaced as he considered this. 'They've got a rough road ahead.'

Moments later Isabel was back on the phone. 'Ms. Somers here,' Isabel said blithely.

'Ms. Somers,' Taylor said with an air of apology, 'I'm sorry to bother you at this late hour, but in today's climate we must check out all stories—'

'The story I gave Larry Grant about my husband, Paul Somers, is true.' Her voice was brisk. 'Nobody knows yet except us and a few close associates. And, of course, Paul and his new associates.' Her voice coated with sarcasm now. 'I'll be happy to have you run the story – quoting me as your source. The voters in this district have a right to know as soon as possible.'

'It'll be on the front page of tomorrow morning's *Enquirer*,' Taylor assured her. He paused for an instant. 'Would you consider giving Larry a personal interview as a follow-up?'

'My pleasure,' she murmured. 'Larry and I will set it up. If you have any questions, just give me a buzz.'

In the spacious dining room of the white colonial that Paul had insisted was the proper background for his political career, Diane sat at the head of the extended dining table. This evening it was serving as a conference table. The atmosphere was tense.

Most of the platters delivered by a local delicatessen had been stripped bare. Empty coffee mugs, soda cans, crumpled paper napkins, plates littered with remains of food were scattered about the table. Everybody attentive as Clark Jackson, head of the district's Democratic committee, summed up their situation.

Everybody reacted with a start when a plate crashed to the floor as Jackson made a sweeping gesture to highlight a point.

'Diane, I'm so sorry,' he apologized.

'Don't be,' she shrugged this away. 'It was a wedding gift from my mother- and father-in-law. I never liked it. Now I can dump the whole set.' A glance at her watch told her they'd been at this for close to three hours. 'Please continue, Clark.'

'All right, we know what we must do,' he repeated. 'We have to bring the Special Primary into action as fast as possible. Send out feelers to possible candidates. Set a deadline for announcing. We should be able to schedule the Special Primary for four weeks from today—'

'Two weeks,' Diane broke in. 'This is the end of July – election day is November seventh. We need every day we can salvage.'

'Two weeks is terribly tight,' Jackson protested.

'We don't have a choice.' Adam Miller was blunt. 'And I suspect we won't be overwhelmed with candidates. Why the hell did that bastard—' He paused, turned in apology to Diane. 'Why did he pull this crap at this late date?'

'Because he's a bastard,' Diane agreed. 'He must have been on this deal for weeks. I was too busy covering his ass – I didn't see the warning signs. The opposition hopes to put us in disarray – instructed him to wait until now.'

'All right,' Jackson capitulated, 'we set the Special Primary for two weeks from now. The date by which prospective candidates must announce.' Jackson frowned in pain as he contemplated this. 'Ballots must be set up at the last possible moment.'

The shrill ring of a phone in the living room beyond was a jarring intrusion. Diane reached for the cordless that sat waiting beside her for such a moment.

'Hello, Diane Somers.'

'Larry,' he said. 'You're set for our TV interview. It'll run live tomorrow morning at ten a.m., be repeated at six p.m. and again after the eleven p.m. news. Let's have a dry run before we head for the studio. Is seven thirty too obnoxious?'

'It's good,' Diane approved. 'At my house—' She gave him the address. 'I'll have coffee standing by.' She turned off the cordless, set it down on the table. Conscious of the air of anticipation of those about the table. 'Larry Grant – the journalist I talked about earlier – will interview me live on our local television station tomorrow at ten a.m. – and it'll be repeated twice in the course of the evening. Everybody in the district will know what's happening. And so will Paul's pals back in Washington. But enough of that,' she wound up briskly.

'Let's get back to business. We'll need some vigorous fund-raising efforts – money to buy television and radio commercials, newspaper ads. This could become a dirty fight.' Not *could*, her mind warned. *Would.*

'This last-minute change of candidates will be a hell of a blow to fund-raising.' Jackson took a long breath. 'Which was never too great. And we may lose some of our people – the ones who figured with an incumbent running we had a good chance of winning. Now—' he spread his hands in doubt, 'they may decide to run from what they think is a sinking ship.'

'In approaching possible candidates,' Liz Franken – whom Diane considered the sharpest head on the committee – said with deceptive calm, 'let's stress that Diane and Joan will continue as campaign managers for whoever wins the Special Primary. Anybody knowledgeable will recognize that Diane's pulled the strings in Paul's political life. That as campaign manager she can do great things for a new candidate.'

'Only my mother recognizes me as co-campaign manager,' Joan interjected good-humoredly. 'I'm here to work with Diane – as always. We're a team.'

'We must expand our promotion—' Thoughts that had been floating about in Diane's head were coming together. 'We don't focus on fighting for funds just in our district.' She leaned forward, excitement building in her. 'We go nationwide.' She paused, sensed doubt in the others.

'I'm not sure we can afford that diversion,' Adam Miller objected, exchanging glances with the others about the table.

'It was a tight squeeze last time,' Joan reminded. 'Guys, we need money!'

'This isn't just a race to put a Democrat from our district into Congress – to fight for our personal needs,' Diane pursued. 'This is a crusade now. A race to help the Democrats take back the House. One vote – the vote of our Congressman – might just be the crucial vote to put across a piece of important legislation.' Her gaze swung about the table. *Good. They're beginning to get the message.*

'It's going to take some doing—' Another committee member seemed inclined to consider this approach. 'It's something to think about—'

'It'll cost a million dollars to put our candidate in Congress,' Liz Franken estimated. 'How do we raise that?'

'That's why we must convince Democrats on a national level that it's important to the party that they help us elect our candidate.' Diane exuded optimism now. 'And with national interest we'll win media attention.'

'We'll be able to place our people on national television news shows—' Joan pushed. 'On radio shows. Grab newspaper space. And all the while we fight to raise money via the Internet.'

'That's good,' Jackson conceded, 'but our primary problem – ' he allowed himself a dramatic pause – 'is to find a viable candidate to replace Paul Somers.'

'What about a woman candidate?' Diane challenged.

'That could be dangerous.' Adam Miller was uncomfortable at the prospect. 'It could turn off a bunch of male voters.'

'Not if they believe she can win,' Diane shot back.

'You got somebody in mind?' Joan asked. Knowing whom Diane had in mind because they'd discussed this at length earlier in the day.

'I was thinking about Fran Logan in the state assembly – she's young, personable, aggressive—' Diane spoke with conviction. She and Fran had worked together in several instances in the past three years. Fran had impressed her with her enthusiasm, her dedication.

'She's only served one term in the assembly,' Miller objected. 'That's a major leap.'

'Paul did it,' Liz Franken pointed out. 'Because he had the right machinery behind him.'

Joan jumped in. 'The same machinery will be behind Fran Logan!'

'She'll have to win in the Special Primary,' another committee member reminded. 'We don't know who will consider running.'

'We can swing that in Logan's direction. Go all out in support of her.' Diane's mind was racing ahead. 'I vote we set the Special Primary in action as quickly as possible, yes – but we talk to Fran Logan right away.' A glint of anticipation in her eyes. 'Tomorrow morning.'

'Ten to one possible male candidates will be wary – it's a rough spot to step into at the last moment this way,' Jackson pointed out.

'But a woman will take chances,' Diane pounced. 'And Fran Logan has been very visible in the state assembly.'

'You talk to her,' Jackson ordered Diane. 'Feel her out.' His eyes swept about the table. Approval in the air. Only Adam Miller seemed dubious. 'If she's willing, we'll be behind her all the way.'

'The assembly is out of session. No time problem there. I'll talk with her first thing tomorrow morning.' Excitement spiraled in Diane. 'Let's send Fran Logan to Congress.' And Paul Somers to oblivion. If he lost, his new party would drop him like yesterday's newspaper.

Ten

In companionable silence – both caught up in the drama of the meeting that had just concluded – Diane and Joan cleared the dining table, carried dishes into the large, square kitchen.

'We made headway,' Joan declared with determined optimism while Diane stacked the dishwasher. 'Sure, we know we'll have a rough fight coming up – but we can deal.'

Diane was contemplative. 'The others suspect we won't be swamped with prospective candidates. I'm not sure of that.'

'Considering the problems of coming into the race as kind of an afterthought?' Joan's eyes were quizzical.

'Consider what the situation offers. Look at what happened in Ohio last year,' Diane challenged. 'In their Democratic Special Primary six candidates were running. To some – male and female – this could appear to be their big chance to move up fast. We'll have candidates.' She nodded in conviction. 'The problem – will there be one with a chance to beat the Republican war chest.'

'That's for us to find out—' Joan smothered a yawn. They'd both been up since 6 a.m., yet were too wired to call it a night just yet.

'Carmen will be in to clean tomorrow,' Diane said, reaching for the dishwasher detergent. She flinched for an instant. 'I may have to give her notice. But she's good,' Diane added defensively. 'She'll pick up those two days a week with no sweat. I'll give her dazzling references.'

'Hey, you're on salary at campaign headquarters as of tomorrow,' Joan reminded. A status arranged just an hour ago. 'I know it's low budget, but you'll manage.'

'I know how to budget.' Diane was grim in recall. What she'd inherited from her parents' estate had gone into promoting Paul's career. 'I've done a lot of that.'

Joan nodded. 'Both of us.'

'I'll keep Carmen for the moment,' Diane decided.

'This is not the time for you to take on the "divorced woman's syndrome." You need Carmen – when have you got time to clean the house?'

'Right.' Diane nodded in agreement. 'I'll manage somehow.' Then she groaned. 'But I've got that huge mortgage payment to face every month—' On her own – with no help from Paul's Congressional salary. 'It was crazy of us to buy this big house.' She'd loved a sprawling contemporary a mile down the road – with huge amounts of glass that brought the outdoors into every room. Paul insisted the colonial had dignity. The right background for a 'young man on the rise in politics.' She suspected he was quoting his mother.

'Paul should split the mortgage payments with you. A chunk of the mortgage went to the down payment on the fancy condo he couldn't survive without,' Joan jeered. 'But you'll let him off the hook, of course.'

'I want him out of my life—' But reality smacked her across the face. 'I can't quite do that just yet, can I? We'll be fighting him every day till election. Joan, we can't let them put Paul back in the House!'

'Keep thinking that way—'

'I'll take one day at a time – except for campaign problems,' Diane rationalized. 'That's the major deal at this point. Paul is dispensable.' She considered this for a moment. 'I thought I was in love with him – back in law school. I think I was in love with his prospective career, that became my career, too.' Only Joan would understand that. 'I don't need a man in my life.'

'That's what I keep telling Mom – "I don't need a man in my life." She doesn't believe me.' Joan's smile was wry. 'I don't believe me. But when do I have time in my crowded existence to join the race?'

'If you were bothered, you'd find time. I've had it with men.' Diane exuded rebellion. 'I'll do very well on my own. Who needs to take on their problems, too?'

'Mom says I'm running away. She was eager to see me walking down the aisle to the Wedding March my first year in college. The only reason she and my old man helped me through the way-out costs of an Ivy League college plus law school was because she was sure I'd find "the right man" there.'

'Meaning a guy who'd be in the big bucks by the time he was thirty,' Diane interpreted.

Joan nodded. 'Now – when she's not trying to fix me up with some friend's son – she's moaning that I'm not out there in private practice, pulling in four hundred bucks an hour.'

'Remember when we went to our tenth college reunion?' Diane reminisced. 'All the girls we were sure would be married before they hit thirty were single—'

'Yeah,' Joan drawled. 'The less fussy ones had at least one kid by then.'

'Thank God, Paul and I didn't have kids. No,' Diane corrected herself. 'Paul decided that we shouldn't have kids.' They'd never even had a pet because Paul was convinced he was allergic. 'Paul said we didn't have time for that.' The career had been their children. And now there was nothing.

'I'd better get home—' Joan sounded reluctant.

'Want to stay over? I can loan you a change of clothes – and I always have extra toothbrushes around.'

Joan shook her head. 'We'll just talk all night and be messes tomorrow. Set your alarm,' she exhorted. 'We've got a tough day ahead.'

Turning off the lights about the house – except for the lamp she always left on in the foyer when she was alone – Diane went into the master bedroom. For a little while the house had ricocheted with heated voices. Now there was a morbid silence.

With Joan's admonition in her head, she reached for her bedside clock, set the alarm for 6 a.m. Now she remembered she was to call Elaine, ask for the name of the attorney who'd handled her last divorce. Set her own divorce in motion.

She sat at the edge of the king-sized bed – remembering all the political moves she and Paul had plotted here. More politics than passion, she jibed at herself, and reached for the phone. It was late to call – but Elaine was a night owl.

Was Elaine in town in this rotten heat? she asked herself while she punched in Elaine's number. They hadn't spoken in almost two weeks. Elaine had talked then about heading soon for her lake house.

The phone rang half a dozen times. Diane was about to

hang up – expecting to get only the answering machine – when Elaine's ever-cheerful voice came to her.

'Hello—'

'Hi, I've got some weird news—' No need to identify herself. 'Our current Congressman from this district is making waves.'

'Darling, I've never been a fan of your Congressman husband,' Elaine drawled. 'What did that fugitive from a B-grade movie pull off now?'

'He's jumping the fence – both from political party and wife—' Diane's voice was casual, betrayed nothing of her inner turmoil. But Elaine would know what initial havoc this must have caused.

'So you're divorcing him.' Elaine was cool. 'Good riddance. You'll have to start circulating. I can—'

'Elaine, he's divorcing me. At my suggestion.' She chuckled at Elaine's grunt of incomprehension. 'Yes, he asked me for the divorce, but for professional reasons.' She amplified, 'I suggested he divorce me rather than the other way round.' A lilt in her voice now. 'That'll cost him women's votes – big time.'

'Baby, you're thinking like a shrewd politician,' Elaine crowed. 'That's good.'

'I need the name of your lawyer – the one who handled your second divorce. Via the U.S. Territory of Guam.'

'I'll give it to you with pleasure,' Elaine purred. 'We'll have a dinner party the day the divorce becomes final.'

'If I'm not all tied up,' Diane hedged. 'We'll be working our butts off with a Special Primary. We have to find a replacement candidate. And when we do,' she pushed, 'I'll expect you to host a fund-raiser for the new candidate.'

'How can I say no to you?'

Off the phone, Diane ordered herself to bed. Knowing sleep would be elusive. She tossed about restlessly, seeking a position conducive to sleep. Her mind overactive despite the hour.

Now she explored her feelings with ruthless candor. Was she ever – in truth – in love with Paul? She'd met him at a painfully vulnerable moment in her life. She was lonely. Her self-confidence at low ebb. He made her feel safe. Important to him. She'd been flattered that he ignored other women, pursued her. Though hardly a great brain, he was ambitious – and he saw her as his winning lottery ticket. She was at the top of their class, on the *Law Review*. She and Joan had fought for him as class president in their senior year – and he won.

With her law-school record she should have gone after a job as a clerk in the office of some top judge, she reproached herself. But that wasn't what she'd wanted. Now Larry Grant's words drifted across her mind:

'*We won't be silent. We'll fight for what's right for everybody. That's what makes this country work.*'

From her freshman year in high school she'd harbored a passion for what her father had derided as 'liberal-mania.' Watching vivid TV reports of unspeakable horrors inflicted on helpless humans about the world, she'd cried. She yearned to be part of making the world a better place in which to live. Her parents had expected her to outgrow this yearning. She hadn't.

At last she fell into troubled sleep, awoke four hours later when her alarm clock shrieked its message. She lay back against the pillows and plotted the day ahead. Larry Grant would be over at 7.30 to block out the interview. Everything must go right. The party must rally support for their new candidate whoever she – or he – might be.

Call Fran Logan around 9 a.m. – she'd be up and running by then. It was too much to expect an immediate answer from her about becoming a candidate, replacing Paul – but let her know the party would be behind her in full strength. That she herself was prepared to fight for their new candidate as she'd fought for Paul. Fran would understand they needed a fast answer.

All at once she felt a flicker of excitement. What about this morning's *Enquirer*? Why was she lying in bed this way? The *Enquirer* must have arrived by now.

She tossed aside the sheet, slid her feet into slippers and – in brief nightie – darted from bedroom to front door. With a hasty glance about to be sure she was unobserved, she opened the door, reached for the *Enquirer*. She scanned the headline as she walked back into the house. Her heart began to pound.

'PAUL SOMERS BOLTS PARTY AND WIFE.'

Larry's article appeared center front page – below a large photograph of Paul and her, taken right after the announcement that he'd won the last election. *God, I look awful. Elaine's right – I need to do something with my hair.*

She read Larry's article with relish. It was great, she told herself with soaring approval. He presented Paul as a scumbag who'd walked out on party and wife because of greedy self-interest. *True.* Every television and radio news program in the country would carry the word.

She hoped – brushed by guilt – that the original candidate had been briefed before Larry's report in the *Enquirer* mushroomed across the country. Paul might represent a district in a small, lightly populated state – but this was the kind of news that captured national attention.

Heady with satisfaction, she rushed to prepare for the day. Wait a bit to call Joan – she'd be commuting from apartment to campaign headquarters. With a hot spray of water pounding her back, she sorted out in her mind just what she meant to convey in the coming television interview.

Larry Grant would be an excellent interviewer, she surmised. He was sharp, exuded charisma. He'd be passionate about any cause he espoused – and he loathed the direction the country was taking.

Somehow, she told herself, the party must bring him into the fold. His causes were the right causes. At the moment he seemed at loose ends, she evaluated. He'd fought in Iraq, had been wounded. He needed time to get his act together.

Was he married or living with someone? Not likely, she surmised – here in Linwood he was living in a studio apartment in his sister's house.

Out of the shower, she debated about what to wear. Elaine scolded her about her generic wardrobe. In truth, she loved smart clothes – but when did she have time – or money – to indulge herself in this? The temperature was soaring, she noted – but the studio would be air-conditioned. Comfortable. She could wear her one smart outfit. The Oscar de la Renta pantsuit.

Public places were air-conditioned to accommodate men in business suits – which was why many women carried a shawl or light jacket when dining out. She'd carry the jacket except on camera. The TV station would have somebody to deal with the proper makeup.

At a few minutes past 7 a.m. she phoned campaign headquarters – guessing Joan would be there.

'Campaign headquarters,' Joan's blithe voice came to her on the first ring. 'Good morning.'

'Have you seen the *Enquirer*?'

'Wow! That'll send shock waves all over. I just this minute taped the front page of the *Enquirer* on one of our windows. Later – when somebody shows up so that I can send out for another copy – I'll tape the article on the other window.'

'Good deal. Larry and I will discuss it – at much length,' she stipulated in satisfaction, 'during our interview.' She hesitated. 'Should I offer to serve Larry breakfast along with coffee when he arrives – ' she checked her watch – 'in about eighteen minutes?'

'Absolutely,' Joan said. 'If it was me, I'd offer him a slight detour – into my bedroom.'

'You talk a lot.' Diane brushed this off with a chuckle.

'It's this damn business – it's doing terrible things to my sex life. But—' Joan's voice was reminiscently blissful, 'I've had my moments. Just nothing that was right on a regular basis. Why are the men that I like most the ones who're dodging commitments?'

'Larry Grant's single,' Diane pointed out. 'Unless he's hiding a bride somewhere in Iraq.'

'He likes you. He felt an instant connection with you. And don't tell me you didn't feel it, too.' Triumph in Joan's voice.

'Now you're a matchmaker?' Diane derided. 'He was just after a great story.' But for a minute there – when she'd told Larry about the divorce and he said, 'He's more stupid than I thought,' she'd felt a flicker of arousal. But he'd been thinking of Paul's political loss. 'Larry Grant can be useful to the campaign.' She struggled to sound professional. 'We've got to figure out how we can bring him into the fold.'

But not into her personal life, Diane warned herself. She knew about the rebound scene. *Not for me. There's no room in my life for a man on a personal level. Don't forget that.*

Eleven

En route to the kitchen, Diane adjusted the CAC thermostat to a lower temperature. Just this morning – in deference to their interview. The way the cost of oil was soaring, everybody except the super-rich was watching energy bills. But she suspected Larry would be wearing a suit. Let the house be comfortably cool.

In the kitchen – conscious of the passage of time – she rushed to put up the coffeemaker, to prepare the waffle mix. Glad she had ground extra coffee beans yesterday. Be ready to serve breakfast immediately if Larry accepted the offer.

Strawberries in the fridge, she recalled. Top the waffles with a mound of sliced strawberries. That was quick and easy. She'd be lazy, leave the waffle iron to be cleaned later.

In minutes the kitchen and adjoining breakfast area were permeated by the savory aroma of coffee brewing. She inspected the wall clock in the breakfast room. It was 7.28 a.m. At the same moment she heard the door chimes sending their melodious message. Why did people always say women were forever late? That applied just as much to men. But not to Larry Grant.

'Good morning—' She greeted him with a dazzling smile. He wore a suit – no tie. A popular rebellion these days. 'I assume you've seen this morning's *Enquirer*?'

'Moments after the newsboy threw it on to the front desk,' he said, striding into the foyer. 'Have you heard the radio or TV morning news yet?' he challenged.

'No,' she admitted. *Does Paul realize what's happening? Somebody from the local Republican campaign office – if anyone is awake this early – must have called him. Wow!* 'I was too busy gloating about the front page of the *Enquirer*.'

'Where's your radio?'

'There's one in the kitchen. I'm sure you're ready for coffee.

What about waffles to go with it?' *Be casual – don't make a
big deal of it.*

He grinned. 'Great. I didn't bother with breakfast—'

In the kitchen he went straight to the radio, fiddled with
the dials. A hyper-masculine voice invaded the room.

'No less than a bombshell . . . the whole district will be
reeling as people awaken—'

Larry dropped into one of the pair of comfortable captain's
chairs that flanked the small table in the breakfast area. His
eyes fastened to the radio – as though trying to visualize the
scene the newscaster was describing. Diane poured batter into
the waffle iron. She, too, was fascinated by the 'breaking news.'

In Rowena Collins's huge, multi-slidered, all-white master
bedroom, Paul sprawled on his face across her king-sized bed.
She lay in fetal position at the far side. Both uttered low
sounds of reproach as a bedside phone burst shrilly into the
early morning silence.

'Paul, pick up,' Ronnie mumbled. 'The phone's on your
side of the bed.'

'Who the hell's calling at this hour of the morning?' But
he picked up. 'Hello—'

'Paul?' A surprised voice. Addison Collins' voice.

'Yes, sir—' All at once he was wide awake. 'I had trouble
with the car,' he improvised, stumbling for words. 'Ronnie
invited me to—'

'You ass!' Addison yelled and Paul pulled the receiver from
his ear for a moment. 'What the hell happened with you and
your wife?'

'I told her I was leaving the party. I—'

'Have you heard the news?' Addison broke in. 'The whole
deal is splashed all over the newspapers back in Linwood. It's
being picked up by all the news services. It's on the radio and
TV news. We didn't want the story to break for a couple of
weeks! This makes us look bad to our constituents!'

'Diane swore she wouldn't say a word—' Now Paul was
the outraged husband. 'The little bitch is using me!'

'Get your butt to my office within the next hour,' Addison
barked. 'We're having an emergency meeting. We can handle
this,' he conceded grimly, 'but the party isn't happy.'

*   *   *

Over waffles and coffee, Diane and Larry labored over what was to be said in the TV interview. The questions he would ask.

'You don't want to play the distraught wife,' he warned, and grinned. There was nothing distraught about Diane this morning. 'Injured, yes – but you can handle it. Play up your shock that he could be a traitor to the party.'

'And stress the party's urgent need for campaign funds,' she added. 'Outline the horrors that could befall this district if the Republicans have their way. I have all the facts and figures memorized. So much at stake – and our candidate's voice on an important issue before Congress could be the deciding vote.' Her face aglow with zeal. 'That's to bring in money from outside the district.'

'Bill Taylor told me a rumor's floating around that the Hall-Stores people have been nosing about town. At least, their plane was sizing up the area a couple of days ago.' Larry shook his head in contempt. 'That's bad news.'

Diane gaped in disbelief. 'They're trying again to move into Linwood?' She was indignant. 'They came into town seven years ago – when Paul was on the Town Council. We fought to keep them out and won.' She frowned in recall. 'But seven years ago we had less registered Republicans in the district than now.'

'Bill said that if they try to open up here, the *Enquirer* will fight to keep them out—' Larry paused. His eyes searched hers. 'How does the party feel about that?'

'We don't want them in this town.' Her voice deepened in defiance. 'They'll kill off local businesses, hire people at low wages, little benefits. Most of them part-timers – with no benefits. We've seen it happen all over this country.'

'We hear about other towns who're keeping them out,' Larry reminded. 'You said Linwood did it seven years ago. Why can't Linwood do it again?' he challenged. 'If enough people get behind it—'

'I'll talk with Bill Taylor about this. If it's true, let's get the ball rolling quick—' Diane exuded determination. In a corner of her mind she remembered hearing that it was routine for Hall-Stores to survey an area by air before going into action.

'Right now, too often big business rules. It's up to people

like us – average Americans, in small towns and in big cities – to change that. We can't just sit back and ignore the facts.' Larry sighed in frustration. 'We've got to make people realize the power of their votes. It's shocking – the number of would-be voters who don't bother to go to the polls.'

'They don't realize it's both a privilege and an obligation. That what happens in elections can change our lives.' Diane debated inwardly for an instant, made an impulsive decision. *The committee will go along with me.* 'I'm sure the district's Democratic committee would like to have you on our team. We'll have to work out something to offer you—' She was groping for words. *Am I taking on too much?* 'Would you be interested?'

'You bet.' He radiated enthusiasm. 'But right now,' he cautioned, 'let's focus on the TV interview.'

Diane glanced at the wall clock. They'd been battering away at this for an hour and a half. It was just past 9 a.m. They'd have to leave for the TV station in a few minutes. 'Let me phone Fran Logan – she's probably awake now.'

'Oh?' Larry raised an eyebrow in query. 'Party business?'

Now she realized he was unaware of what had occurred at last night's emergency meeting. It was all right to brief him – he was going to work with them. Unless she'd spoken too impulsively. 'The Committee would like her to run against Paul. We see Fran Logan as a strong contender. She's a passionate crusader – she's what this district needs in Congress. Of course, she has to win in the Special Primary.' But the party would be behind her.

'What's her background?' Larry asked. 'Can she win?' For all his laid-back attitude, Diane thought, he went straight for the jugular.

Diane summed up Fran's background in a few words, then pounced on a new angle. 'Fran will make fighting against Hall-Stores a campaign promise. Her brother and sister-in-law run a popular local hardware store. I'll warn her about this new possible invasion. She knows what Hall-Stores does to small businesses.'

'Have her talk with Bill Taylor, work with him,' Larry advised. 'If she agrees to run. But let's get this ball rolling.'

Diane reached for the cordless phone that hung in its nest beside the breakfast table. She'd found Fran's home number in her address book last night, scribbled it on the memo pad that was fastened to the refrigerator. Now she sought out the number, called Fran.

'Hello—' Fran's always upbeat voice.

'Fran, this is Diane Somers. Have you seen this morning's *Enquirer* – or heard the radio or TV news?'

'Oh, wow!' Fran's voice was electric. 'I couldn't believe it! It's rotten.' Her voice softened. 'But for you, Diane, it's good riddance. You don't need a man like that.'

'True. And it'll cost Paul votes,' Diane pointed out.

'Has the committee come up with a replacement candidate yet – or is it too early?' Fran was solicitous.

'We figure we can rush through a Special Primary in about two weeks.' Diane strived to appear cool. 'Of course, the Primary will make the final selection – but the committee is prepared to back you if you're willing to run.' She heard the startled gasp at the other end.

'Di, am I hearing you right?' Fran was startled, elated – in shock.

'The committee is prepared to fight for you.' Diane's heart was pounding. Fran was their best bet. 'It'll be my major assignment to promote you.'

'I should discuss it first with Brad—' Fran was ambivalent – for a moment. 'But I know what my husband will say,' she decided in joyous decision. 'We've talked about my running for a seat in the House in about six or eight years. I don't know if I can draw enough votes to pull it off,' she conceded. 'But yes, I'll be thrilled to run against Paul!'

'Great.' Diane felt a surge of adrenaline. 'Oh, a bulletin. Remember when Hall-Stores tried to move into town? Well, we hear they may be at it again.'

'We'll fight them every inch of the way!' Fran was outraged. 'They'd wreck our local economy—'

Larry's face lighted up when Diane switched off the cordless. 'She agreed to run?'

'She'll run,' Diane confirmed. 'Now we must dig up the votes to put her across the finish line.' Plus the money to plug her as a winning candidate.

'Obstacle Course One,' Larry pointed out. 'Can she finish first in the Special Primary?'

Twelve

In Addison Collins's palatial suite in one of Washington D.C.'s most prestigious office buildings, Paul Somers sat with a shaky air of bravado as the half-dozen expensively suited men debated about how to handle the bombshell attack of the morning.

'Paul, you don't talk without being scripted,' Jason Kerrigan – a high-level party member – exhorted. 'We screen reporters who attend your next press briefing – ' he glanced at his watch – 'which will be in about three hours. We give them a list of questions they may ask. You'll know how to respond.'

'You expect them to observe that?' Another member of the group was skeptical. 'This isn't the Bush White House.'

'They'll observe it.' Kerrigan was crisp. 'They know if they don't, they'll be barred from all of our press conferences – all the way to the top,' he added significantly.

'Paul, go to another room with Gerald—' Addison instructed. His staff assistant, who was standing by. 'You make damn sure you memorize the script. Gerald will coach you.'

'Sure.' Paul managed to exude a confidence he didn't feel. The damn press conference was being televised! He liked talking to groups of chosen voters – basking in their admiration. He hated reporters. Always trying to throw him off base.

'Play up your "man of the people" image,' Kerrigan picked up. 'You're one of them, fighting for their causes.'

'You handle that well,' Addison emphasized. 'Use it. Make them believe every word you say.'

'Yes, sir,' Paul agreed. The old confidence rising to the surface. He wouldn't let that little bitch Diane wreck his career. How could she, when he had the whole party behind him? They saw him as the heir to the Ronnie and Bush II votes. Another 'man of the people.' 'I'll play it up big, sir.'

'All right.' Addison Collins was brusque now. 'Paul, go with

Gerald.' He turned to the others about the conference table. 'Let's go into the screening room. Our people in Linwood taped Diane's local TV interview at ten a.m. They had a private jet standing by to fly the tape to me. Let's see how much damage she's done to us.' He allowed himself a smug smile. 'She wants to play dirty, that's fine with us. When we get through with her and the opposition, they'll be toast.'

Diane and Larry sat with Joan in the one truly private room in campaign headquarters – normally used only for high-level conferences. Diane warned herself the high she felt was temporary. They faced a rough road ahead. But the atmosphere when she and Larry had walked into headquarters had been exhilarating. The whole staff had leapt to their feet and applauded. The TV interview had gone well.

'I need to bring the finished copy of our *Enquirer* interview to Bill Taylor first thing tomorrow morning,' Larry reminded Diane in low tones because Joan was on a conference call with Clark Jackson and Liz Franken. 'Are you clear to work with me this afternoon?'

'We'll have lunch and move right to it,' Diane promised. She glanced up with a smile when Robin, their enthusiastic all-round administrative assistant, hurried into the room with sandwiches and coffee from the restaurant next door.

'Alice said they turned on the TV set there, and everybody watched the whole interview. Only one creep complained,' Robin reported.

Diane and Larry reached eagerly for the sandwiches and coffee. Joan completed her conference call to join them.

'Everybody seems happy that Fran Logan's joining the fold,' Joan reported. 'We'll start sending out press releases right away.'

'You checked it out with her?' Diane probed. 'It's now official?'

'Oh, sure, I called back to confirm,' Joan soothed. 'She faxed me back, so it's on record.' She frowned in irritation. 'Oh, hell, I didn't get a chance to tell you. Our great publicist – sans retainer,' she admitted drily, 'called to resign as of immediately. She's been offered a job with an agency in New York.'

'Now she leaves?' Diane was upset – for a moment. With

a brilliant smile she turned to Larry. 'You've worked in public relations. You can handle press releases—'

'Sure—' He waited for follow-up. Wary. *He's not about to be a volunteer. He can't afford it.*

'I can't guarantee until the committee approves, but would you consider joining the team as staff writer and publicist? Our budget is low,' she warned, her eyes apologetic but hopeful. 'I can come up with a figure by tomorrow morning—'

'Let's talk tomorrow morning—' He chuckled. 'I'm at loose ends. My expenses are low. I'm living rent free. And I'm spoiling for a real fight. But for right now, I'll get on to the press releases.'

With a light knock to proceed her, Jill opened the door. A cordless phone in hand.

'There's a call,' she said. A glint of curiosity in her eyes. 'For Larry—'

'I said to buzz me here if I wasn't home,' he explained, reaching for the phone. 'This guy from the TV station—' He focused now on his call. 'Hi, Larry Grant here.' He listened intently for a few moments while the others watched. Jill, too, lingered. 'Thanks, old boy. I owe you.'

'A mole at the TV station?' Joan asked, exchanging a loaded glance with Diane.

'This cameraman,' Larry explained. 'Hal Watson. He had a brother in Iraq – in my company—' Larry's face was unfamiliarly terse. 'We got hit by the same land mine. He didn't make it.' Larry took a deep breath. 'Hal and I talked a bit. He promised to clue me in if anything happened that would interest us. He says the opposition just tied up a deal to buy a lot of airtime. They're rushing through a bunch of TV commercials backing Paul Somers.'

'We should have expected that,' Diane shrugged it off. But she was unhappy.

'We're having a replay of the interview twice this evening,' Larry chortled. 'That's stronger than a dozen thirty-second commercials.'

'We'll talk to the committee about approving commercials for Fran Logan. It'll make a dent in the budget – but necessary.' Joan turned to Diane. 'Let's do it quick,' she stressed. 'I'll tell Fran to stand by.'

'What about the local radio station?' Larry asked.

'What about it?' But Diane's mind was juggling figures in her head. TV time cost big – but between now and the date of the Special Primary they needed to saturate both TV and radio.

'Push the radio people to focus on the TV interview in their news briefs,' Larry prodded. 'Alert listeners to the reruns this evening.'

'We might manage a quickie—' Joan sounded doubtful. 'The local radio station is not on our side of the fence. They've given me a rough time in the past.'

'Offer them an interview with an American soldier just returned from Iraq – recovering from wounds,' Diane suggested.

'Wait a minute—' Larry held up a hand, frowned in concentration. 'Isn't the local radio station owned by a guy named Alex Thompson?'

'Right—' Diane's mind zeroed in on this. 'The real-estate mogul.'

'Then it's no deal.' Larry was terse. 'From what Andrea – my sister – tells me, he's a rabid conservative Republican.'

'Right—' Diane grunted in distaste.

'Andrea's had a running battle with him about the tiny abortion clinic in town. She's a social worker,' he explained. 'She steered a fourteen-year-old girl abused by her father and pregnant by him to the clinic. Thompson tried to get her fired from her job.'

'But he doesn't know you,' Joan objected.

'He knows me,' Larry admitted. 'I wrote a nasty "Letter to the Editor" from Baghdad – which the *Enquirer* published on the front page. Thompson responded – mad as hell.' He chuckled. 'That was my "in" to Bill Taylor.'

'The radio station will be plugging Paul from now till election day,' Diane surmised, 'but the station can't turn down cold cash if we buy airtime for commercials.'

'What dirt do you have on Paul?' Larry asked. Diane gaped at him in shock. 'I mean, if he starts talking low down and dirty, let's be prepared.'

Diane was startled. 'I'm not running for office!'

'He needs to clear himself of the charge of throwing aside a wife of ten years. You can be damn sure he's going to try to push your face in the dirt. He – or whoever's calling the shots for him – will want to win back women voters.' Larry's face was compassionate. 'But it won't last long – he'll want to move on to more vital problems.'

'If Fran Logan comes out ahead in the Special Primary – and with any luck at all we can handle that – we'll be in a good position. They won't be able to dig up dirt on Fran. She was born and raised in this town – without a spot on her record. A bright young lawyer, married to a popular pediatrician. A solid marriage,' she emphasized.

'Diane, don't be naive,' Larry scolded. 'They'll manufacture dirt. We see that all the time. Look what they did to John Kerry with those "Swift Boat" lies. But let's put it on a back burner. We've got to do an interview for Sunday's *Enquirer.*'

The setting sun dropped a rosy glow over the oceanfront Southampton estate built twenty-seven years ago by Carl Somers – Paul's father. The beach deserted at this hour except for a pair of exuberant Labrador retrievers darting in and out of the blue Atlantic. A serene seascape that Carl called his refuge from the insanity of Washington.

Carl liked to boast that his two-acre oceanfront estate was worth four times what it had cost him to build. The spectacular mahogany-decked Mediterranean-style manor contained six bedrooms, seven bathrooms, an exercise room, a magnificent living room, a formal dining room, and an eat-in kitchen plus a breakfast room. It had been built closer to the ocean than town zoning would permit at the present time.

Ten years ago – when he left Congress to form his prestigious lobbying firm – Carl had added a wing to be used as his office when in Southampton. Now he stood by a window wall and gazed out at the spectacular view of waves crashing against the white sandy beach. Appearing to ignore the tableau being performed a few feet away.

Two hours ago his private jet had flown what he liked to call 'my team' – along with Paul – from Washington to Southampton. Here at regular intervals he and his wife Cora entertained clients of his lobbying firm. At critical moments he summoned his 'team' here for embattled conferences.

Paul knew his father wasn't missing a word of what was transpiring now. He knew and he was sweating – despite the central air-conditioning. The hastily called press conference in D.C. earlier today had been a disaster. Only a handful of reporters had bothered to appear. Gerald and his crew hadn't pulled their usual stuff. The damn reporters threw embarrassing questions at him.

It would be OK, though, Paul told himself in a surge of defiance. Right away Dad had gone into action, called his top team together, flown everybody out here. His lobbying firm's high-salaried publicists had gone into action, set up a last-minute cable TV appearance. Tomorrow at 6 p.m. He'd be prepared this time. No goof-ups.

'Paul, you can't afford to screw up this television interview tomorrow,' Kerrigan warned. An unspoken reference to the badly attended Washington press conference – where he'd floundered like a petulant schoolboy called up before his principal. 'When you go into that TV studio, everything must go the way we're working it out.'

'I'll handle it,' Paul said with a confidence he didn't feel. Still, this was a great start to the new campaign, he told himself. A television interview on cable TV. He'd be getting national coverage. Heady stuff.

'We open with the grand reconciliation scene between you and your father,' Gerald – his father's special assistant – picked up. 'Be warm, touched by this poignant moment. Make the viewers feel how much this means to you.'

'A tear or two in your eyes wouldn't hurt,' another member of the group contributed. 'You and your father were separated by party – and this was painful for both of you. Very emotional. Every prospective voter out there must feel for you.'

'That'll lead into your explaining how you came to return to the fold,' Gerald continued. 'The big embrace with your dad – the way you've rehearsed – then you talk about your disillusionment with your former party—'

'I got it—' Paul nodded. Fighting impatience.

'Then comes the business where you win over any women voters who might be upset about your divorcing your wife of ten years,' Kerrigan added. 'That could be a lot of votes.'

'It was a heartbreaking decision,' Paul parroted, turning on the histrionics. 'I love my wife – I thought she loved me. But she was a party girl – she liked big-time nightlife. I like to be asleep by nine thirty p.m. – so I can wake up at five a.m., fresh and ready to fight for what I believe is right for my constituents. I had to choose between my wife and the people I'd sworn to serve. I—'

'Focus on that attitude,' Carl approved. 'Let's go through the whole action again. Be real,' he exhorted Paul. 'Make the people out there believe every word you say. Make them see your wife – soon to be your ex-wife – as a woman who was determined to come between you and the dedication you feel to the people of your district.'

'We've been through it four times, Dad.' *Why is the old man such a tyrant? Enough is enough.*

'We'll go through it four more times!' Carl yelled. 'Damn it, do you want to win this election?' His eyes clashed with Paul's. Paul lowered his eyes, took a deep breath.

'OK, let's rehearse.' Paul exuded fresh determination.

I'll win this election, damn it. I have the whole party machine behind me. What chance do Diane and her creeps have against us?

Thirteen

Diane spent a heated hour on a conference call with members of the committee this Thursday morning. She emerged with a deal she felt confident Larry would accept. He'd be an asset. And they needed all the help they could muster.

'Diane, have you heard?' Jill – exuding excitement – hovered at the entrance to her cubicle.

Diane swung around to face her. 'Heard what?'

'Paul's scheduled for a six p.m. interview on cable TV. "To explain his switch in parties," ' Jill quoted with vitriolic sarcasm. 'It's being plugged on the morning news.'

'We'll watch,' Diane decreed. The powers-that-be had decided he had to try to cover his ass. 'The opposition's first shot.' Paul had left a message on her answering machine yesterday – at a time he knew she wouldn't be home. He'd spoken with Elaine's attorney. The divorce was on schedule. Good. 'What about the Hall-Stores deal?' Concentrate on something more important. 'Could you dig up any more information?'

'I just discovered that the zoning board is holding a special meeting tonight.' A triumphant glint in Jill's eyes. 'Very hush-hush. Two officials from Hall-Stores will be there,' she added with a significant smile.

'The Hall-Stores characters are here in Linwood?'

'You said their plane was seen flying over town,' Jill reminded. 'So I checked with hotel reservation clerks.' *Nice to have them on our side.* 'The Hall-Stores guys checked in at the Palace Hotel about twenty minutes ago. Like I said, it's all hush-hush.'

'Not for long,' Diane promised and reached for her phone. She punched in Fran Logan's office number. They needed to get word in the *Enquirer* quickly that Fran was about to toss her hat into the ring. That she would run in the Special Primary. And Fran must take a stand against the proposed invasion of a Hall-Stores superstore. That would be a major local issue.

'Good morning,' a cheery feminine voice chirped. 'The law office of Fran Logan.'

'Sheila, this is Diane Somers. Is Fran in the office?'

'One minute,' Sheila said.

'Hi, Diane—' Fran's voice came over the line. 'Something up? Am I still your favorite candidate?'

'Honey, you're it,' Diane reassured her with warmth. 'I need to brief you about the town zoning board. The word is there's a special meeting this evening, and,' she stressed, 'two Hall-Stores officials checked into the Palace Hotel a little while ago. I suspect Hall-Stores's off and running again.'

'Not good—' Fran was suddenly somber. 'I have to leave for a real-estate closing in about ten minutes, but I'll rush right back to the office. I'll call Bill Taylor, suggest a blistering article for the *Enquirer* about Hall-Stores trying to move in again.' She took a deep, audible breath. 'My brother and sister-in-law will be real pissed. They figure they'd go under in about a year if Hall-Stores ever comes into town. Throwing eight employees out of work.'

'We must keep Hall-Stores out of this area.' Diane's mind was charging ahead. 'They're bad news. Oh, Fran, we have a new publicist joining the team—' *Larry won't turn down the deal. We're facing the kind of battle he relishes.* 'He's just back from serving in Iraq and spoiling for a fight. What about my sending him over to work with you on the article – and maybe on follow-up? That's a strong issue for you—'

'That'll be great. I should be back in the office by two o'clock – if that's OK with him.'

'I'll have him buzz you. His name's Larry Grant. He has a public-relations background.' Among other fields. *Am I jumping too fast? Joan's always warning me about acting on impulse.*

Off the phone, Diane's mind strayed into personal problems. The first of the month was uncomfortably close. She had that huge mortgage payment to meet – plus all the other household expenses. She had her half of their joint checking account balance – a piddling amount. She'd cashed the check already. That would be a meager help. Thank God, she was on salary now at campaign headquarters. A very modest salary. But Joan managed. So would she.

With an unnerving jolt she realized she'd be losing her health insurance as of August 1st. Tuesday. Damn, she'd better stay healthy! She felt a recurrent surge of frustration. How could a country like this deny its people the security of health insurance? Millions of Americans lived in dread of some illness. Now she was one of them.

Stop griping, she ordered herself. Focus on the work at hand. When the hell was Larry coming in? She needed to know he was set for their team. She was working on the premise that he would accept their offer.

Now sounds beyond her cubicle caught her attention. Larry was here. Kibitzing with their volunteers. People reacted well to him, she told herself in approval. Yes, he'd be an asset to the party.

Joan's remark about him filtered unwarily into her mind: *'He likes you. He felt an instant connection. You two are a lot alike. And don't tell me you didn't feel it, too.'*

Joan was such a romantic at heart. But she wasn't about to fall into a rebound relationship, Diane promised herself. Even though she was conscious of Larry's disconcerting way of gazing at her at odd moments. He'd be passionate yet tender, she thought unwarily.

'Hi—' Larry smiled down at her from the entrance to her cubicle. With *that* look. *He's probably used it hundreds of times. But I'm not some impressionable twenty-something.*

'Hi.' *Be cool. I want him on the team. Not in my life.* 'Sit down,' she said briskly. 'I've worked out a deal I think you'll find acceptable. Remembering,' she stipulated, 'that we don't have a Republican-style budget.'

Diane outlined what the committee had approved, what they expected of him.

'That's the deal,' she wound up. 'Are you in?'

'I'm in.' His eyes were serious. 'I'm not sure we can win – in this era where elections are too often bought – but we'll put up one hell of a fight.'

'We can win,' Diane defied him. 'We've got the Power Upstairs on our side.'

Their eyes carried on a momentary conversation far removed from politics, then Diane glanced away – as though checking on voices beyond. *Why am I feeling this way? I'm reacting to the divorce – I feel rejected.*

'I've talked with Fran Logan this morning.' She was crisp, impersonal now. 'If you have no conflict, be at her office at two this afternoon. She needs help on an article about Hall-Stores to go to the *Enquirer*.' She sighed. 'It seems Hall-Stores is off and running again. The zoning board is holding a special meeting this evening – to talk with them.'

'What's the situation with the zoning board? Are they apt to cave?'

'We kept Hall-Stores out seven years ago when the Town Council passed a ruling that nothing larger than thirty thousand square feet could be constructed within the city limits. Their minimum seems to be about a hundred thousand square feet.'

'So they'll be looking to change the zoning rules—'

'They didn't make it last time – but then we put up a furious fight.' Diane was uncomfortable with this new effort. 'I suspect they wouldn't be making this second effort if they didn't have some hidden agenda.' She forced a smile. 'But get together with Fran Logan – she'll be expecting to hear from you.'

He was contemplative for a moment. 'We're announcing our support for Logan right away?'

'No need to delay it.' Her voice was a challenge.

'It might have more strength to delay until other candidates announce,' he suggested. 'Top them with Logan and what she has to offer.'

'Point taken,' she agreed. *He's right.* 'But get together with Fran – the article about Hall-Stores should hit the *Enquirer* tomorrow morning. Bill will run it. We'll hold up her announcing her entry into the Special Primary.'

'You've heard about Paul Somers being interviewed on cable TV today?'

'At six p.m.' Diane was conscious of a tic in one eyelid. Stress. 'We'll all be watching.'

At minutes before 6 p.m. – with the switch in shifts at campaign headquarters lending a spurious air of emptiness – Diane and Joan sat before the huge TV set. Sound muted. Waiting for Paul to appear.

Larry strode into headquarters, back to the TV area.

'News,' he reported. 'Tomorrow's *Evening News* will carry word that Alex Thompson is entering the Special Primary.' His face was eloquent. 'Now the richest guy in the state wants to be a Congressman.'

Diane was astonished. 'He's a Republican.' Somebody else jumping parties?

'Why would Thompson run?' Joan was suspicious. 'His big deal is real estate. He's never held any public office. Why run for office now?' she asked again. 'And what does he have to offer?'

'Unlimited campaign funds,' Diane pointed out drily.

'With no political background – no war record – he's trying for a seat in the House?' Larry was skeptical. 'What's he trying to promote?'

'Most of the time he keeps a low profile—' Diane gestured in confusion.

'You described him before as a real-estate mogul,' Larry recalled. 'Has he got some major project he wants to promote? A political campaign would give him a pulpit. Maybe he doesn't give a damn about winning – he just wants public exposure.'

'I heard somewhere that he owns that huge stretch of vacant land at the edge of town – across from the Linwood Mall.' Diane's eyes held Larry's in mutual comprehension.

'Where Hall-Stores would like to build,' Larry pounced. 'They always like to be at the outer limits.'

'Thompson doesn't care about winning the Primary,' Diane pinpointed. 'He'll use the campaign to promote what Hall-Stores can do for this town – as he sees it. He'll claim it's to the town's advantage to have Hall-Stores here. More jobs, more sales taxes, huge new property taxes. Never mind the damage—'

'I can't believe Thompson's jumping into the Special Primary just because he'll make a bundle on the land sale. Why is he praising Hall-Stores to the skies?' Larry's eyes moved from Diane to Joan.

'He holds a chunk of Hall-Stores stock?' Diane surmised.

'Let me ask Bill Taylor.' Larry reached for the phone. 'He's fourth generation in Linwood.'

'Put the call on speaker phone,' Joan urged.

The three of them waited impatiently until Bill Taylor was located.

'Bill Taylor—' His voice was brisk. 'What's up?'

'We're trying to put together a full picture of Alex Thompson,' Larry began.

'Everybody in town's talking,' Bill broke in. 'The brass of the bastard – to try to run for Congress with no qualifications!'

'Look what we've got in Washington these days,' Joan drawled.

'We heard rumors that he owns that large undeveloped acreage across from Linwood Mall – which would be an ideal locale for a Hall-Stores store.'

'That's right,' Bill confirmed. 'And he's got other interests in Hall-Stores. He's the richest man in this state because his father bought a chunk of Hall-Stores stock when the company went public back in 1972. The old man bought at five cents a share—'

'Wow!' Larry was awestruck. 'What's it worth today?'

'About fifty dollars a share. When Thompson's father died seven years ago, the stock was divided among the old man's three kids – including Alex. You can bet he wants to see that store open here in his own home town.'

'Any word leaking through to you about the zoning board's reaction to this Hall-Stores business?' Larry asked.

'They'd have to re-zone the area, of course. We beat it once—'

'Any difference this time?' Larry asked.

'Yeah.' Bill's tone was scathing. 'Hall-Stores will have more support in town this time. Our current Congressman is on their side.'

Diane sat upright. 'That's new!'

'Hey, I have to run,' Bill apologized, 'some problem with our computer line-up.'

'What was that last bit about?' Joan demanded.

'Bill says our current Congressman is on the side of Hall-Stores. He'll be pushing for them to open up here.' Larry shrugged. 'So shouldn't we have expected that? Big business sticks together.'

Jill rushed into view. 'Chow time,' she said with a flourish and smiled at Larry. 'You're included – Robin figured you'd show by now. Roast-turkey sandwiches, salads, and coffee. Come and get it.' She distributed paper plates, plastic cutlery, and napkins.

The three women and Larry huddled before the TV set. The atmosphere tense. The TV muted while they ate. The conversation caustic.

'After air-conditioning,' Diane declared, 'the best invention of all time is the mute button on the TV remote.'

'OK, here it comes—' Larry reached for the remote, switched off the mute button. Sound filled the room.

'My guest tonight,' the host intoned, 'is Congressman Paul Somers. We're also honored to have four-term former Congressman Carl Somers with us—'

Eating ceased. All eyes were glued to the TV screen.

'They're feeding us the whole enchilada,' Diane interpreted as they watched. Her face scornful. 'The great father–son reunion.'

'There should be a string section playing in the background,' Joan murmured while they watched the well-rehearsed encounter between Paul and his father. 'Something depressing, classical.'

'I made a horrific mistake,' Paul said, striving for an air of humility. 'I was rebelling against my dad. But I thank God that I've seen the light. I'm returning to home base. Stepping in to replace our fine candidate, who must withdraw because of illness in his family.' *Oh, sure! That must have taken a lot of arm-twisting.*

'We've heard rumors,' the cable TV interviewer began, almost apologetic, 'that you and your wife don't agree on this change in party. That you're on the point of divorce.' *He's been given a list of questions he can ask. It's typical White House policy.*

'It was a heartbreaking decision. We've been married for ten years. I love my wife – I thought she loved me.' Paul took a deep breath, as though in pain. *The bastard's been well coached!* 'But she's a party girl – she likes big-time nightlife. I have to choose between my wife and the people I've sworn to serve.'

'I like nightlife?' Diane hissed. 'I'll kill him!'

'Then the rumor about a divorce is true,' the interviewer pushed. His voice sympathetic.

'I'd hoped we could make adjustments – but there was no chance of that. It's sad. Very sad.' A break in Paul's voice – no doubt planned.

'Turn it off,' Diane ordered and snatched the remote from Joan's hand. The screen went black – just as the first of the night-time volunteers came into headquarters. 'I have to catch up with my nightlife.'

'Yeah,' Jill agreed, 'your second shift at campaign head-quarters.'

'Larry, reply to that travesty we just saw,' Diane snapped. 'Paul won't get away with that pack of lies.'

'It'll be smarter if you write a brief denial, to be published in the *Enquirer*,' Larry said gently. 'Shocked, hurt at such lies – and quote your night-time schedule for these past months.'

'Right,' Diane approved. 'I won't stoop to his level.' But her smile was devious. 'Not yet.'

Fourteen

Diane glanced at the wall clock. Past 10 p.m. – the last of the volunteers were leaving for the night. So sweet, so supportive, she thought, about her break-up with Paul. They were anxious about Paul's replacement as their Democratic candidate for Congress.

None of them knew that Fran would enter the Special Primary by the first of next week. Fran was well liked. Their best bet to win against Paul. Their major problem – to raise funds to fight a far stronger war chest.

Joan was switching off lights, Diane noted. Ever conscious of their tight budget – and with prices on everything rising. They ought to call it a night – it'd been a rough day. But Larry had said he'd pop in after his go-round with Bill at the *Enquirer*.

Every sound seemed magnified in the near-deserted campaign headquarters. The low lighting lent a ghostlike quality. Now Diane heard the staccato click of Joan's heels as she approached her cubicle.

Why did women – including Joan – punish themselves by shoving their feet into shoes with four-inch heels? Because high heels did great things for feminine legs, she derided. Men thought high heels were sexy.

'Enough already.' Joan hovered at the doorway, kicked off her shoes. 'My feet can't take any more of this. Let me rest up for a few minutes, then let's get out of here for the night—'

'Larry said he'd drop by after his session with Bill,' Diane reminded and stopped short. Larry was striding towards them now. 'Hi—' She managed a faint smile. 'Do we make tomorrow morning's *Enquirer*?'

Larry grinned. 'You knew Bill would pull something off the front page for your announcement. "CONGRESSMAN SOMERS' WIFE OF TEN YEARS STUNNED. SHOCKED

THAT STRANGERS KNEW BEFORE SHE DID ABOUT DIVORCE." He used a few obscene words to describe our Congressman. Oh, two more hopefuls are signing up for the Special Primary. I gather from Bill they won't be heavy hitters.'

'That's four now – not counting Fran Logan,' Joan summed up.

'We'll break Fran's entry in the Sunday newspapers – that's the day of their largest readerships,' Diane plotted. 'On Monday she'll make it official. You take it from there, Larry.'

'Right.'

Joan stifled a yawn. 'Let's close up for the night and get some sleep. We need to build ourselves into fighting trim.'

Diane drove home. In record time she was in bed but suspecting sleep would be slow in coming. She lay against a pair of pillows and stared into the darkness.

Why did she feel so shaken at her approaching divorce? Deep inside she'd known for a long time that their marriage was dead. But the career was vital, demanding. Exciting. Paul's career was her career. She harbored deep commitments that were meant to bear fruit through Paul's political role.

If Paul is re-elected, is that the end of the road for me? For Joan and me? Will we be just a pair of local lawyers handling real-estate closings, civil suits, and divorce cases? All these years have been for nothing?

She started at the jarring shriek of the telephone in the night silence. Elaine, she surmised, and reached to pick up.

'Hi, don't you ever sleep?' she jibed.

'I figured you'd be awake.' Elaine chuckled. 'I drove by – with my current male – at past ten, and the lights were still on at headquarters. What do you hear about the Guam divorce mill?'

'As far as I know, Paul's working with your lawyer. He's pissed, of course, that I broke the story ahead of their schedule. It wasn't supposed to be public news until after election day.'

'It's the best thing that ever happened to you. Now maybe you'll come out of the shadows and remember you're a woman. Divorce isn't the end of the line.' Elaine's voice softened. 'Darling, you aren't moping about joining the parade of divorced women? Statistics show that fifty per cent of marriages end in divorce.'

'I knew – almost from the beginning,' Diane admitted, 'that ours wasn't one of the great marriages. What we had going for us was the common goal. To be part of the public-service world.'

'Your goal,' Elaine corrected. 'Paul wanted to make a splash, show his old man he could match him professionally.'

'I know – most women settle for less than a perfect marriage.' Diane forced herself to be honest. 'Some women are scared of being out there on their own. Even in the twenty-first century.'

'My aunt Minnie has been married for forty-three years – and she and her husband haven't stopped bickering since their honeymoon. But they stay together because neither wants to be out there alone. It's kind of a self-inflicted prison sentence. And for other women – it's a job. They run the house, raise the kids, do volunteer work. And wrestle under the sheets with no real passion. Just part of the job.'

'Your parents weren't like that,' Diane reminded. 'Nor were mine.' Though, in truth, she suspected there'd been little passion in her parents' lives in her growing-up years. It was a comfortable arrangement.

'It's makeover time,' Elaine summed up. 'I've got this terrific hair stylist who'll—'

'Not just yet,' Diane interrupted. 'I've got a tough three-plus months ahead. I'll kill myself if we can't unseat Paul.' She managed a giggle. 'So I exaggerate. But I mean to put up one hell of a fight. No time for your terrific hair stylist who does great makeovers.'

By 8 a.m. Friday morning – as usual, already at campaign headquarters – Diane was on the phone with Fran.

'Larry will be at your office around ten a.m., with a photographer from the *Enquirer*. Bill wants photos to accompany the article about your signing up on Monday morning for the Special Primary. OK?'

'I'll be at my office by nine a.m. – I'll be there till noon. No problem,' Fran assured her.

'Wear something smart,' Diane urged.

'A pantsuit,' Fran decided. 'With a tailored blouse.' Her voice exuberant. *She'll be a strong candidate – telegenic, bright, fast on her feet.* 'And I'll hit hard on the Hall-Stores situation. You and I were both active in keeping them out on their last attempt,' she recalled.

'And we'll be there fighting again.'

'My brother and sister-in-law are working on bringing together a group of merchants to fight their coming into town.'

'Great!'

'Brad's college roommate's father had a large manufacturing outfit. Hall-Stores drove him out of business. They're so powerful – like Fascist dictators.' Fran's voice deepened in rage. 'They go into a supplier, demand to see their financial records—'

Diane was astounded. 'Suppliers go along with this?'

'Hall-Stores can make or break a supplier,' Fran reminded. 'Suppliers don't dare object. The Hall-Stores people squeeze them to drop their prices – or be frozen out. All Hall-Stores cares about is getting lower prices. Suppliers have to fire employees – and outsource – to make that happen. A lot of them are driven into bankruptcy.'

'Suppliers don't fight back?' Diane challenged.

'Fight Hall-Stores?' Fran scoffed. 'Brad says if they open up in this town, most of the small local businesses will be out within a year. And all those employees they've dumped will be buying nothing except bare essentials. Sales-tax revenues drop. Money is siphoned out of town. We see a flock of empty stores.'

'Hall-Stores's not unionized,' Diane remembered somberly. 'And I'll bet the turnover is high—'

'If a union approaches a store, Hall-Stores threatens to close it. Employees are scared to lose even their seven-dollars-an-hour jobs,' Fran said flatly. 'We don't want Hall-Stores here. We don't want their bargains, made by child labor working for pennies an hour!'

Diane's 'call waiting' was signaling her. 'Fran, hold on – I have another call coming in.' She signaled for the switch. 'Hello—'

'Di, it's me—' Larry was terse. 'My sister hates the *Evening News*, but she subscribes to be able to swear at it. I just saw last evening's edition. Alex Thompson took out a full-page ad – praising Hall-Stores like mad. Including – among other sugar-coated deals – their contribution of five million dollars to charity last year. Which means nothing to Hall-Stores,' Larry said through gritted teeth. 'A minuscule fraction of their billions in profits last year. Plus the latest – I hear they're running a series of commercials, with supposed employees expressing their delight with Hall-Stores as their boss.'

'Trying to polish their image,' Diane interpreted, feeling a cold shock wave. 'Alex Thompson's ad is meant to persuade the zoning board to change the code to allow Hall-Stores to open one of their monster stores in this town.'

'And there'll be members of the zoning board who'll swallow their garbage,' Larry suspected.

'Considering this business with Alex Thompson—'

'You know the plot,' Larry broke in. 'He'll spend a fortune trying to be the Democratic candidate – and if he gets in, he'll throw the election to Paul. Hall-Stores will come in – Thompson sells them his acreage at some astronomical price. Plus he foresees more profits from his stock.'

'Maybe we should push Fran to announce earlier—' Diane's mind was charging ahead. 'She'll be a diversion. Oh, I have her on hold,' Diane realized. 'Let me tell her about the ad and about shoving our schedule ahead—'

'It'll be a sharp move to have her announce earlier,' Larry approved. 'Tell her I'll be at her office by ten a.m. – with an *Enquirer* photographer. We'll move up her entrance into the Special Primary with a TV "news break" tomorrow morning. I'll work it out – and check with Bill about the change in schedule. People will be talking about Fran. Alex Thompson will fade into the background.'

'We'll have Fran issue a statement – the "news break" you'll deliver to the TV people early tomorrow morning,' Diane picked up.

'Follow up with a TV interview tomorrow evening – provided I can set it up,' Larry plotted. 'The Sunday *Enquirer* will wrap it up.'

'Go,' Diane urged. 'Now let me get back to Fran.' She pushed the proper button, spoke to Fran. 'I'm sorry – we've got a change in plan – but it's good.' She reported on Alex Thompson's ad in the *Evening News*, the change in timing.

'Sounds good,' Fran approved.

'Larry will be at your office at ten a.m. The *Enquirer* photographer will take some shots for the Sunday paper. Larry will work with you on the statement he'll deliver tomorrow morning to the local TV news desk, then try to set up an interview for you tomorrow evening. That should be a snap. Hopefully, Larry can set it for six p.m. – before people go out for Saturday dinner or whatever.'

'Great,' Fran approved.

'He and Joan will work with you on the interview – provided he can set it up, of course. Some time today – whatever fits in with your schedule.'

'Any time they choose,' Fran said. 'Everything else goes on hold. I think we should hit the Hall-Stores situation hard. My brother worked fourteen hours a day for years to get his business off and running. If Hall-Stores comes in, his business goes down the drain.'

'We've got two objectives. To keep Hall-Stores out of Linwood, and to stop Alex Thompson from winning the Special Primary and throwing the election to Paul.' Diane was grim. 'Over our dead bodies will that happen!'

Fifteen

Larry glanced at his watch. It was almost 5 p.m. He and Joan had huddled with Fran earlier in the day. Now he must take care of personal business, he told himself with a tender smile. Andrea had warned him – 'Be at the house no later than seven p.m.' For Claire's birthday dinner.

It was hard to believe Claire was nine years old today – and Joey almost seven. Where did all the time go? He remembered Claire as that tiny 'preemie' that they were all praying would survive.

Everything was under control on the campaign front. He'd deliver Fran's statement to the TV newspeople by 6.30 a.m. tomorrow morning – as promised. It would hit the 7 a.m. news. Her candidacy under wraps until then.

In the course of the next two hours he'd hear from the TV station about Fran's interview – which should be scheduled at 6 p.m., per his request. They'd talked about having their top anchorwoman handle the interview – if it was approved. Bill was set for the big story – with photos – in the Sunday edition of the *Enquirer*.

Now he headed for the mall to choose Claire's birthday present at the jewelry shop he'd noticed earlier in the day. Young as she was, Claire was nutty about tennis. He'd buy her a tennis bracelet. So it was an item for a teen girl – it would make Claire feel grown up. She'd love it.

In the small jewelry store he debated about which to buy, accepted the advice of the friendly saleswoman.

'She'll love this one,' the saleswoman was confident. 'The opal and diamonds – well, zircons,' she conceded with a chuckle, 'will be a big hit. And have her bring it in and we'll adjust the size to fit her.'

Larry drove home. Pleased with his purchase. He parked in the garage, walked up to the front door – open, as usual, in daylight hours. He heard Andrea singing in the kitchen. Their mother's much-loved 'Leaving On A Jet Plane.' He remembered hearing a relief worker singing it to a group of enthralled little Iraqi kids.

Savory aromas filtered into the foyer. Sounds from the living room told him Jimmy was watching the news on TV. He glanced into the room. Claire and Joey were sprawled on the floor, each involved in a five-hundred-piece puzzle that Andrea – a pack rat – had saved through the years. Their latest craze.

'Hey, don't I get a kiss from the birthday girl?' he called out in reproach, and Claire rushed to him.

'You bought me a present, Uncle Larry!' she gloated, clamoring for the parcel he made a pretense of hiding behind his back.

'Kiss first!' he ordered and welcomed the kiss she deposited on his forehead.

It felt so good, being here with Andrea and Jimmy and the kids, he thought with a surge of pleasure. And he remembered the kids in Iraq – so poignantly delighted with the smallest gift. A pencil, a notebook, a cookie.

'It's a tennis bracelet!' Claire shrieked joyously. 'Oh, Uncle Larry, thank you! Thank you!'

In minutes Andrea was summoning them to the dinner table. Claire and Joey bubbling over with talk about the birthday cake to come. Unwarily, Larry thought about Diane. She and that creep of a husband never had kids. He'd bet she loved kids.

Why did Diane have this insidious way of seeping into his thoughts? Let him remember – there was no place in his life for a full-time relationship. Yet sitting here at a family dinner, he was conscious of a yearning to hold Diane in his arms. To make passionate love with her. But face it, he warned himself – Diane was all career woman. No room in her life for a man.

'How're things going with the Special Primary?' Andrea asked Larry while Claire and Joey – along with Jimmy – dug into their apple cider glazed pork tenderloin with sounds of bliss.

'Hectic,' Larry admitted. 'Watch the seven a.m. TV news tomorrow morning.'

'What's happening?' Jimmy stopped eating – forkful of pork tenderloin in midair.

'The candidates so far are not impressive.' Andrea was blunt.

'You mean, somebody new will be announcing tomorrow morning!'

'I can't tell you who it'll be. I'm sworn to secrecy—' Larry grinned. 'But it may be Fran Logan.'

'Thank God—' Andrea exhaled in relief. 'Fran's great. I've campaigned for her in earlier races.'

'I can't understand how we were so misled by Paul Somers.' Jimmy grunted in distaste.

'He was a puppet.' Andrea shrugged in dismissal. 'That wife of his was our real Representative. I heard her speak a few times – she's real.'

'Diane's great,' Larry said and was suddenly self-conscious as he saw the glint in Andrea's eyes.

'How'd you get involved so fast in the campaign?' Jimmy was curious.

'It's in the blood,' Andrea joshed. 'You never knew our parents, Jimmy—'

Jimmy chuckled. 'I feel as though I did. Your father fought in Vietnam,' he recalled. 'He came home – like John Kerry – to fight to stop the war. Your mother was a college peacenik. I wasn't too surprised when you enlisted, Larry.'

'I went to Iraq to learn.' Larry was honest. 'We must come out of our personal lives, become involved in the country's problems.'

'What about Diane Somers?' Andrea probed. 'What's she like?'

'She's bright, compassionate – and a fighter. Whatever Paul Somers accomplished – before he jumped the fence, it was Diane's doing. He's a dumb jerk.' Larry grimaced in contempt.

'She sounds like your kind of woman—' Andrea's smile was dazzling.

'You're way off track,' Larry dismissed this. 'Diane and I are operating on the same wavelength – career-wise. Nothing personal between us. Neither one of us has the time – nor inclination – for that.'

Remember that. No room in my life for commitment to any woman. Not even Diane. I have things to accomplish and places to go.

Sixteen

At a few minutes before 8 a.m. on Saturday morning Diane sat with Joan and Larry in the private conference room at the rear. Except for Jill and Robin, staff had not yet arrived. Robin was online, checking blogs. Jill was manning the phones. The television set was on but muted.

A copy of the morning's *Enquirer* lay across the conference table. At this hour on a Saturday morning, Diane surmised, only a handful of readers had seen the newspaper's headline: popular assemblywoman joins the race.

'The "break" should come through on the eight a.m. news.' Larry sat in tense alertness, remote in hand. 'I worked that out early this morning.'

Diane leaned forward. 'The news is on! Larry, kill the mute—'

They listened impatiently to a roundup of the international and national news. Now the newscaster was moving on to the local scene.

'Word has just come through that Assemblywoman Fran Logan is entering the Special Primary to choose this district's Representative in the House—'

The three in the conference room listened in high excitement as Fran's credentials were described.

'Assemblywoman Logan will be interviewed on this station at six p.m. this evening,' he wound up this segment. 'Her entrance brings to six the number of prospective candidates in the race.'

'The *Evening News* will try to rip Fran to shreds, heap praise on Alex Thompson,' Joan predicted.

'They won't be able to do much damage.' Diane allowed herself a glow of triumph. 'Fran's record is impeccable.'

'They'll lie – you know the score. Let's try to anticipate them,' Larry urged.

'Both Fran and Brad – her pediatrician husband,' Diane

explained, 'have campaigned for all the good causes in this town. Fran's a fighter.' *Why is he looking at me that way again? As though we were alone in a room and he can't wait to make passionate love to me. Why do I want that, too? I'm out of my mind. The damn rebound thing. I won't fall into that trap.* 'She was very active in Paul's campaign for Congress—' Diane forced her eyes away from Larry. 'His first campaign—'

'This could become a dirty fight,' Larry warned – and Diane recalled his saying this earlier.

'We can fight dirty, too—' Joan's smile was dazzling. 'When necessary—'

'Whatever it takes,' Diane vowed, 'we'll fight to keep Paul out of Congress. We need Fran Logan in his seat.'

Paul was sullen as he settled in his seat aboard Addison Collins' private jet on this dismal Saturday morning. What the hell was this crap about him having to spend the next two weeks in the Linwood area? Damn, dull town! And why couldn't Ronnie come with him? He could say she was his personal assistant.

'Relax, Paul.' Gerald Adams – who had become his shadow, at Addison's orders – sounded sympathetic. Gerald wasn't looking forward to two weeks in the Linwood area, Paul surmised. Campaigning to a bunch of redneck would-be voters. 'Be natural – one of the guys. Casual clothes,' he exhorted. 'Chinos or jeans, T-shirt and sneakers. You packed them?' All at once he was wary.

'Yeah.' Paul shrugged. Standard routine – as ordered by Diane.

'We'll eat in the local diners. No room service. Be "one of the guys." Their man in Congress.' A cajoling tone infiltrated his voice now. 'I've set up meetings with small local groups – all on our side.'

'I don't want to run in to Diane,' Paul said self-consciously. 'She can be vicious. Look at the way she attacked me about the divorce! And she lied – she promised she'd be quiet about it until after the election.'

'She's history,' Gerald soothed. 'Without you she's nobody. Just "the Congressman's ex-wife." Nobody'll remember what she said—'

'She was trying to make me look bad. We have to keep a watch out for her,' Paul warned. 'She's smart—'

'She'll disappear into the woodwork.' Gerald shrugged. 'Without you she's nobody.'

'What's this deal Addison keeps throwing at me about Hall-Stores?' Paul was wary.

'It's a major issue locally,' Gerald explained. 'It just popped out into the open. A group in town is already fighting it. They can't see the big picture. That a major chain – an international chain,' he emphasized, 'is coming into town to provide residents with the best bargains to be had anywhere. Look at the jobs they'll bring into the district. And don't forget the extra tax revenue the town will earn.'

'Sure.' Paul's face lighted – for an instant. 'But how does that affect my running for Congress?'

'You need votes to keep you in Congress.' Gerald was blunt. 'It was a tight squeeze the last go-round. You back up something that's great for the town – like Hall-Stores. The people who anticipate buying all those bargains there will vote for you. All the people who don't have jobs but hope to find work at Hall-Stores will vote for you.'

'Addison owns stock in Hall-Stores?' Paul grinned. 'I'll bet my old man does, too.'

'When you're talking to folks in the district,' Gerald cautioned, 'you don't say a bad word against Alex Thompson, who's running in the Special Primary.'

Paul was startled. 'I thought he was on our side.'

'He is.' Gerald's smile was enigmatic. 'He just keeps that to himself. At the moment he's running for a spot on the Democratic ticket – and telling everybody that Linwood and the surrounding area needs Hall-Stores to open up here.'

'Alex Thompson is as rich as Bill Gates,' Paul added with infinite respect. 'Well, almost—'

'Sharp, too,' Gerald said. 'Plus he knows where all the bodies are buried in this district. I suspect he'll come up with a lot of surprises in the next couple of weeks before special-primary day.'

Their plane landed at the small Linwood Airport. A chauffeur-driven limousine was waiting to whisk them off to their hotel. Paul gaped in astonishment when the limo swung into the circular driveway before the modest Racine Hotel.

'We're staying here?' Paul was indignant. 'It's a dump. Why not a first-class hotel like the Palace or Linwood Court?'

'The image, Paul,' Gerald scolded. 'The Racine's favored by the budget-watchers. The ones we want to add to our party membership.'

'They don't even have suites here.' Paul emerged from the limo in distaste. 'I didn't stay in dives in my earlier campaigns.'

'You need more votes than you had in earlier campaigns,' Gerald reminded. 'We don't want to gamble on your just sneaking through.'

His face radiating injury, Paul strode beside Gerry into the tiny hotel lobby to register for their room. The clerk's face lighted when he recognized their Congressman. *He'll be bragging about how I stayed at his dump. How's this crap going to win votes?*

Gerry carried on a genial conversation with the clerk – signaling to Paul to join in. Now he prodded Paul from the registration desk to follow the bellhop to their room.

When they were alone, Paul sent a swift glance about their modestly furnished room, stared at Gerry in rebellion. 'This stinks! Our campaign headquarters is opening up in the ballroom of the Palace Hotel – and I'm sleeping in a dump like this?'

Gerry refused to be ruffled. 'It's clean, comfortable. There're two beds and a private bath. It's perfectly acceptable to the average traveler.'

'I'm not the average traveler,' Paul shot back. 'I'm Congressman Paul Somers.'

'And you'd like to hold on to that status,' Gerry pointed out. 'Which means getting your butt out there and winning votes. When Perón was having problems with people, his wife Eva told him to take off his tie, take off his jacket, go out there, and be one of the people.'

'She sounds like my ex-wife. Almost ex-wife,' Paul conceded. 'Wasn't there a Broadway musical about her? Eva Perón, I mean—'

'Paul, I'm here to make you appear to be an average Joe, to help you win votes to keep you in Congress. Campaign headquarters can afford to be splashy – that's to woo volunteers. They'll be served fancy snacks from the hotel kitchen, be provided with canned music.'

'And I'm supposed to live like somebody on welfare?' Paul was indignant.

'That's a bad choice of words.' Gerry clucked in disapproval. 'Our volunteers – our voters – see this as a real democracy. A country where everybody is on his own. To hell with social benefits – if you're sharp, you'll get ahead. Why should we pay high taxes for people too lazy or too dumb to earn their own keep?'

'Yeah—' Paul nodded in agreement. 'Like my old man always says.'

'But volunteers – and voters – have to see you as some-body prepared to fight for them. You'll vote against spiraling benefits. You'll vote for tax cuts.' Gerry's voice took on fresh authority. 'You do what I tell you, Paul. That's orders from the top. Remember that.'

'My father didn't go through this crap to stay in the House for six terms,' Paul complained – slightly defiant – and sat on one of the double beds. 'Hey, they didn't clean up this room. Somebody left a newspaper behind.'

'That's today's Linwood *Enquirer*—' It was clear Gerry was straining for patience. 'It's a service. Like the chocolate mint on the pillows of each of our beds.'

'What's this stuff about Fran Logan?' All at once – reading the headline of the *Enquirer* – Paul was suddenly alert. 'She's after my seat in the House?'

'You know this Fran Logan?' Gerry reached for the news-paper, scanned the front-page article.

'She's been following my tracks. She took my seat in the Town Council, then in the state assembly!' Paul radiated a blend of anger and alarm. 'Now she thinks she's moving into the House?'

'She's running in the Special Primary,' Gerry conceded. 'She'll be interviewed on local TV at six p.m. We'll watch.'

'She's bad news.' Paul was on his feet now. Began to pace. 'Dig up dirt on her, make her look lousy!'

'Why does she scare you?' Gerry was calm, but Paul sensed his mind was charging into action. *They'll fix her wagon, run her out of the Primary. They know how to do these things.*

'Fran Logan fights like a male Rottweiler after a bitch in heat! If she wins the Special Primary, we're facing a big headache.' Paul stopped pacing. 'I remember now – she was active in keeping Hall-Stores out of town a few years ago, when they made their move. You said that's a big issue again.'

'But we're on Hall-Stores's side,' Gerry reminded, deceptively calm. 'You want Hall-Stores to bring their cheap merchandise, their jobs to Linwood.'

'Right.' But Paul felt a surge of unease. He'd been part of that scene in the last go-round. In the wrong direction, according to his new party. *Diane pushed me into all the wrong deals – but voters know I've changed. I've come home again. Back in the right party.*

'So you feel Fran Logan is the strongest contender.' Gerry was unimpressed. 'Let's not overlook Alex Thompson. He's willing to spend whatever it takes to win that Primary. And with Thompson as opposition, you'll be in a great position.' He frowned at Paul's blank stare. 'Alex doesn't want a seat in the House – he's running to give you a break. He's interested in selling acreage to Hall-Stores – and making sure this becomes a total red state.'

'Diane's behind Fran Logan's running for my seat. She's out to get me!' Paul began to pace again. 'I don't trust Di. She'll try anything to mess me up.'

'Nobody can do that except you,' Gerry said drily. 'You've got our whole machine behind you. Do what we tell you, Paul – and you're a shoo-in.'

Seventeen

Around noon, Diane and Joan settled themselves in Diane's office for sandwiches and coffee. They'd just inspected photos in the *Evening News* of the newly organized campaign headquarters of the opposition.

'They must have a pipeline to Fort Knox,' Joan jeered. 'Can you imagine what they're paying for that ballroom at the Palace Hotel – from now through election day?'

'So they'll outspend us.' Diane made an almost believable pretense of shrugging this off. 'Can they bring in the votes?'

'They're pulling in volunteers,' Joan admitted, 'with their promise of campaigning as a nonstop party situation. The word is they're setting up a series of headquarters throughout the Congressional district.'

'But our volunteers are committed,' Diane said softly. 'They know they're fighting for what's best not only for our district but for the whole country.'

They glanced up in wary inquiry as Jill strode into the room with her 'have I got news' aura.

Diane tensed. 'What's up?'

'Our mole at the airport just buzzed me. Guess who arrived in town about an hour ago? Your almost-ex,' Jill said, without waiting for a reply. 'Our Congressman of the moment.'

'On the campaign trail,' Joan interpreted. 'We expected that, didn't we?'

'On a private jet, with an entourage,' Diane guessed. 'They're out for blood.'

'We're prepared.' Joan refused to be disturbed. 'They'll trot Paul around to small, selected groups – and along the line somewhere he'll hold a press conference for chosen reporters – with pre-approved questions. You know the routine.'

'I'm going back to work,' Jill said. 'Fran will make mincemeat out of him.'

'Where's Larry this morning?' Joan asked and continued before Diane could reply, 'Yeah, he's with Fran. Working with her on the six p.m. TV interview.'

'We should have expected Paul to show up about now.' Diane was somber. 'His people must have heard about Fran coming into the race.'

'The first break came on the eight a.m. news this morning.' Joan was dubious. 'They threw him on to a plane and flew him straight here to campaign?'

'Their local spies heard the news, called Washington. They jumped into action,' Diane surmised. 'Paul got orders to come to the district and play his role. He's got a seat in the House to protect.' Unexpectedly she chuckled. 'He realizes Fran is a formidable opponent. Only in the past, Fran was fighting for him.'

'Jill's got a crew out pinning up circulars about Fran's TV interview this evening,' Joan recalled. 'Everybody in the area will tune in.'

Diane's private line was a sharp intrusion. She reached to pick up. 'Diane Somers—'

'Di, it's me.' Larry was terse. 'You know where I am? Just answer yes or no,' he added quickly.

'Yes.' Alarm signals shot up in Diane's mind. *He's with Fran at her home office now. What's happening?*

'Drop whatever you're doing and come right over. We have a problem.'

'I'll be there in five minutes—' Diane's heart began to pound. *Paul's in town – and all at once this weird call from Larry.*

'What was that all about?' Joan sensed this was a crisis.

'I don't know—' Diane dug into a drawer for her purse, pulled out car keys. 'He was afraid to talk on the phone, told me to rush right over.'

'Shall I go with you?' Joan was on her feet.

'Hold the fort here. I'll buzz you as soon as I hear something that makes sense.'

Driving to Fran's house in the town's upper-middle-class suburb, Diane searched her mind for what could have caused this mysterious summons. Were Paul and the opposition launching some vicious attack on Fran? Sometimes Fran refused to recognize the fact that outrageous lies were part of the political game.

She turned into Magnolia Lane – Fran's road. So deceptively serene this morning. But she geared herself for fearful
news as she swung into the driveway and parked behind Larry's
car. *Whatever it is, we'll deal with it.*

Larry was pulling the front door wide as she approached.
He and Fran had heard the car.

'I came as fast as I could—' she said breathlessly, rushing
to the house. Larry's face a somber mask – telling her nothing.

'We've got work to do—' He drew her into the foyer.

Fran was at the entrance to the living room. 'Diane, I feel
so awful about putting you in this spot – but there's no other
way. I talked it over in depth with Brad – and he agreed.'

'Where's Brad?' *When will somebody tell me what's
happening?*

'He's making a house call—' Fran's smile was tender. 'He's
one of the few pediatricians in the country who makes house
calls. He says he doesn't want to drag a really sick kid into
the office – and he doesn't want to expose other kids to the
sick one.'

'All right, what's going on?' Diane was brusque in her impatience.

'I'm pregnant—' For an instant Fran glowed. 'Brad and I
have been married for nine years. We'd thought it would never
happen.' Her joy was suffused with apology.

'All of a sudden this morning you know you're pregnant?'
Diane's head was reeling. Should this make a difference in
Fran's running for another public office? 'Just like that?'

'I was sure I was late – it's happened before. Then Brad
went out to pick up shaving cream or something – before he
knew about the house call. And – ' Fran was struggling to
continue – 'he brought home a pregnancy test. Not one test
– two. To make sure.' She took a deep breath. 'Both were
positive.'

'We've had pregnant women in Congress,' Diane protested.
'Even a governor a couple of years ago—'

'Fran's not running.' Larry was firm. 'We have to deal with
this. We'll—'

'Why can't you run?' Diane challenged Fran. This was the
twenty-first century – women had children and careers. 'We
can set up a schedule that won't be too demanding. We—'

'Di, if I should be elected, I'd be almost five months pregnant when I'd be sworn in. It won't work. Brad's against my running – and I have to agree with him. We don't know what we're getting into – it could be a difficult pregnancy. We've wanted children so desperately. We can't take chances now.'

'All right, let's sit down and figure out where we go from here.' Larry prodded the two women on to the sofa, dropped into a chair facing them.

'I'll have to issue a statement explaining I'm withdrawing from the Special Primary.' Fran was searching for words. 'That I'll continue as a member of the state assembly.' Basically a part-time job. 'Soon enough,' she added with a wry smile, 'those who know me will realize why I'm withdrawing.'

'Sit down at your computer, write out the statement,' Larry told Fran. 'I'll deliver it in person, remind them that they'll have to reschedule the six p.m. slot this evening.' He turned to Diane. 'Any ideas about a replacement candidate?'

'None at the moment,' Diane admitted and tensed in sudden realization. 'Oh God, Jill's got people out putting up fliers about the TV interview this evening! Fran, where's a phone?' Her eyes shot about the room.

'On the table in the corner there.' Fran pointed. 'I'll go to our computer room and type up the statement.'

Diane punched in Joan's private line, waited impatiently for her to respond.

'Joan Rubin, campaign headquarters—' The usual lilt in her voice.

'Joan, instruct Jill to arrange to have those fliers pulled down as fast as possible,' Diane began. 'And shred them!'

'Tell me I'm not hearing right,' Joan gasped. 'Does that mean what I think it means?'

'It does.' Diane strived for calm. *Be cool. This isn't a moment to panic.* 'Call every member of the district committee. Whatever they have planned for this evening, have them cancel it. We're meeting in an emergency session at six thirty p.m.' She ignored Joan's murmur of reproach at the early hour. 'No excuses accepted. Set it up as before.'

'A six thirty p.m. emergency meeting at your house. Dinner brought from the deli at seven p.m.?'

'That'll be about right,' Diane approved.

'You're anticipating a long meeting,' Joan interpreted with an air of resignation.

'When word leaks out, Paul and his crew will be gloating. Fran was our best shot against him.'

'Hey, we're not giving up on this Primary,' Joan scolded. 'The battle's just warming up.'

'And we're low on ammunition.' Diane was blunt. 'We need a master plan to find ourselves a candidate to beat Paul. All we have now are minnows. We need a big fish!'

Eighteen

Diane charged into campaign headquarters. From the disconcerted smiles of the volunteers, she understood Joan had already spread the word – '*We don't have a candidate with a chance of winning.*'

'Don't be upset,' she called to them with contrived optimism while striding to her cubicle. 'We're putting a Democrat in Paul Somers' seat!'

'Here's coffee.' Joan followed her into her cubicle. 'The real thing – we need it right now.'

'Driving back here, I searched my mind—' Diane sighed. 'We may have to approach Judge Winston – he's as bright as they come, but he likes his judgeship.'

'Wasn't he approached in the last go-round? Before Paul entered the Primary?'

'Right. He said he wasn't enthralled at the prospect of moving to Washington,' Diane confirmed. 'He complained that Washington was a jungle. The three of us were debating about whether to throw Paul into the ring – or if it was premature.' Bringing in Paul, acting as his campaign managers had lifted her and Joan into their current strong position in the district.

'OK.' Joan was brisk. 'Do you or I approach Judge Winston? It might be stronger if you did it—' She was reflective. 'Now.'

'Before the meeting this evening,' Diane agreed and reached for the phone. 'Oh, what's his number?' She reached for her address book, found the number, called Judge Winston.

'Judge Winston's residence,' a friendly voice responded.

'May I speak with Judge Winston, please. This is Diane Somers.'

'Hi, Mrs. Somers—' Recognition in the voice at the other end. *Someone I know? Probably not – she knows my name from the political scene.* 'The judge is at the hospital with Mrs. Winston – he gets special visiting hours.'

'Oh, I didn't know Mrs. Winston was ill.' Diane was shocked. 'I wouldn't have bothered him.'

'She had a fall – she has a slight fracture in her right ankle. She'll be home in a few days.'

'That's good. But no need to tell the judge I was trying to reach him,' she said quickly. 'I was just reporting some political gossip.'

This was not the time to try to persuade Judge Winston to enter the Special Primary. Everyone knew how devoted he was to his wife. And this wasn't the first fall she'd suffered.

'So his wife is sick.' Joan was philosophical. 'Take him off the list. Where do we go from here?'

'It's not good.' Diane frowned in thought, dredged three more names from her mind. 'What about Ted Munson? Or Alec Jamison or Bill Monroe?'

Joan was doubtful. 'To pit against Paul and the Republican Party? For state office, yes. But for Congress?'

'We may have to run with one of them—'

'We discussed the three of them at the last emergency meeting,' Joan recalled. 'Discarded them in favor of Fran.'

'We should feel them out,' Diane decided. 'Let them know if they run in the Special Primary, we're behind them.'

'It'll take a miracle for any of them to beat Paul and the Republican machine.'

'Pray for a miracle,' Diane ordered. 'Pray hard.'

'But right now get on the phone – we need names to present to the committee,' Joan pointed out. 'You tackle Ted Munson. I'll go for Alec Jamison. We'll toss for Bill Monroe.'

Diane reached for her private line. 'All before six thirty p.m. this evening—'

Now the two women realized it was a steamy hot Saturday afternoon. An answering machine at the Munson house informed Diane that the Munsons were at their lake house for the next week. The answering machine at the Jamison house repeated a similar message.

'Don't they know that's a serious invitation to burglars?' Joan scoffed when she compared phone calls with Diane.

'You call Bill Monroe,' Diane ordered Joan. 'You said

your father runs into him on occasion at the major race-tracks.'

'They're not exactly buddies – except at the Kentucky Derby and in Saratoga Springs,' Joan told her. 'But I'll try.'

Moments later Florence Monroe reported that her husband had just taken off for Saratoga Springs. 'He likes to settle in a few days before the races begin.'

'This is kind of important,' Joan pushed. 'Could you give us a phone number in Saratoga Springs?'

Florence Monroe chuckled, 'Honey, that would be grounds for divorce. Anyhow, he's never in his room up there except to sleep.'

'We're not doing too well,' Diane conceded when Joan was off the phone.

'Maybe somebody on the committee will have a brainstorm. Damn, why can't we find some great woman candidate? That would make my day.'

They heard Larry in somber conversation with a group of volunteers in the area beyond Diane's cubicle.

'Don't be downcast,' he rebuked them. 'That's the wrong attitude. Think positive. We're keeping a Democrat in that seat in the House.'

'You delivered the bad news to the TV people?' Joan greeted him.

'I did.' He dropped into an empty chair. 'They're scrambling to fill the six p.m. slot. Any brainstorms around here about a prospective candidate?' His gaze swung from Joan to Diane.

'We made three calls. We forgot – this is summer. An especially hot summer. All three men are out of town,' Diane told him.

'The Special Primary is breathing down our necks. Push – try to contact them wherever they are,' Larry urged.

'Not one of the three has a chance of winning,' Joan admitted. 'Maybe – just maybe – somebody at the meeting tonight will come up with a new name. Somebody we've stupidly overlooked.'

'Larry, I want you to be at that meeting,' Diane told Larry. *He's part of our team now.* 'Another emergency meeting of the committee. At my house. Be there at six thirty p.m. It's going to be a battlefield.'

* * *

'Come on, Paul,' Gerry insisted, coaxing him from the booth at a local diner where he'd been holding court. 'We have to get back to the hotel.'

'What's the rush?' Paul grumbled when they were out on the street. 'I was making friends there. Working – even though the food was lousy.'

'We need to see that interview of your possible competition.' Gerry was terse. 'What's her name? Fran Logan,' he recalled.

'Oh, yeah—' Some of Paul's ebullience evaporated. 'She's smart.' But now a condescending tone seeped into his voice. 'How the hell could she go to Washington?'

'The usual way. By plane.' Gerry prodded him in the direction of the hotel when he paused to ogle a stacked teenager.

'Wanna bet she won't make it?' Paul grinned. 'Her husband's a popular pediatrician in this town. You think he's going to give up his practice to follow her to Washington?'

'There have been Congressmen – and Congresswomen – who've managed that hurdle. One remains back home, the Congress member flies home for weekends.'

'OK, a point for you,' Paul conceded. Diane had spent a lot of time back home – more than in Washington. 'But we can latch on to the line that she'll be a part-time member of the House,' he said in triumph. 'Folks in this district will feel cheated.'

'We'll keep that point in mind,' Gerry promised, and Paul glowed.

'Let's pick up some beers before we go back to the hotel.' Paul was ebullient. Feeling himself in control of the situation. 'Nothing to do in this fleabag town on a Saturday night except to watch TV.'

They arrived in their room only seconds before the scheduled 6 p.m. interview. Paul dropped on to the bed, reached for a can of beer. Gerry flipped on the TV set.

The previous program was signing off. A moment later Paul and Gerry snapped to attention.

'A late statement from Assemblywoman Fran Logan announces that she is withdrawing from the Special Primary as a Democratic candidate in the race to replace Congressman

Paul Somers. Therefore, the interview scheduled for this time has been canceled—'

Paul leapt to his feet, switched off the set. 'That's a break,' he chortled. 'Now who will they dig out to run against me?'

Nineteen

L arry hurried out of the shower, rushed to dress. He knew
the meeting was scheduled for 6.30 p.m., but he meant
to be there early to talk with Diane and Joan. He hadn't returned
to campaign headquarters after he'd delivered Fran's statement to the TV people. He'd lingered to go out with Hal for
a very late lunch.

How would the committee react if he made an effort to
offer suggestions – or was he to be there just as an observer?
That's what he had to clear with Diane.

He grunted in annoyance at the chirping of his cell phone,
crossed to pick it up. He'd avoided – thus far – Andrea's
suggestion that she have a phone installed in his apartment.
That indicated permanence. Was he ready for that?

'Hello—'

'Larry, it's me – Hal Watson.'

'Long time no see,' Larry drawled, checking his watch.
'Something up?'

'I picked up something I thought might interest you,' Hal
said. 'The jumping-ship Congressman is here in town.'

'Paul Somers?' *Does Diane know about this?*

'That's it. With an entourage of one – so far. He's here to
speak to the Chamber of Commerce next Wednesday evening.
And I heard something about a visit to a senior-citizens group
tomorrow afternoon.'

'Hal, thanks. I have to rush now to a meeting. But keep
feeding me what you hear. We appreciate it.'

Larry finished dressing. Chinos, T-shirt, and sneakers replaced
by a business suit and shoes. The men on the committee, he
assumed, wouldn't wear casual clothes. But no tie, he rejected.
That was the current rebellion.

Diane's house had central air-conditioning, he recalled.

They'd be comfortable in suits. And she'd said not to bother with an early dinner – they'd have cold cuts for the meeting.

With a final glance in the mirror to reassure himself he looked respectable, Larry hurried from his apartment and to his car. If he was going to stay in town, he ought to do something about a rental, he chastised himself. It was rough for Andrea and Jimmy to deal with one car.

'Hi—' Andrea called to him from the deck. 'We're having a cookout tonight. Interested?'

'It sounds great, but I can't make it. I'm headed over to Diane's house for—'

'Ah-hah!' she broke in with a triumphant smile, inspected what Jimmy called his 'serious business' attire. 'That sounds promising.'

'Down, girl,' Larry chided. 'This is serious business. Diane's called a meeting of the district's Democratic committee. I've been instructed to attend.'

'That was rough about Fran Logan's pulling out.' Andrea was somber now. As of five minutes ago, much of the town must know. 'What's going to happen now? I never did like that Paul Somers. His ex-wife –' she emphasized the 'ex' – 'is a doll.' An approving glint in her eyes.

'She's cool.' Larry was casual. Andrea was back to her old matchmaking tricks. 'A great boss.' *Andrea thinks Diane and I have something going. What gave her that idea?* 'Happy cookout.'

Larry slid behind the wheel, drove away from the house. Twice he'd been involved in serious relationships. Each time – at the critical moment – he'd broken away. This wasn't the time to become involved again. But every time he was with Diane, he felt this connection between them. This was something new in his life. Unlike his previous, near-serious relationships.

Linda, he'd discovered in shock, had a drug problem – and refused treatment. Nadine had rebelled against his involvement in political causes. He chuckled in recall. *'Damn it, Larry! You care more about your damn causes than you do about me!'*

He'd never known anyone like Diane. They thought alike. She was warm, appealing, passionate about the same things

as he. And each time they were together, he wanted to pull
her into his arms and hold her.

*Knock it off, Larry. You sound like a character in a B-grade
TV movie! Diane's in love with her career. I've got things to
accomplish. No room in her life or mine for romantic compli-
cations.*

Diane struggled to insert the extension panels into the
dining-table top. She'd bought the table, she recalled, when
Paul was running for the town-council seat. Joan had suggested
they do some serious entertaining. A smart investment.

Joan came into the dining room with a chair clutched under
each arm. 'Why must you be a one-woman band?' she scolded
Diane. 'Let me help with that.' She managed to extricate herself
from the two chairs, crossed to take one side of a panel in
hand.

'I think the table's getting warped,' Diane said in disgust.
'I shudder when I think what we paid for it.'

'Nothing wrong with the table. You're uptight. Not without
reason,' Joan acknowledged, abandoning her earlier air of
confidence. 'Unless somebody comes up with a name out of
left field, we're in bad shape.'

'I can't believe we could lose that seat in the House!'
Frustration lent an unfamiliar sharpness to Diane's voice.
'Now, when it's so important—' She started at the sound of
the door chimes.

'They're coming already?' Joan flinched in reproach.

'Probably Larry,' Diane guessed. 'I'll go to the door.' He
wanted to be here early – to talk about his place at the meeting,
she suspected. She'd given the committee a strong recom-
mendation for hiring him – and the fact that he was an Iraq
vet had been a factor. There were a lot of yellow ribbons on
display in this town.

'Hi—' Larry's casualness refuted any anxiety about the
meeting this evening. 'I come early – with gossip.'

'Give,' Joan ordered, dealing with the other panels on her
own.

'Paul's in town,' he began and the other two nodded. 'He's
meeting with the Chamber of Commerce and a senior-citizens
group.'

'They're moving into heavy campaigning.' Diane shrugged.

'That's to be expected. They heard this morning about Fran's entering the Special Primary, and suddenly realized they had a battle on their hands—'

'Now they're gloating because she's out,' Joan added.

'The mob will be descending in a few minutes,' Larry surmised. 'They won't balk at my presence?'

'Hey, you're a member of our team,' Joan reminded.

'Am I free to enter discussions?' Larry glanced from Joan to Diane. 'To say what's on my mind?'

'All clear.' Diane was emphatic. Joan nodded in agreement.

'OK, what can I do to help now?' He glanced at the table, surrounded at this point by four chairs. 'What about other chairs?'

'Come with me,' Joan ordered. 'We also dust and vacuum.'

At 6.36 those in the house heard two cars pull up outside. Diane hurried to the door. Clark Jackson and Adam Miller had arrived seconds apart, were approaching now.

'What was so urgent that I had to break my weekend and come home from the lake?' Jackson grumbled as Diane pulled the door wide in welcome.

'Yeah. This better be urgent.' Miller was acerbic. 'My wife is pissed.'

'You haven't been watching TV,' Diane gathered as they walked into the house and headed for the improvised conference room.

'We don't watch the news,' Jackson admitted. 'My wife's cardinal rule when we're at the lake house.' But he was on alert, Diane noted.

'Our TV has been out of order for two days – I considered it a gift,' Miller said.

'Let me brief you quickly.' Diane reported on Fran's withdrawal.

'Oh shit,' Jackson groaned. 'We're back to square one.'

Now other cars were heard pulling up outside. Other members of the committee surged into the house within minutes of one another. They had watched the 6 p.m. telecast, knew that Fran had withdrawn. They gathered about the dining table with grim faces.

Clark Jackson waded into the problem.

'While Diane was chasing after Fran Logan,' he admitted, 'I made a few calls on my own to other possibilities. The smart guys don't want to tangle with the Republican war chest.'

'Alex Thompson is the strongest candidate so far,' another committee member pointed out. 'And we know he won't launch a real campaign against Paul Somers if he should win the Primary. All he gives a damn about at this point is to persuade the zoning board to change the code to allow Hall-Stores to open one of their killer stores here in Linwood.' *But the zoning board is just the first major step – the Town Council still must approve.* 'His running in the Special Primary is a gift to the Republican Party.'

'And we have residents who're dying to see Hall-Stores open up here in town,' Liz Franken warned. 'All they see are the bargain prices that'll be available to them. They don't see the local businesses that'll be pushed out, the poverty-level jobs that will be offered. The traffic congestion – the road repairs required.'

'We're not here to argue about Hall-Stores.' Adam Miller was testy. Diane suspected he was part of the new group being organized in support of Hall-Stores. 'We have to find a candidate to run for a seat in the House. Somebody with a chance of defeating Paul Somers.'

'I was on the phone for two hours after you called me, Diane,' Liz Franken told her. 'Trying to bring in a possible candidate that in normal circumstances we wouldn't consider – and you know what I got?' She spread her hands in a gesture of defeat. '"The opposition is too strong – I'd be wasting my time."'

'May I make a suggestion?' Larry was diffident. *He knows there are egos here to be handled with care.*

'Suggest,' Jackson instructed. But he was wary.

'First, let's discuss what we need in a candidate.' Larry's tone was ingratiating. 'We need an individual with much exposure in the district—'

'Essential,' Liz Franken agreed.

'Our candidate must have a background of fighting for the principles of the Democratic Party. Be passionate about this. It's an asset if the candidate has a reputation as a bright, compassionate person – and an advantage to be physically attractive, telegenic.'

'Where are you heading with this?' Adam Miller was annoyed.

'I'm about to point out a very strong candidate to fight Paul Somers,' Larry said, his gaze turning to Diane. 'And you're looking at her.'

Twenty

Diane gaped in shock. *Larry's serious. But the committee will ridicule him. How did he dream up this fantasy?* And yet – at the same time she felt a rush of excitement. Somers v. Somers. Could that happen?

The moment of startled silence was broken now. 'I know we're in desperate straits – but Diane's never run for public office,' Adam Miller protested. 'Not even for Town Council.'

'Most people in the district – and in the House,' Larry picked up, 'are aware that Diane pulled the strings on Paul Somers. She was his voice. He was her puppet. It was Diane Somers – not Paul Somers – who fought for this district. Let her come out into the open, continue to fight for us. Be another voice to turn this country in the right direction.'

'He's absolutely right.' Liz Franken was resolute. 'We were blind not to see this before. We've all known for years that it was Diane who called the shots. From his election to Town Council to the seat in the House.'

'Somers v. Somers.' Jackson's face reflected his satisfaction. 'That'll make a splash in the media! Do I hear any dissenting votes?' he demanded.

Diane sat silent in an aura of disbelief while the members of the committee elaborated on the new approach. Could she win the Special Primary – and the election in November?

'Paul Somers will be out of his mind when Diane wins the Special Primary,' Larry said quietly. 'Because who among us can doubt that she'll win?'

'The battle will be between Diane and Alex Thompson.' Joan exchanged a loaded glance with Diane. 'Now let's figure out how we handle that.'

The sound of the door chimes was a sudden intrusion.

'The caterer from the deli.' Diane identified the caller and headed for the door. 'We'll have an early dinner.'

'Count me out.' Diane heard Adam Miller's apology as she hurried to admit the caterer. 'I have some mending to do at home.' *That's right – he said his wife was pissed at being brought back into town. Why do I get the feeling he's not happy about this solution?*

The caterer and a helper dispensed cans of soda, brought out platters of corned beef, pastrami, smoked turkey, and a variety of side dishes from insulated bags, then took off. Diane and Joan handed around plastic plates, paper napkins, and utensils. After a whispered conference with Joan, Larry headed for the kitchen, returned with a tray of glasses in hand and with a magnum of champagne clutched perilously under one arm.

He saw it there on the top shelf. Waiting for some very special occasion. I guess this is it.

'We'll get this show on the road with class,' he announced and proceeded to uncork the champagne. *I'd expected to serve this in November – provided Paul was re-elected. Will the others think I'm expressing over-confidence?*

There was a momentary pause while they drank to Diane's election. Yet Diane was conscious of an air of uncertainty about the dinner table. She deciphered some doubt about their future. They'd approved her because there was no other choice.

Dinner talk was monopolized by discussion between Liz Franken and Clark Jackson – both focused on the need to eliminate Alex Thompson as a rival. Adam Miller had disliked her as a candidate because she was a woman, Diane interpreted. He'd been tepid about Fran.

With the committee members gone and the table cleared – with Larry pitching in to help – Joan phoned headquarters to speak with Jill.

'Jill and Robin are probably nervous wrecks,' Diane told Larry with a wry smile. 'We should have called earlier.'

In the current situation volunteers were on duty even on Saturday evening. They, too, would be nervous, Diane thought compassionately. If they didn't approve of their new candidate, would they desert the campaign?

'Di and I will be there in about twenty minutes,' Joan told Jill. 'Don't ask questions now – but have we got news!'

'Going back to headquarters with us?' Diane asked Larry. Still reeling from the startling change in events.

Larry gazed at her in mock reproach. 'Of course – we've got work to do.'

They left the house. Diane and Joan hurried to Joan's car, Larry to his. They stood there in brief conversation.

'I still can't believe this is happening – it's unreal.' Diane shook her head, as though to clear it. 'What happens if I don't win in the Special Primary? If Alex Thompson buys it? How do we deal with that?'

'We won't let that happen.' Joan exuded conviction.

'Larry, I heard you say all those things about me.' Her voice rich with tenderness. 'I hope I can live up to them.'

'You're the only candidate who gives us a chance,' he said calmly. 'Think positive, Di.'

'We'll have a rough time ahead.' Her smile simultaneously fearful and defiant.

OK, I get the message. I'm the only port in the storm. Great for my ego. But why is he looking at me that way? As though – if we were alone – he'd take me in his arms.

'Come on,' Joan ordered Diane and Larry. 'Let's beat it back to headquarters. Let Jill and Robin and the volunteers on duty all know what's going down!'

Back at headquarters, Diane realized that Jill had clued in the volunteers to some dramatic change. She'd done that, Diane realized, to make it easier when they were told. Expectant faces greeted the new arrivals. Unexpectedly Larry took charge.

'Ladies and gentlemen,' he said, reaching for Diane's hand, lifting it aloft with his own. 'Welcome the next Representative from our district. Congresswoman-to-be Diane Somers!'

Thunderous applause rent the air. *They're surprised – but they approve!*

Thirty minutes later Larry sat in Bill Taylor's office. He'd summoned Bill from a Saturday-evening family dinner to meet him at the *Enquirer*.

'This better be good,' Bill warned, swiveling in his chair in wary anticipation. 'I walked out on my sister and brother-in-law's twenty-fifth-wedding-anniversary dinner party.'

'The district's Democratic Party has a new candidate to support – at least, we expect her to win in the Special Primary.'

'Her?' Bill leaned forward, eyes bright. 'Fran changed her mind?'

'Not exactly. For family reasons she has to withdraw. But the committee agrees it's chosen the best possible candidate in the field.' Larry allowed himself a dramatic pause. 'Diane Somers.'

'Wow, that's news! I don't remember when we've had a week like this one!' But it was clear Bill approved of the latest change in plans. 'So Diane's never run for public office—' He zeroed in on the likely complaint in some quarters, dismissed it with a shrug. 'Most people in the district know her as well as Paul – if not better. So when will it be announced?'

'What about in tomorrow morning's *Enquirer*?' Larry challenged. 'Along with a TV news break around seven a.m. tomorrow.' *The radio station won't cooperate.*

'You've got to be kidding!' Bill glared in disbelief. 'It's almost nine p.m. on Saturday night!'

'All you'll have to do is pull the main section.' Larry refused to lose his cool at Bill's eloquent grunt. 'Cut some deal on the front page. Just make the simple announcement that Diane's running in the Special Primary a week from Monday.'

'We can't cut a front-page story!' Bill objected. But Larry sensed the wheels racing in his head.

'A few lines to spread the word,' Larry cajoled. 'You know how to do it!'

Bill reached for the phone. 'I don't believe I'm doing this. But you'd better have a sizzling article for me to run on Monday morning as payback!'

What Joan labeled the 'ferocious four' – Diane, Joan, Larry, and Jill – huddled in the conference room at campaign headquarters. The volunteers, then Robin long gone. Diane glanced at her watch as Joan and Larry debated a campaign slogan. It was close to midnight.

'We're all beat—' Larry radiated compassion. 'Let's call it a night. We'll think clearer after a few hours' sleep.'

Joan nodded in agreement. 'And Di has that TV interview tomorrow evening – we need to work on that.'

'We have to lay the groundwork for our campaign.' Diane was conscious of a fresh surge of excitement. 'Stress the urgent local issues – yet remind voters of the importance of our vote in the House. Especially in current times.'

'It's great that Liz Franken agreed – on such short notice – to appear in the TV interview with you. Two dynamic women,' Jill said with relish. 'Alex Thompson is about to be hit with a steamroller.'

'Let's not forget – a lot of elections in recent years have been bought.' Diane refused to become complacent. 'First, we've got the battle to win against Thompson – and all his money. And if we win, then comes the battle against Paul and the machine behind him.' *Will Larry be around for the long haul? How can I feel this way about a man I've just met?*

'Honey, you'll make mincemeat out of Paul,' Joan predicted.

'We won't be fighting just against Paul.' Diane ordered herself to remain realistic, not to assume the aura of optimism that surrounded the other three. 'We'll be battling the opposition party – and the money they can raise.' Her eyes eloquent.

'That's going to be a less painful obstacle in the future.' Larry refused to back down. 'More average Americans are realizing this country is veering off into the wrong direction. They're making themselves heard. They're contributing money. In small amounts, yes – but the number of them is impressive.'

'And the Internet is essential,' Diane said in satisfaction. 'A whole new route of reaching voters has been activated now. But that doesn't mean we don't have the battle of our lives ahead of us,' she retreated.

'No more battles for now.' Joan was decisive. 'Let's call it a night.'

Diane drove home through night-darkened streets. Here and there loud sounds erupted from an open tavern. She slowed down to allow a pair of drunks to cross the street in safety. She'd sleep late tomorrow morning, she promised herself. So she'd miss the morning breaking news on TV. She must look fresh for the evening TV appearance with Liz Franken. Have a clear head.

At 10 a.m. she'd huddle with Larry and Joan about what to stress in the interview. Then she was meeting Liz for a Sunday brunch at noon. They had to pull their act together, make the voters of their district understand the urgency of the

Special Primary. That Alex Thompson was just a front for the opposition. He'd disappear into the woodwork at the November elections, leave Paul with no real opposition.

How do we convince voters that this is true?

Twenty-One

In a double room at the Racine Hotel, Paul slept – blanket-enveloped, arms embracing a pillow – in the bed closest to the air-conditioner. Relishing the December coolness of the room. He'd ignored Gerry's pleas to lessen that coolness.

He grunted in annoyance at the shrill intrusion of the phone. The intrusion continuing. Why in hell wasn't Gerry answering? He swung about, saw Gerry reaching to pick up. Damn, what now?

'Hello—' Gerry was terse. 'Yes, this is Gerry—' His eyes closed, he listened to the voice at the other end.

Paul glanced at the travel clock on the night table between the two beds. Damn! It was just minutes past 8 a.m. Who had the nerve to wake them up at this hour on a Sunday morning? But now alarm set in. Why did Gerry look like that?

'Thanks for bringing us up to date. We'll deal—' Now Gerry was cool again – just listening. 'Yeah, see you at church around ten o'clock.'

Paul frowned. Why did they have to go to church this morning? 'What was that all about?' He tried to sound casual.

'Fran Logan is out,' Gerry began.

'I know.' Paul brushed this aside. *That was good. Fran Logan could be tough.* 'So?'

'She's already been replaced. A new entry in the Special Primary.'

'They couldn't wait much longer,' Paul jeered. 'Who's the new sucker?'

'You're not going to like this,' Gerry warned.

'What's the difference?' A condescending note in Paul's voice now. 'Alex Thompson will win.'

'I wouldn't count on that. He'll have a real battle to fight. No matter how much he spends.' Gerry paused. 'The new candidate is your soon-to-be ex-wife.'

'Diane?' Paul sat upright. His face disbelieving. 'That's plain crazy!'

'Believe it,' Gerry said drily. 'Alex Thompson could lose in the Special Primary. You may be running for re-election against Diane.'

'What chance has she got?' All at once Paul was cocky. 'She's never run for office in her life! She's a nobody!'

'She's smart. She knows all the angles. And she's had tremendous exposure. Much of it,' Gerry needled him, 'when she had to cover for you. Party time's over, Paul. We've got one rough campaign ahead of us.'

Paul gaped in alarm. 'We could lose?'

'No.' Gerry allowed himself an indulgent smile. 'We'll just have to work harder. And pull out every trick we know—'

Despite her determination to sleep at least until 9 a.m., Diane had awakened – as usual – at minutes past 6 a.m. But only now – at close to 9 a.m. – had she deserted her bed. At intervals she'd drowsed. Life was moving with frightening speed – with so much at stake.

With a need to talk with Joan, she reached for the phone, punched in her number. Joan would be awake by now.

'Good Sunday morning,' Joan greeted her. 'How're you doing?' Guessing the caller was Diane.

'I'm trying to keep my feet on the ground. This is such a turnabout—'

'It's the right way to go.' Joan was crisp, reassuring.

'Why did I stay with that creep all these years?' Diane demanded. 'Because I liked being the Power Behind the Throne?' she jeered at herself.

'You liked pushing what you thought was right for the country – and you didn't trust yourself to do it on your own. You hadn't understood woman power,' Joan clucked. 'You were a late learner.'

'Paul's going to be nasty,' Diane surmised. 'That was always his instinct. I had to cool him down regularly.'

'Yeah,' Joan drawled. 'Voters had to see him as just a regular guy.'

'I've been searching my mind for what he knows about me that could be harmful to my candidacy. I came up with nothing.' Diane gestured broadly. 'What about you? Do you remember any dark spots I've forgot about through the years?'

'Di, stop being naive. They'll lie like hell, with Paul going along. And we'll come right back at them.'

'The other party follows the advertising-agency code – say something often enough and people will believe it.' Diane took a deep breath. 'We've seen that often enough. We'd better be prepared for the worst.'

'We'll win the Special Primary, no matter how much Alex Thompson spends. And we'll win the election in November. We'll be living in Washington by next January,' Joan gloated. 'My mother will be torn. She'll be thrilled that I'll be meeting "important guys" – but she'll moan about not seeing me at least once a week.'

'They have phones in Washington,' Diane reminded. 'Arrange for unlimited state-to-state calls.'

'Let me get off the phone and dress. And have coffee ready,' Joan ordered. 'We've got a whirlwind campaign to launch. A week from Monday this district goes to the polls to choose its Democratic candidate.' She shuddered for a moment. 'Who could believe we'd have to go to the racetrack on such short notice?'

'Joan—' Diane hesitated a moment. 'Do you think Larry will stay with us? I mean, go the full route? If we win—'

'We'll win,' Joan repeated, 'and a herd of bulls couldn't keep Larry away from you. When the hell does your divorce come through?'

'Oh, shut up,' Diane ordered. 'Dress and get over here.'

Diane showered, dressed in her home-at-work outfit – jeans, T-shirt, and sneakers – and went downstairs. Joan would be here shortly, Larry at 10 a.m. 'Don't make breakfast for us,' Joan had said last night, and Larry agreed. All right, have coffee now. Brunch with Liz at noon. And pick up the Sunday *Enquirer* at the door.

En route to the door, she stopped to lower the thermostat on the air-conditioning side. Flinching as she remembered the soaring energy costs. But already the day was hot – let them be comfortable.

Her heart pounding, she stooped to pick up the newspaper. Her eyes drawn instantly to the tiny headlined segment on the front page. DIANE SOMERS ENTERS SPECIAL PRIMARY. Below, a very brief article about her. There'd be much more tomorrow.

It was real – she was fighting to replace Paul as the district's

Representative in Congress. Paul was here in town to campaign for his re-election. Prepare, she warned herself – their paths were sure to cross. Prepare for some low blows.

Be sweet, she exhorted herself. More shocked than reproachful at Paul's jumping the fence when questions were fired at her during this evening's interview. Jill said he and his cohort were staying at the Racine. A giggle escaped her. That must annoy Paul. So entranced by his so-called stature as a Congressman.

She carried the Sunday newspaper into the kitchen. Too tense to move past the front page this morning. So much to be done! She brought down the twelve-cup coffeemaker, reached for the coffee grinder. Instinct told her they'd be drinking a lot of coffee this morning.

Jill and Robin would handle the volunteers at campaign headquarters – officially opening at noon on Sundays. Larry had talked with them last evening. Jill and Robin knew to update their blog, schedule fliers to be delivered by hand, arrange to have posters printed and posted. Two months of campaigning must be pushed into the next eight days.

Mug of coffee in hand, she went up to the master bedroom to consider what to wear for the TV interview. Opening the first of the array of louvered doors that led to closet space, she realized that she had not yet rid the house of Paul's clothing. So sad, she told herself with a flicker of laughter. She'd take care of it after the Special Primary.

Elaine was right, she reproached herself. She must update her wardrobe, do something about her hair and makeup. She was moving into a new world. And the prospect was exciting. Larry's presence in that new world helped to make it exciting.

Now she laid out her turquoise silk pantsuit – worn on special occasions only – and a low-cut matching top that Joan had labeled 'sexy.' Frowning in rejection but determined to wear them, she brought down a pair of high-heeled, off-white sandals.

She heard the door chimes sounding. Did Joan fly over by helicopter? She rushed downstairs to respond, pulled the door wide.

'Hi,' Larry greeted her. His eyes somber. Apologetic. 'Do you mind that I'm early?'

'No way. We're both compulsive about being early.' Her smile tender. They were alike in so many ways. But that didn't indicate an emotional relationship between them. The road she meant to travel was best traveled alone.

'I wanted to get over to tell you before you saw it on the TV news,' he began.

'What's happening?' she broke in. Instantly fearful.

'Not a tragedy,' he comforted, 'but one of our two Republican Senators and our Republican Governor will be in town on Wednesday – when Paul's scheduled to speak to the Chamber of Commerce. I gather they'll appear with him.'

'They figure we're a threat!' Diane's face glowed. 'That Paul's chances are shaky!'

'Don't jump,' Larry cautioned. His outer cool was defied by the rage in his eyes. 'The Governor, the Senator will be on a panel with Paul to explore the Hall-Stores situation.'

'You mean it's out in the open that Hall-Stores's actively seeking to come here?' Diane was taken aback. It was supposed to be hush-hush. But how long could that last in a small town like Linwood?

'It's out in the open – the zoning board was approached. It's considering the Hall-Stores offer. Paul's speech has suddenly become a town meeting,' Larry derided. 'Alex Thompson – supposedly Paul's chief rival for the seat in Congress – is joining the panel.'

'How do you know this?' Diane was breathless with shock.

'Hal Watson at the TV station called me about twenty minutes ago.' Larry walked with her to the kitchen. 'Alex Thompson was in a conference with the powers-that-be. He was demanding TV coverage of the town meeting.'

'A town meeting is, by nature, nonpartisan.' Diane protested. 'It's a place where both sides are argued.'

'Alex Thompson is to represent our side,' Larry said derisively. 'Di, think about it. Thompson – running as a Democrat in the Special Primary – will be their straight man. He'll bring up points they're sure they can refute. It'll be rehearsed until the four of them – Paul, the Senator, and the Governor on one side, Thompson on the other – are as smooth as sweet cream pouring over strawberries.'

'Larry, we have to make that a real town meeting! Real discussions! Both sides equally represented.' Her mind searched for an angle. 'Let's demand that Liz Franken be on that panel along with the Mayor.' She paused. 'No way they'll allow me to be part of it.'

Larry chuckled. 'You and Paul on the same panel? Wow, I'd love to see that! You'd beat him to a pulp. But no,' he conceded, 'it'd be considered explosive. A personal battle between the two of you rather than politics.'

'Let's alert our people to be there at that meeting.' Diane was fighting desperation. 'And brief them on questions to ask—'

'We'll try,' Larry soothed, 'but it's too late. You can be damn sure they'll load the auditorium with their people.'

'How can the zoning board even consider changing the rules for Hall-Stores?' Diane churned with frustration. 'They've seen what happens to towns that allow a Hall-Stores to open up. Longtime local businesses are forced to close. Decent paying jobs replaced with seven-dollar-an-hour jobs – often part-time. Hall-Stores creates traffic jams. Suddenly road repairs are necessary. And money that should remain in town is shipped off to sweeten Hall-Stores profits. They've seen it happen to other towns,' she repeated. 'Why do they think we'll be safe?'

Twenty-Two

Paul sprawled on one of the beds while Gerry fiddled with the TV set. He didn't want to see this interview with Diane and some local big shot, damn it! What a rotten way to spend a Sunday.

First, he was awakened practically at dawn to hear that insanity about Diane running in the Special Primary, then sweating it out in church for what seemed to be hours. And after church, meeting with that senior-citizens group. Gerry's voice echoing in his mind:

'Remember, play the average Joe, a guy they'd welcome for a son-in-law. Look what it did for Ronnie and George. Follow the same script, Paul. Keep that in mind everywhere you go in the district. Show yourself as a regular guy. It's the road to re-election.'

Paul's face brightened in recall. That group at the church lapped it up like a cat before a plate of caviar when he said he'd gone into politics because God told him he must do that. God wanted him to fight for them.

'Here it comes—' Gerry's voice punctured his reverie. 'Listen up, Paul.'

He gritted his teeth and watched while Diane and somebody named Liz Franken were introduced. Now the woman interviewer was questioning the two, alternating between Diane and Franken.

'Routine stuff,' Paul scoffed after a few minutes, was hushed by Gerry.

'You'll need to be able to rip down their platform.' Gerry was scribbling notes on a legal-sized pad while the interview grew more passionate in tone. 'We'll work on that tonight.' *Damn, why can't Gerry get off my back? I play 'one of the guys' – people love it.*

Then all at once the tone of the interview changed.

'I know it must be difficult to discuss this,' the interviewer said gently, 'but how do you feel about your divorce in progress?'

'Oh, shit!' Paul leapt into a sitting position. 'What's Diane going to pull now?'

'Shut up and listen,' Gerry ordered. Intent on hearing every word of Diane's response.

'I was shocked—' Diane was somber, wistful. 'I hadn't seen it coming. I was all wrapped up in working for Paul's re-election. And then I realized – I didn't know him at all. He'd accepted my advice all through the ten years of our marriage – and now he was moving to the other side. The man who was concerned for the well-being of the average American had disappeared. He returned to his father's fold – the corporate structure, Wall Street—' Her voice trailed off with the skill of a well-trained actress.

'The bitch!' Paul screeched, charged for the remote, hit the mute button. 'She's trying to ruin me!'

'Grow up, Paul.' Gerry grasped the remote from him, restored sound. 'We need to hear every word she and Liz Franken utter!'

'Why?' Paul was outraged.

'Because we don't want Diane Somers to win this Special Primary,' Gerry hissed. 'We don't want to have to fight her in the general election.' But all at once he regained his cool. 'Of course, we know how to make her lose.'

Like homing pigeons, Diane, Joan, and Larry headed for campaign headquarters after the interview. Volunteers and Jill had watched. They applauded exuberantly as the three walked into headquarters. Diane exchanged brief, lively conversation with them, Larry and Joan joining in.

'That was a voter-getter,' Jill crowed to Diane 'You made Paul look a class-A heel!'

'He is,' Joan shot back.

'Oh, your mother called,' Jill told Joan. 'She said she needed to talk with you. It's important—'

'She watched the television interview,' Joan guessed. 'She's got comments.'

'Call her,' Diane said. 'She's probably sitting by the phone—'

'Jill, they have delivery service at the restaurant next door, don't they?' Larry asked. 'We're all famished. Or could you send somebody over?'

'Give me a list – one of the volunteers will be happy to pick up for you. That'll be faster.' Jill exuded triumph. 'Everybody's so pleased about the interview.'

The other three huddled over dinner choices. Larry reached into his pocket. Joan waved this away.

'Campaign expense account,' she decreed. 'Seldom used.'

They settled in Diane's cubicle. With an air of apology Joan reached for the phone. 'Let me call Mom—'

Moments later Diane and Larry abandoned talking to eavesdrop.

'Yeah, Mom,' Joan said. 'We know Paul's here to campaign.' She paused to listen. 'No, we didn't know that.' She turned to the others. 'Somebody on the Republican committee just arranged for a hotel suite for Paul – on an annual basis. He needs to establish residence.' She rushed back to the phone. 'Yeah, Mom, I'm listening. We know senior-citizens groups are his favorite places for campaigning.' As she listened, her jaw dropped in astonishment. 'Mom, you've always said that group was so conservative they made Rush Limbaugh seem a way-out liberal. Are you sure you want to do this?' A pause again. 'Sure, Mom, we'll appreciate the effort.'

'What was that all about?' Diane asked when Joan put down the phone.

'My mother's closest friend – except when they discuss politics – told her that Paul's visiting her senior group tomorrow afternoon. Mom asked if we'd like to have a mole checking in.' Joan giggled. 'She's seeing herself as a member of the CIA, undercover.'

'Sure, we want to know what lies Paul will be circulating,' Larry approved. 'We'll know what to refute. But let's not forget.' He turned to Diane. 'You're waging a double campaign here. One against Alex Thompson and the other against Paul, because we're convinced you'll beat Alex and face Paul in November.'

'Somers v. Somers. That has a gorgeous ring to it.' Joan pantomimed her approval. 'It'll create big interest – not just in the district but nationwide. And it'll help in fund-raising. Somers v. Somers will move us into the national spotlight.'

'If we mow down Alex Thompson.' Diane alternated between euphoria and fear. 'You know how he's spending. All those damn commercials.'

'But he's going to cut his throat sponsoring that town meeting to sell Hall-Stores,' Larry predicted. 'Local groups are being very vocal about their objections. Thompson will face a lot of opposition.'

'Plus the rumor's circulating that Thompson only wants Hall-Stores to come to town because he figures on selling them that sixteen-acre plot he owns across from the mall.' Joan's smile was smug. 'Isn't it amazing how rumors spread in this town?'

'The next eight days are going to be insane,' Larry warned. 'We've got a hell of a lot of work to do.'

'You two will probably have to wheel me to the polls to vote,' Joan surmised. 'And what do you know, Mom's going to vote again.'

'I know we've all had a rough day,' Larry consoled, 'but we've got to get those eight days scheduled right now. On my side, I'll make sure Bill Taylor has a front-page story every day. I'll beat up on the TV stations and radio stations in the area. Joan, make sure Diane has at least three appearances – formal or informal – for each day. Minimum,' he emphasized. 'Remember, we have to cover the whole district.'

'Food for hungry workers.' Jill appeared, flourishing an insulated bag. 'You'll need it. I suspect it's going to be a late night.'

Joan distributed dinner. The three of them settled down to combine eating with heated discussion.

'The town meeting,' Diane began, 'may seem a local matter, but we'll see people popping in from other areas in the district. It's meant to seem just an appeal to bring Hall-Stores into Linwood – but Paul's going to be there, campaigning like crazy.'

'In jeans, shirt open at the neck, and no tie,' Joan drawled. 'Just a "regular Joe." Like you taught him, Di.'

'A guy who likes to go to bed at nine thirty p.m. – while his wife loves the nightlife scene—' Larry quoted Paul. Diane grunted in disgust. 'Which leads me to believe the opposition will stay on the "family values" bandwagon.' He frowned in thought. 'Di, search your memory. Is there anything Paul and his crew can latch on to to refute your respect for "family values?"'

'No,' Diane dismissed this. 'Remember, he's the one who's suing for divorce.'

'What about kids?' Larry probed. 'Will he come out and claim you put career before family?'

'He may claim it, but it'd be a damn lie!' Diane flared. 'Whenever I tried to broach the subject, he said, "Kids grow up to be teenagers – they embarrass the hell out of their parents,"' she mimicked. '"In politics that's bad."'

'Right,' Joan picked up, her smile effervescent. 'It's the Democrats who have children who stay out of the headlines. Think Amy Carter, Chelsea Clinton.'

'The administration makes big noises about "family values,"' Larry pursued. 'I've got a gut feeling it's trickled down to lower-level campaigning in a big way. They're going to zero in on that area. Di, try to think back,' he urged. 'Dig anything up – no matter how small. Did you ever run away from home? Ever get caught smoking pot?'

'I never smoked pot,' Diane recalled and smiled in recall. 'During my rebellious years I had a minor respiratory problem. I knew pot would cause me big trouble. And I never once ran away from home.'

'God, I'd love to be a fly on the wall in that hotel room where Paul and the character with him are plotting their next steps – in a conference call with the party bigwigs,' Joan fantasized, then sighed. 'But I don't suppose we could arrange that.'

'What a dump this is,' Paul complained. Ignoring that Gerry was on a call with Addison Collins and two party big wheels. 'Not even room service!'

He paced about the room while Gerry debated with the others. It was almost midnight – they'd had dinner before 7 p.m. Because that was popular among the locals, he derided. He was hungry, damn it.

Now Gerry was off the phone. His demeanor complacent. 'We'll keep on the "family values" shtick,' he told Paul. 'That's a big deal these days. Straight down from the President to Congress. Why didn't you and Diane ever have kids? You're thirty-five. How old is she? A year younger?'

'Right – but we had no time for kids—' Paul stopped dead at the sight of pain on Gerry's face. Paul switched gears. 'It made me feel awful. Diane refused to have kids – no matter how often I tried to change her thinking.' His voice plaintive now – in the mode drilled into him by Diane. 'She wouldn't allow me to have a dog—'

Twenty-Three

Diane had been at campaign headquarters since 7 a.m. this Monday morning. She struggled for an air of high spirits, verve. She couldn't afford to be tired or depressed at this stage of the game, she told herself. A week from tomorrow voters in their district went to the polls to vote in the Special Primary.

They were sending out both snail-mail and e-mail 'alerts' about the town meeting the day after tomorrow. Urging attendance, though Larry warned the opposition would find ways to keep out those who were forming the 'Keep Hall-Stores Out of Linwood' group. Fran's sister-in-law and Larry's sister Andrea had leapt in to promote this faction.

Reluctantly Diane had allowed Joan to make an appointment for her at 6 p.m. that evening with Elaine's highly praised hair stylist, Jacques, at the Oasis. Beyond her budget in normal circumstances. The Oasis catered to the wealthy social set and high-level professional women. But Joan had been insistent.

'Di, the time has come – you've got to have your hair restyled. You need to look sharp on public appearances.'

Joan said women waited a month for an appointment. But all at once she was a local celebrity. Jacques would be delighted to do her hair. At least 6 p.m. was a good time, Diane told herself defensively. From 6 p.m. to 7 p.m. she had nothing scheduled.

She glanced at her watch. It was almost 9 a.m. At 10 a.m. she was to speak to a group of young mothers about the need to upgrade the local school system. At noon she was to attend a hastily arranged luncheon sponsored by the local Women for the Environment. She checked her schedule – at 3 p.m. she'd speak to a senior-citizens group in another community that was part of their district.

She looked up with a start when Joan burst into her cubicle.

'Get your butt to the TV set,' she ordered. 'Paul's being interviewed at the Olympic Diner!'

Diane hurried to join Joan, Jill, and the handful of volunteers who'd already arrived for a shift. The camera had zoomed in on Paul, sitting at the table with the Olympic's owner – a dyed-in-the-wool Republican, Diane recalled.

A few people sat around at the tables and in booths. Four male senior citizens in one booth – elated at television exposure. A pair of young mothers, with strollers strategically parked. Suppressing giggles, yet appearing to be fascinated at the experience.

'We hear you'll be moving into a local hotel, now that you and your wife have separated,' the male commentator said. 'Have you made your choice yet?'

'That'll probably have to wait until after the election.' Paul flashed his 'I'm kind of shy' smile. 'Much to do until then. I mean, the bust-up of my marriage hit me hard—'

'Oh yeah!' Joan hissed at the TV set.

'Half the town knows he's established residence with a hotel suite here in Linwood,' Diane derided.

'How would it feel to be fighting against your ex-wife for your seat in Congress?' the commentator pursued.

'Hey, she hasn't won the Special Primary,' the owner of the Olympia intervened. 'He may be fighting Alex Thompson – or one of the others.'

'I wish her well.' Paul was demure. 'But I suppose you'd say it was a matter of "a woman scorned." I mean, she'll miss the excitement of living in a wonderful place like Washington. Meeting all those people who're working to keep this the greatest country in the world. Of course, I've missed living in Linwood the last two years,' he rushed in to declare. 'Still, I've managed to get home a lot. I need to talk with my people, know what they want for our district. I'm here to serve – and with your help – and God's – I'll go back for another two years.'

'Over our dead bodies!' Diane glared at the TV set.

'You were married ten years—' The commentator's tone was casual, but Paul seemed tense.

'That's right. We were just out of law school—' Paul strived for a wistful demeanor. 'I worked hard at the marriage – but I guess I just didn't have what it takes to keep it alive.'

'You never had children?' A deceptive casualness that put Paul on guard.

'No.' He contrived a sigh. 'Diane refused to have kids,' he improvised. 'No matter how many times I tried to change her thinking.' His voice plaintive now. 'Diane didn't want children. She wouldn't even allow me to have a dog—'

'Turn that thing off!' Diane yelled in rage. 'I won't listen to that pack of lies!'

'This is all part of his "family values campaign,"' Larry pointed out. Diane glanced up in surprise. She hadn't been aware that he'd arrived. 'We should have expected something like this. Don't worry, we'll talk back,' he soothed.

'Diane will deny it.' Joan's voice was venomous. 'And that crap about Diane not allowing him to have a dog!'

'I had a dog all my life – until I went off to college. I love almost everything on four feet.' Diane fought for calm. 'We didn't have a dog for the ten years we were together because Paul always insisted he's allergic to dogs. "It's been my problem since I was three,"' she mimicked. 'And he said he was allergic to cats as well. Where does he get the nerve to say I deprived him of a dog?'

'Did you refuse to have children?' Larry asked. His voice gentle, as though anticipating a negative reply.

Diane closed her eyes for a moment in anguish. 'I was dying to have a family. Paul said, "No way. Kids can wreck a career. Who needs them?"'

'He's going to use this gimmick straight through to election day,' Joan predicted. 'He didn't dream it up—' Her smile scathing. 'He doesn't have the brains for that.'

'No matter what I say, he'll deny it.' Diane searched her mind for a way to handle this situation. 'And for some prospective voters that makes me appear a hard, calculating woman whose "family values" are non-existent.'

'There's just one way to beat it.' Larry refused to be downcast. 'First, let's consider this bit about Paul's being allergic to animals. What proof do you have that he was allergic?' he challenged Diane.

'It was just something he always said.' Diane shrugged. 'I never thought about questioning it.'

'Think back,' Larry prodded. 'Do you remember any occasion when Paul was exposed to dogs – and had a bad reaction?'

Diane squinted in thought for a moment. 'No—' *Why all this excitement about Paul's being allergic to dogs? It's his creepy claim I didn't want kids that'll do the real damage.* 'We were never around dogs.'

'Wait a minute!' Joan glowed in triumph. 'I remember Paul being a judge at a dog show in Maryland about a year ago! You were here in town with a case of the flu. I set up the deal. Paul didn't complain about it – I heard nothing about a bad reaction.'

'He's a liar!' Larry pinpointed. 'And once we can prove it people will suspect he lied about your not wanting children.'

'We're going to do this in eight days?' Diane was skeptical.

'Not in eight days,' Larry brushed this aside. 'Between now and November seventh.'

'What about the Special Primary?' Diane protested. 'How do I win that?'

Larry dismissed this with an eloquent gesture. 'You're going to win that Special Primary. What Paul said at that diner won't circulate fast enough to throw the Primary to Alex Thompson. We'll have Liz Franken call another town meeting on Friday – to refute whatever dirt the opposition throws out at the Wednesday town meeting. And it won't be stacked with Thompson supporters. The big question at the moment: Do we allow Hall-Stores to open up in this town?'

'If it's a real town meeting, there'll be dissent,' Diane pointed out, nodding in approval. 'But we can handle that—'

'Liz Franken, flanked by several concerned local citizens, will remind people what horrors can develop in our town if we allow Hall-Stores to operate here. She'll back it up with facts.' Joan was emphatic. 'Liz and her cohorts will knock down whatever hogwash the other side throws back.'

Larry nodded in vigorous agreement. 'We'll keep Hall-Stores out of town.'

'We did it before, we'll do it again.' Diane was defiant, though at unwary moments she harbored fears.

'People will vote against Alex Thompson as our candidate for Congress – despite all the money he's spending on TV and radio commercials. We'll see Somers v. Somers in November. And before then,' Larry vowed, 'we'll find a way to convince the voting public that Diane Somers' family values are real and to their liking. And that Paul Somers is a lying skunk!'

Twenty-Four

Diane suspected the next few days would charge past like a category-five hurricane – and she wasn't wrong. The Wednesday town meeting was packed with opposition supporters. Admittance had been announced for 8 p.m. Would-be attendees arrived at 7 p.m. Strong rumors indicated this had been prearranged to assure a friendly audience. Thursday morning's *Enquirer* was scathing in its report of the town meeting's performance.

'*A town meeting implies that both sides have equal time to express their views. This did not apply to last evening's meeting. Shame on the Chamber of Commerce for sponsoring it.*'

On Thursday the *Evening News* applauded the efforts of the panel, but conceded that earlier in the day the zoning board had rejected the Hall-Stores offer.

'*Hall-Stores – ever generous in its efforts – is preparing an offer more acceptable to our finicky zoning board. This fine organization will be a great addition to our town.*'

On Friday evening – with the zoning board making no statement about a just-received fresh proposal – the second town meeting drew a record crowd. The familiar points were pressed. Heavy emphasis was placed, also, on the urgency to vote for Diane Somers in the approaching Special Primary.

Each morning at 7 a.m. Diane huddled with Larry and Joan over breakfast brought in by Jill. They checked the day's schedule. After a hurried conference they dashed off on their separate ways. Jill would deal with the now-frenzied activities of the volunteers.

By 11 p.m. each day they were back at campaign headquarters to confer on the day's efforts. The current objective to defeat Alex Thompson – and at the same time cut back the chances of Hall-Stores opening in town. The approval of the zoning board was just the first hurdle, Diane reiterated with shaky confidence. If the board approved, then the Hall-Stores proposal would go to the Town Council.

Commercials for Thompson dominated the district's radio and television. He appeared on endless street corners to shake hands with prospective voters. His supporters handed out leaflets that simultaneously promoted his campaign and the efforts of Hall-Stores to locate in the Linwood area.

At the same time – with the November elections in mind – Paul was on a daily round of speeches to special groups. In open-throated sport shirt, jeans, and sneakers, he ate his meals – accompanied by Gerry – in the local diner or local-favored fast-food spots.

'Guess who I just saw at the restaurant next door?' Jill drawled, bringing in breakfast for the other three of the 'Ferocious Four' on the Saturday morning before the Special Primary. 'Our current Congressman,' she said without waiting for a reply.

'Paul awake and in action by seven ten in the morning?' Diane jeered. 'What's he on?'

'He was holding court from a stool at the counter. Being "one of the guys." Inviting people to some barbecue tomorrow afternoon.' Jill gestured incomprehension.

Joan's mother – exhilarated by her first venture into politics – had ferreted out the tenor of Paul's speeches.

'*He's a scumbag! He's still hammering on how Diane was a party girl, never wanted kids, wouldn't let him have a pup!*'

'Maybe I should have rushed in and showed Paul up for being a liar,' Diane moaned while the 'Ferocious Four' gathered for a near-midnight snack and conference on Saturday evening.

'How?' Larry challenged.

'Telling them Paul's lying!' Diane shot back, then stopped dead. 'That's not enough—'

'Right.' Larry's face was grim.

'How do I convince voters I love kids? I want a family!' *Why is Larry looking at me that way? With such tenderness.*

'It comes down to what we've said before,' Jill picked up. 'Family values are going to dominate this district's Congressional election. And Paul will ride it to the bitter end.'

'But that business about his being allergic to dogs.' Larry seemed suddenly invigorated despite the hour. 'Joan, you said

when we talked about this before that he'd been a judge at a
dog show in Maryland. And he showed no signs at that time
of an allergic reaction.'

'He could have been lying to me,' Diane admitted. 'I've
always suspected he didn't like dogs – or cats. He's been
known to lie when it's convenient.' She paused for a moment.
'We need to go back and check on that dog show—'

'For beginners,' Joan pounced. 'If he's allergic, he must
have left a trail. I mean, doctors' reports, medication—'

'If Paul is really lying,' Diane said sardonically, 'we need
a way to prove it. It'll show him up for the man he really
is.'

'We dig in right after the Primary,' Larry said. 'Right now
that's on the back burner.'

'My mother's going to the barbecue tomorrow,' Joan
reported. 'With her best friend. The one who's her bitter enemy
when they talk politics. But not tomorrow.'

'The polls show that Thompson is running neck and neck
with me.' Diane forced herself to be realistic.

Jill was somber. 'Because of all those damn commercials
on radio and TV.'

'Oh hell, I forgot to call Bill Taylor!' Larry lunged for the
phone. 'My cell phone went dead this morning, but I picked
up my messages on Andrea's answering machine about five
hours ago.' He punched in Taylor's private number, waited.
Drummed impatiently on the table with one hand.

'It's late,' Jill warned. 'He could have left for the night.'

'Not at a crucial time like this,' Joan rejected. 'And hit
speakerphone.'

'Hello. Bill Taylor here.' Sounding grumpy, exhausted.

'Sorry not to have called earlier,' Larry apologized.
'What's up?'

'Read tomorrow morning's *Enquirer*.' Grumpy no longer.
Bill was smug. 'A couple of my guys – who loathe Alex
Thompson – got together to upset his applecart. They took
photos – half a dozen of them – of Thompson on a drinking
spree with Paul Somers at some gin mill in the next community.' Bill was almost convulsed with laughter. 'Somers escaped
his keeper for a couple of hours of playtime. That's going to
cost Thompson a lot of votes!'

*　　*　　*

With rain threatening on Sunday morning, Larry learned that the barbecue would be held in a huge tent. Rain or not, he warned the others, the attendance would be large.

'It's for free,' he pointed out as the 'Ferocious Four' gathered for breakfast. 'And with the Governor, the Senator, and our Congressman there again, it'll bring out a crowd,' he predicted and grinned. 'But this morning's edition of the *Enquirer* will cause a lot of talking! None favorable to Alex Thompson.'

'That seems to be a failing among the opposition,' Diane said, her smile shaky. 'You caught Paul with the Republican bigwigs at some fancy restaurant. Now Bill's reporters caught Alex Thompson playing buddy-buddy with Paul.'

'We're going to win the Primary on Tuesday,' Larry said yet again. *Diane's scared. She's seen enough of dirty politics to be scared.* 'But our work will just be beginning. Di, Paul grew up in this town, didn't he?' Larry's mind was charging ahead.

'Except for the eight years his father was in Congress.' Her eyes searched his. *She knows where I'm going – we think alike in so many ways.* 'And then he went away to college. His parents hadn't been truly residents of Linwood since Paul was in college,' she recalled. 'They keep a suite at the Linwood Court on a yearly basis – which gives them local residency. And you can figure that out,' she said knowingly.

'Right. There's no state income tax here. They save themselves a nice chunk of cash.'

'Paul and I – and Joan – came back to Linwood after law school. It was going to be the jumping-off point for his career – and ours. A team effort. But when you try to track down his supposed allergy problem—' Diane shook her head in doubt.

'I know, doctors can't reveal patients' medical records.' Larry brushed this aside. 'But there are ways of checking out if Paul's lying about being allergic to dogs. We prove he's lying about that, then people will suspect he's lying about your refusing to have kids.' *She didn't – she wants a family. I look at Andrea and Jimmy and their kids – and I know I want that, too.* 'That'll shoot a hole in his big family-values package.'

'If I win the Special Primary, Paul will play the wistful, denied fatherhood role right up to November seventh.' Diane was insistent. 'Again, the old advertising mantra. "Say it often enough, people will believe it."'

Twenty-Five

On Tuesday – the morning of the Special Primary – Diane awoke with a sense of zooming downward through space. Instantly aware that she faced a major hurdle today. Her heart began to pound as she anticipated the day ahead – and the possible results at the end of the day.

If she won the Special Primary, she'd move on to fight Paul for his seat in Congress. If she lost, she and Joan would have no option but to set up law practice here in Linwood. Their political ambitions – their determination 'to make a difference' at a dead end.

Early morning sun pushed its way through her bedroom drapes, laid a ribbon of gold across her bed. The weather was fine – that meant people would go to the polls, she told herself. A plus for their side.

She reached to switch on the night-table radio – cringing at the likelihood of being assaulted by yet another Alex Thompson commercial – abandoned this to pick up the phone. Its ring shrill in the 6 a.m. quiet.

'I'm awake and en route to the voting booth,' she announced. Confident the caller was Joan. 'But first, I'll shower and dress—'

'That's advisable. I'll pick you up in thirty minutes. We'll go out for breakfast – by then the polls will be open.' Joan's voice vibrant with high spirits. 'Jill's setting up volunteers with brochures at every corner close to the polls.'

'I can't believe Larry's optimism.' Diane's laugh was shaky. 'He said last night that he'd spend this morning working on my acceptance speech for tonight.'

'Mom was threatening to parade routes to the polls – wearing a sandwich sign reading "Moms for Diane." I persuaded her to abandon that and just phone all her on-the-fence friends to vote for you.'

'It's a changing world – when your mother sees the need to vote. It took a lot of years for you to get her there.'

Joan chuckled. 'It wasn't me. She saw the light when Bush talked about redesigning social security. Now Mom's decided if I go to live in Washington, I'm sure to meet "some rich thirty-year-old who knows he needs a sharp wife to make it in politics." I reminded her I'll be thirty-five in four months.'

'This is the twenty-first century – life goes on past thirty-five. But enough yakking – let me shower and dress. Pick me up in thirty minutes. Let just one of us be a gas guzzler.'

Twenty minutes later Diane heard the front-door chimes, hurried downstairs and to the door.

'You're early,' she told Joan in mock reproach. 'I haven't put on my shoes yet.'

'And get out of those jeans and that T-shirt.' Joan clucked in disapproval. 'You'll be appearing as a Congresswoman-in-waiting.'

'Nobody's going to be there at this hour.'

'I figured you'd say that. Back up to your bedroom. Change into your silk pantsuit and a turquoise shell,' Joan ordered.

'It's a warm day—' Diane clucked in reproach. But she was climbing the stairs. Joan was right – she ought to dress like a winner. *I'm not fighting for Paul now. I'm fighting for me.*

The polls opened at 7 a.m. At 7.06 a.m. Diane and Joan sauntered into the ghost-like area of the neighborhood school that served as a polling center. One person in a booth, one woman waiting to vote. The other two tables, manned by people Diane recalled from earlier elections, devoid of action. No voters as yet.

'OK, go vote,' Joan said blithely and prodded Diane towards the table that serviced Diane's address.

'This is a great morning for an election—' Larry's deep, charismatic voice spun them around. He was striding into the room along with a cameraman poised for action. The call letters of the local TV station emblazoned on the cameraman's shirt. 'Let's get a shot of the winning candidate as she prepares to vote!'

Diane smiled for the cameraman – a hand aloft in the victory sign – as she entered the booth. Joan and Larry – and the cameraman – waited for Diane to vote, then to pull aside the polling booth curtains and emerge. Several more shots of Diane. Larry and the cameraman exchanged brief conversation. Now the cameraman moved away to take photos at another table.

Diane smiled graciously at a sprinkling of voters who appeared now. *The voting's starting early. That means it'll be a heavy turnout.* She'd been through this scene before with Paul – yet today it was so different, she mused. She was conscious of emotional turmoil. So much depended on the outcome of the Primary. This was the first rung of her personal political ladder.

'I'll find time to vote later in the day,' Larry murmured. His eyes everywhere. The atmosphere charged with an aura of excitement as voters began to arrive in surprising numbers, considering the hour. 'Joan and I vote at different schools,' he reminded Diane.

'All right, let's get moving,' Joan effervesced, then froze. Diane and Larry followed her gaze. The cameraman was rushing into action. Flanked on his right by a grim, thirty-ish man, Paul was walking towards the table where minutes ago Diane had signed to vote. The home they once shared was still his legal residence. Until the divorce came through.

Diane's heart began to pound. She hadn't seen Paul since that unreal encounter in the condo. Now he was ten feet away – and scowling at her.

How could I have been so blind for ten years? I let ambition blind my eyes! Paul was going to be my voice. My way to 'make a difference.'

She felt Larry's protective hand at her elbow – guiding her away from a head-on encounter with Paul. But the cameraman was taking a flood of shots. To be seen, no doubt, on this evening's TV news. High drama – the encounter of the spurned wife who was daring to challenge the incumbent Congressman.

Larry positioned himself between Diane and Joan, prodded them to the doorway. 'OK, let's head for breakfast.'

'Joan and I have had breakfast,' Diane said like a stubborn five-year-old.

'You need another,' Larry insisted. 'You probably settled for tea and a bagel.'

'You got it,' Joan admitted. 'I'm ready for something more

substantial.' *Larry and Joan know how upset I am at running into Paul this way. Why am I upset? I'm glad about the divorce.* 'We have a long, rough day ahead.'

'Oh, it's sure to be rough.' Larry's voice at a volume calculated to carry back to the arriving opposition. 'And I have to see the caterer about a late dinner party at campaign headquarters this evening. We'll be celebrating till dawn!'

Walking into the near-crowded restaurant next to campaign headquarters with Joan and Larry, Diane flashed a dazzling smile for the three truckers who straddled stools at the lunch counter and turned to applaud her appearance.

'The way to go, Di,' one called out. 'You go to Congress and fight for what we need!'

But a middle-aged couple in a rear booth glared in disapproval. This was going to be one of the longest days of her life, Diane warned herself. The longest day would be – provided she won the Special Primary – when she waited to hear the vote count for the seat in the House now held by Paul.

'Over here!' Alice – their political-minded waitress – waved a menu at a booth that was part of her station. She was removing dishes, cleaning the table. 'I voted ten minutes ago,' she said with relish as they approached. 'I wish I could vote a hundred times.'

'Don't try that, Alice.' Joan giggled. 'Who'll take care of us here if you're in the slammer?'

They settled down to order. Alice made suggestions.

'That's it,' Larry summed up, and Alice headed for the kitchen with her usual sassy walk.

'It feels so peculiar not to be rushing around like crazy.' Diane struggled for calm. *It'll be midnight before the votes are counted.*

'We have stuff to do yet.' Larry's tone was casual. His eyes said his mind was racing. 'Joan, you and I have to pick up two senior-citizens groups,' he reminded. 'Providing rides to the polls. Somewhere along the line, Di – you and I need to go over your victory speech.'

'Larry!' *How could he be so confident? Everybody knows this will be a close race. Thompson's outspent us by four hundred per cent.*

'I have to huddle with Jill about which caterer to use.

We have to arrange a party for a huge bunch of happy volunteers.' Larry refused to be deflated.

Diane moaned in protest. 'Alex Thompson has had our Senator, our Governor, and our current Representative out there plugging for him. He's—'

'Come on,' Larry broke in. 'Thompson's running on the Democratic ticket.'

'In a backhanded way they were campaigning for Thompson,' Diane insisted. 'Let's be realistic.' She avoided Larry's reproachful eyes. 'We don't know who'll win this Primary. Not until the last vote is counted.'

'It won't be the end of the world if we lose.' Diane was startled by the compassion in Larry's eyes now. 'There'll be another race two years from now.' Under the table his foot brushed hers. *No accident. Why am I reacting this way? And what is he saying? That he'll be around two years from now?* 'We're in this for the long haul.' His eyes held hers. Saying much more than he'd ever put into words.

Diane pretended to be unaware of the under-the-table communication. She launched into a diatribe against Paul. This was safe territory.

The day passed with agonizing slowness. Reporters from the *Enquirer* and the *Evening News* issued contradictory exit-poll figures on frequent radio and TV news breaks. Diane and Joan checked in with Jill or Robin at campaign headquarters at intervals. In late afternoon Larry corralled Diane to work on her 'victory speech.'

'What about a "conceding the election" speech?' Diane defied him.

'Think positive,' Larry insisted.

The polls closed at 9 p.m. Back at headquarters again, Diane glanced about at the jostling crowd of volunteers. The mood switching from moment to moment. Applause at appropriate TV news breaks. Already the caterer's people had arrived to set up tables against one wall.

'We're not losing this race.' Joan was defiant. 'People in this district are wising up. They look around and know it's time for change.'

'And for some,' Larry said with an ironic smile, 'there's all that glamour in a race that'll pit wife against husband. People are going to take sides in a very vocal way.'

Now the local TV station was the focus of attention. Figures were beginning to come in. Thompson was in the lead, then Diane. The figures jumped back and forth between them. Reports advised that the turnout had, indeed, been heavy.

'They're reporting a record voting!' Larry chortled. 'But the way things are moving we ought to have an answer by midnight.'

The caterer's helpers were jostling towards the newly set-up tables with trays of food. The atmosphere heated. All at once the figures were climbing on Diane's side. Victory cries rent the air. Two minutes before midnight the TV newscaster announced the final count:

'It's Diane Somers! By nine per cent!' he yelled in excitement, and joyous voices of volunteers almost drowned out his next words. 'In November our seat in the House will be fought for by Somers v. Somers!'

Press from various parts of the Congressional district – standing by in both camps – rushed to interview Diane. TV cameras shot endless pictures.

'We did it!' Larry exulted, hugging Diane and Joan while a pair of reporters questioned Jill about the coming campaign. 'And we'll do it again on November seventh!'

Twenty-Six

In the elegant private dining room at the Colonial Inn – where a flat-panel 42-inch TV graced one wall for the convenience of important guests – the atmosphere was mixed. The Governor and the Senator refused to be disturbed by reports that Diane Somers was the winner of the Special Primary.

'So she won the sympathy of some of our women voters because Paul's divorcing her.' The Governor dismissed this with a shrug. 'In a week or ten days they'll forget it.' He directed an encouraging smile towards Paul.

'Insiders in Washington know her as shrewd and hard-working,' the Senator conceded. 'But we've got the machinery to mow her down.'

Addison Collins stared into space. His face revealing his rage. Paul Somers was furious but forced into silence by sharp eye contact with Gerry.

'Addison, stop looking as though we'd lost control of the House over this "nothing" Primary,' the Governor cajoled. 'It might be to our advantage that Diane Somers won. Consider the drama of the situation—' He turned to Paul with an indulgent smile. 'An ex-wife daring to challenge her ex-husband for a seat in Congress! You'll be in the national spotlight from now to November seventh. Use it well.' Now a warning note in the Governor's voice. 'We need that seat.'

'We'll make her wish she'd never entered the Primary,' Addison Collins vowed. 'We'll go all out on the "family values" issues. That's damned important to every voter in this district. Paul, you go back in your memory, ferret out every derogatory incident you can recall.' He paused. 'And invent what you need.'

'Every family with kids will loathe Diane for refusing to have children.' Gerry exuded triumph. 'Not even to let the poor guy have a dog.'

'Of course she didn't want children,' Collins' head lobbyist picked up. 'Look at the hours she keeps – she's plugging away at the career scene from seven a.m. to midnight seven days a week!'

'You know this for a fact?' Collins demanded.

'We've got a man on her tail.' The lobbyist smirked. 'We go everywhere she goes – except to the ladies' room.'

'See if you can pin down a man in her life,' Collins ordered and Paul gaped in shock. 'If you can't find one, manufacture one. We must set her up as a hard, greedy, overly ambitious bitch who's fighting now for revenge because her poor, suffering husband wanted out. Not someone suitable to represent the American people in Congress.'

Paul was impatient for the group to disperse. He was off the hook for the next three days. A break before the wild race to election day. Saturday he was scheduled for another of those corny barbecues in a nearby community that was part of his district. From there on it would be a daily grind of chasing votes.

Right now he was churning to escape from Gerry's clutches and drive to Ronnie's house in Arlington. He forced himself to listen with the proper show of deference while the others wished him good luck in the days ahead.

'We're winning this election,' Collins reiterated as they headed off in separate directions. 'No dumb broad is going to change our plans.' Addison Collins was heading back to his Southampton estate in his private jet. A charter flight had been arranged to take Paul and Gerry to Washington. 'Don't you forget that for a minute.'

'No, sir,' Paul agreed enthusiastically. Because this was expected of him. *But I don't trust Diane – she's smart. How do we know what she'll pull off?*

'I'll pick you up at your condo around half past seven on Saturday morning,' Gerry told him. Eyes warning him to be available. 'We'll fly to Linwood on Addison's jet. He's coming with us.'

'Right, Gerry. We've got a campaign schedule to follow.' Radiating confidence because this was reassurance for Gerry. At times he suspected Gerry wasn't thrilled at being his 'personal assistant.'

By 3 a.m. Paul was on his own – behind the wheel of his

Lincoln Town Car. Business suit replaced by tight jeans and black T-shirt. What Ronnie called his 'bad boy' look. She'd wriggle up against him and whisper how 'bad boy' always made her passionate. He reached to switch on the air-conditioning. It was damn hot again – even at 3 a.m. He'd trade the Lincoln in for a red Jaguar now that Diane was off his back, he promised himself. And in a little while Ronnie would be on her back. Welcoming him in the way he preferred.

Ronnie was gorgeous – and hot as a California forest fire. And she was all his! Every straight guy on the planet would be jealous of him. Ronnie wasn't always giving him orders. Do this, do that! And she wouldn't give a damn that Diane had won the Special Primary.

Despite the hour – as he'd anticipated – Ronnie's Arlington estate was lighted up as though awaiting a horde of guests. The staff would be tucked away for the night in their wing at the rear of the house. And they knew to stay there until morning.

Churning with impatience now, he pulled up before the entrance of the multi-glassed contemporary, reached on the back-seat for his luggage. The front door swung wide. Ronnie stood there – in a black chiffon nightie that left nothing to the imagination.

All his, he gloated. And knowing this made him hot. She'd be the sexiest First Lady ever to live in the White House! Addison Collins had a ten-year plan. And the money and the machine to carry it out. Diane couldn't have done this for him.

'What took you so long?' Ronnie pretended to pout. 'I was considering heading out for Southampton for a few days.'

'You don't want to do that,' he clucked, hurrying into the house. Luggage dropped to the floor while he reached to pull her close.

His first wife had been chosen because she was sharp. Ronnie had Daddy Dear to push him up the ladder. And the fringe benefits were sensational.

Twenty-Seven

Except for Diane, Larry, and Joan, the last of the celebrants had left campaign headquarters half an hour ago. An eerie silence hung over the area. It was past 3 a.m., Diane noted – still reluctant, along with Larry and Joan – to call it a night. Too caught up in the excitement of this first victory. But this was just a first step up the ladder, she cautioned herself. The roughest road lay ahead.

'We've cleaned up as much as we can for tonight – or this morning,' Larry corrected himself with a wry chuckle. 'We've loaded the headquarters' refrigerator with the remains of the caterer's spread, cleaned up the remaining debris of plastic plates, utensils, cups, napkins. In a few hours caterer workers will arrive to take away the tables.'

'It was a great night,' Joan said, exhausted yet triumphant. 'We may be the only Democratic district in this state – but tonight proves we plan to stay that way.'

'Joan, be realistic,' Diane derided. 'This was a Democratic Primary. What were we proving?'

'We chose the candidate who can beat Paul.' Joan refused to be ruffled. 'A lot of voters realized Alex Thompson was just a shill for Paul.'

'Let's spread the word.' Despite the hour Larry was enthusiastic. 'There's change in the wind.'

'I know – tomorrow's a short work day for the three of us,' Diane conceded, 'but we should head home and grab a few hours' sleep.' She was still grasping at reality. *I won the Special Primary. I'll be running for Paul's seat in Congress.*

'I'll drive you home,' Larry told her. Now she remembered that Joan had picked her up this morning. Her car – her nine-year-old Dodge Stratus – was sitting in the garage. 'I go right past your house.'

'We won today.' All at once Joan was somber. 'But the real

battle's coming up. And it's going to be dirty.' Her face was eloquent.

'We've learned to expect that since the 2000 elections.' *Am I a nut case to think I can win that seat? I'm not just fighting Paul – I'm fighting the whole opposition party.*

'But like I said before—' Larry's smile was whimsical. 'The winds, they are a-changing.'

'So let's put on full battle gear,' Joan challenged. 'We can't afford to lose that seat in the House. Not just for this district,' she pointed out. 'Our vote could be the crucial vote in critical legislation.'

'Off the soapbox,' Larry clucked in mock reproach. 'We need to refuel on sleep.'

They left campaign headquarters in a blend of triumph and wariness. The next three months would rush past – every moment threatening defeat.

'Jill's opening at noon,' Joan reminded Diane and Larry as she pulled open the door of her car. 'I'll probably be a no-show until one p.m. It may be my last chance between now and November seventh to get a decent night's sleep.'

'Sleep well,' Diane said tenderly. Without Joan and Larry, could she have survived these last frenzied days?

'See you in the morning.' Larry was brisk now. 'Di, in the car. I don't want you falling asleep standing up.'

'I'll be lucky if I fall asleep at all. I'm too wired.'

In Larry's car – still on loan from his sister – he slid behind the wheel, reached to switch on the radio. Diane settled herself beside him. Traffic almost non-existent at this hour.

It was as though the whole world slept except for them, Diane thought – and was oddly disturbed at this unspoken assumption.

On an all-night radio program, a newscaster began to recall the events of the evening.

'Do we have to listen to that?' Diane protested. 'Again?'

'No—' His voice indulgent, Larry reached to fiddle with the dial, settled for a medley of Cole Porter tunes.

'Oh, I love Cole Porter.' She leaned back in pleased anticipation.

'So do I.' Larry reached to squeeze her hand for a moment. She was conscious of a surge of excitement – as though her life was about to move in a new direction.

'We'd better get some sleep tonight – because, as Joan warned, we won't be sleeping much for the next few weeks.' She struggled to appear casual. *Why did I react that way when Larry reached for my hand? It was just a comforting gesture.*

'We can handle it,' Larry said quietly.

'Larry—' All at once Diane felt close to panic. 'You'll be there with me? You're with us for the long haul?'

His eyes left the road for an instant. 'I'll be there,' he promised.

Why did I ask that? Will Larry take it the wrong way?

'Paul must be fuming. He's been so sure that Republican money would buy whatever the party wanted. And we know the Republicans meant for Alex Thompson to win – to leave the field wide open for Paul's taking. They probably figure me for a loser.'

'They figure wrong. You're not a loser, Di.' Again, his hand reached out for hers. 'I knew that minutes after we met.'

'I'll fight,' Diane vowed. Simultaneously relieved and disappointed when Larry's hand left hers to return to the wheel. *How can I feel this way about a man I've known such a little while? It's rebound – that's all it is. That's what Elaine would tell me.* 'But we'll never be able to raise the kind of funds that'll be there for Paul.'

'You want to bet?' His voice all at once rich with confidence. 'We've got technology on our side. We'll—'

'Buy every voter a computer?' It was dangerous to be over-confident.

Larry ignored her interruption. 'Now that you've won the Primary, we hit the Internet. We'll solicit money in every state in the Union. Because this isn't a race just to see who represents our district. We're—'

'"We're fighting to hold on to every seat we have in the House. When important legislation comes up, ours could be the crucial vote." I know the mantra.'

'Hey, where's that fighting spirit?' he demanded, pulling up before her house. 'Where's the gorgeous dynamo I knew?' He reached to grasp her by the shoulders. *He called me gorgeous?* 'You're going to win this race. Don't you dare consider anything else!'

All at once he was pulling her close. His mouth reaching

for hers. Her arms about his shoulders. *This is insane. What's happening to us?*

Diane came awake slowly. Aware of rain pounding on the roof. Of lightning zigzagging across the sky. All at once aware that she wasn't alone in bed. She stiffened in shock – recalling the passionate encounter with Larry. So marvelous, she thought – she'd never felt so alive!

'Di—' Larry, too, had emerged from the brief moments of slumber.

'We were out of our minds—' In the darkness she slipped out of bed, fumbled for the robe that always lay at the foot of the bed. *Where is it? Oh, here on the floor* – 'We had too much champagne—'

'Di, we weren't drunk. It was wonderful and—'

'We were overtired,' she jumped in. 'Overstimulated from the day's excitement.' Her words tumbled over one another as she pulled on the robe, fastened it about her waist. 'We'll forget this ever happened.'

'Whatever you say.' His voice gentle. *He's humoring me – as though I was a demented small child.*

She sensed that he was reaching for the bedside lamp. 'Don't turn on the light,' she ordered. Her mind in chaos. *Yes, it had been wonderful – but absurd. I'm in the midst of a divorce. I won't fall for the first good-looking man that makes a pass.* 'Please, just dress and leave. We'll pretend tonight never happened. I'll see you tomorrow at campaign headquarters.'

'Right, boss.' Teasing yet tender.

'This won't change our working relationship?' Her heart was pounding. She didn't want Larry to walk out on the campaign. She didn't want him to walk out of her life. *He called me gorgeous.*

'I wouldn't miss this campaign for the world.' His voice was a caress. 'I'll be at headquarters somewhere between noon and one p.m. We've got a hell of a lot of work to do. We have a campaign to win.'

In silent swiftness Larry dressed, headed in the darkness for the door. 'See you later—'

'Right.' Diane's voice barely above a whisper.

She lay on her side, clutching a pillow. Her heart racing. Listening for the sound of the front door closing, then Larry's car pulling out of the driveway. Rain pounding on the roof. Thunder rumbling overhead.

Can things be the same for Larry and me as they were before tonight? I'm not ready for anything more. But I need Larry in my life.

Twenty-Eight

Diane awoke from troubled slumber, was instantly assaulted by recall of her last waking hours. How had she allowed that to happen? It was the excitement of the election returns, she told herself yet again. Willing herself to believe this. It was just that both of them had been so wired. *It won't happen again. Larry understands that.*

She turned to glance at the clock on the night table. Wow! Minutes past 8 a.m. When was the last time she'd slept this late? But today was a semi-working day. Jill wouldn't be opening up until noon. The volunteers – bless them – would be pouring in after that.

Last evening's dreary rain had given way to a glorious, sunlit morning. But before she went into campaign head-quarters, she needed to talk with Elaine – with whom she'd shared many critical situations.

She waited until past 9 a.m. to phone Elaine. Suspecting Elaine might be still asleep, but too impatient to delay any longer.

'Hello—' Elaine suppressed a yawn.

'I hope I didn't wake you.' Diane was wistfully apologetic.

'I was awake,' Elaine soothed. 'Gearing myself to go in to shower and dress. Congratulations, baby. We'll have to sit down and plot a fund-raiser.'

'Meet me for breakfast?' Diane strived for casualness. 'I need to cry on your shoulder.'

'Breakfast at ten sharp. But what's this crap about crying on my shoulder?' Elaine scolded. 'You're a woman on her way to Congress.'

'My personal life has become complicated. I know – it's the "woman on the rebound" syndrome. But, Elaine, I've never felt this way about any man – and I know I mustn't let myself become involved with him.'

'Tell Mommie the story over breakfast,' Elaine crooned. 'Let's live it up – have breakfast at Cecile's.'

At five minutes before 10 a.m. Diane was seated at a table for two at ultra-expensive Cecile's – the morning gathering spot for the corporate elite of Linwood. Instinct told her that Elaine had chosen Cecile's as the proper setting for a Congressional candidate.

At 10 a.m. sharp Elaine – tall, currently blonde, attractive, smartly dressed – strode into Cecile's, was escorted to Diane's table.

'I can't believe this room is mobbed at seven thirty,' Elaine drawled, settling in the chair opposite Diane. 'I used to think top-level men and women executives kept short hours, took long vacations. Not so, darling. For them it's the seventy-hour work week and only weekend vacations – interrupted by endless business calls.'

'Sweetened by seven- and eight-figure bonuses,' Diane reminded. 'I'm not crying for them.' She glanced about the room – lightly populated at this late hour. In her brief tenure in Washington she'd learned about the frequency of 7 a.m. meetings – all the way to the top.

A deferential waiter appeared. Diane and Elaine focused on ordering. Diane ignored the astronomical cost of even a traditional breakfast. She knew Elaine would insist on picking up the check. She'd write it off as a contribution to the party.

A local real-estate entrepreneur whom Diane knew by sight sauntered over to their table on his way out of the room.

'Congratulations, Diane,' he murmured with a warm smile. *Why are you on first-name basis the minute you're a candidate?* 'We expect to see you heading for Washington in January.'

'Thank you, we're working for that.'

'He's probably a heavy contributor to Paul's campaign,' Elaine murmured when he was out of hearing. 'But he'll contribute some to yours, too. You know, covering his ass.'

'I was on a committee fighting him last year on an "eminent domain" case,' Diane recalled. Her face brightened. 'We won.'

'All right, baby – what's bothering you?' Elaine oozed sympathy.

In succinct terms Diane explained the situation with Larry.

'I know – it's the old rebound scene. I gather my divorce

will be final in about three weeks. My Territory of Guam divorce.'

'It's legal.' Elaine glowed with triumph. 'Nobody can prove otherwise.'

'I know.' Diane struggled to appear cool. 'Paul's almost out of my life.' She took a deep, anguished breath. 'But I've never felt this way about any man—' *Why do I keep saying that?*

'Allow yourself a casual affair,' Elaine ordered. *It could never be casual with Larry – we're both too intense.* 'You deserve it after ten years with that heel. I could never understand why you married him.'

Elaine and Joan had been their witnesses at their very private civil ceremony. They'd had no time for a traditional wedding, sought an escape from the disapproval of Paul's parents.

'I was lonely – and flattered,' Diane said after a moment. 'He was so good-looking – he could have had anybody in the student body. But he wanted me. I know,' she went on before Elaine could pick up, 'he was vowing to outdo his father politically – and he figured I was sharp. I'd help him up the ladder.'

'And you did. You created that "man of the people" character people see in Paul. They don't see the spoiled brat who's always had somebody to fight his battles for him. But now you kick him out on his butt,' Elaine urged. 'How does he have the balls to light into you the way he did on that TV interview? You fight the bastard. You win!'

'I'm afraid an affair with Larry would get out of hand,' Diane admitted. 'I never felt about Paul the way I feel about Larry.'

Elaine's smile was knowing. 'He was great in bed—'

Diane nodded. 'And we think alike in so many ways. All the important ways,' she pinpointed, and sighed. 'But I have no room in my life – the way I want to go – for that kind of distraction. I don't want to be derailed.' *Paul was no distraction. We worked together on a common goal.*

'Then stay the course – if that's what'll make you happy. But,' Elaine continued with resolve, 'I still think you ought to allow yourself an affair. This guy is clearly special.'

'I'll think about it,' Diane promised. *I can't – because an affair would get out of hand.*

'And do something about your makeup,' Elaine pushed.

'You're going to be in the public eye! I know this marvelous—'

'Elaine, I'm not running for Miss America—'

Elaine ignored the interruption. 'We'll sit down and do something about your makeup.'

'I'm wearing lipstick and powder,' Diane countered defensively. 'And there's a makeup person at the major TV stations.'

'You're never to leave your bedroom except in full battle gear,' Elaine instructed. 'And yes, it does make a difference,' she rushed on as Diane was about to protest. 'This race – Somers v. Somers – will be an attention-grabber. You're going to be interviewed on television, appearing before large groups. It's important for you to look your best even if you're just walking into a supermarket to buy a container of milk. How you look shouldn't matter,' she conceded. 'But it does.'

Walking into campaign headquarters – heart pounding – Diane geared herself to face Larry. Maybe he wouldn't be in until late, she comforted herself. With a surge of relief she saw only a cluster of jubilant volunteers and Jill. Neither Joan nor Larry in sight.

She paused to accept congratulations from volunteers, in turn thanked them for their dedicated efforts.

'Without all of you, we'd never have made it,' she assured them.

'We've got a long way to go yet,' an elderly man who had gone through many local campaigns cautioned now. 'But we'll do it!' he said in a burst of optimism.

'Diane,' Jill drew her away now, 'Joan and Larry are waiting to talk with you in the conference room.' The one truly private spot in campaign headquarters. 'One of his sources came up with some news.' Her face serious now.

'OK—' Bad news? 'I'm on my way.'

Tensing at the prospect of facing Larry, Diane strode back to the conference room, opened the door.

'Hi, Madame Candidate,' Larry greeted her. Casual, gently joshing. *It's going to be all right – we can carry this off.* 'We've got word of the initial attacks from the opposition.' More serious now.

'Bad?' She sat in the chair next to Joan – across from Larry.

Why is my heart going a zillion miles a minute? He's dismissed what happened last night from his mind.

'We knew this wasn't going to be a picnic,' Joan pointed out. *But she's nervous.*

'A group of four of your former college cronies – as they call themselves – ' Larry dripped sarcasm – 'have come out to sympathize with Paul. They claim not only have you refused to have children – you had an abortion in your senior year—'

'What?' Diane shrieked.

'I know – it's a lie,' Larry soothed.

Diane gaped in shock. 'I don't believe this! Who are these women? Who's paying them off?'

'Here're the names—' Larry handed her a sheet of paper. 'They're featured on a TV commercial to be released beginning tomorrow.'

Diane stared at the names. 'I don't know these women!' She turned from Larry to Joan, back to Larry. 'I've never heard of them.'

'They were in your graduating class,' Larry admitted. 'I checked them out as soon as I heard.'

'There were over two hundred women in my graduating class,' Diane lashed back. Already it was a dirty, lying campaign on Paul's side. *No, he didn't come up with this. It's the inner circle around him – determined to keep his seat in Congress.* 'Where did you get this information?'

'Hal Watson,' Larry told her. 'The cameraman at our local TV station.' *The one whose brother was in Larry's company in Iraq.* 'I asked him to be on the lookout for us. I figure they were afraid you might win, decided to be prepared with ammunition right away if it happened. This is part of the "family values" package they're throwing at the voters.'

'Then we'll do a commercial branding them liars!' Diane's mind shifted into high gear. She rose to her feet, began to pace. 'These women may have been at college with me, but I don't even know them!' She paused. 'All they have to offer is a blatant lie. No proof. They have a doctor who'll lie for them?' she scoffed.

'If pushed, they might come up with some creep,' Larry conceded. 'Supposedly, these women have nothing to do with Paul's personal campaign.' He allowed himself a slight grin at Diane and Joan's grunts of disbelief. 'They're disgruntled conservatives, fighting for "family values."'

'Can't we prove – medically – that you never had an abortion?' Joan was groping for a solution.

'I'm not stooping to anything like that.' Diane was indignant. 'I'm not having some doctor poking around to check this out. I won't give those lying women that much recognition!'

'Let's stay cool,' Larry soothed. 'We'll handle it in a dignified manner. You have never been pregnant – never had an abortion—'

'Thank God, I never had a baby with Paul.' Diane began to pace again. 'I don't know how I could ever have wished for that.'

Her eyes met Larry's, swung away. *Having a baby with Larry would be so right. But how do I know what I feel for him now is real? I can't get away from the rebound deal. That's all this could be.*

'They'll run that damn commercial until – they hope – people will begin to believe it.' Joan gestured her frustration. 'Where do we go from here?'

Unexpectedly Larry chuckled. 'Wouldn't it be wild if we discovered Paul can't have kids? That would dump his campaign right down the drain!'

'Come back to earth,' Diane scolded. 'How do we convince the voters – the very divided voters – in this Congressional district that I never refused to have children, never had an abortion – and I never told Paul he couldn't have a dog?'

Twenty-Nine

With election day barely ninety days away Diane knew that every waking hour must be packed with campaign efforts. Joan would be scheduling endless personal appearances for her. Larry would focus on print and Internet publicity. The three of them were working already on the Diane Somers blog. There would be many late-evening meetings with the district committee, with Liz Franken – bless her – furiously active.

Foremost in Diane's mind was the urgency to refute the malicious claim that she'd had an abortion. Because this would prove Paul was a liar, demolish his claim that she'd refused to have a family. That her 'family values' were non-existent. Sure, she considered it every woman's right to have an abortion – but she'd never been confronted with the need for this.

On this Friday morning after the Special Primary she awoke before her alarm clock screeched its 6 a.m. wake-up call. Sleep broken at intervals by the news from Hal Watson that the first TV commercial attacking her would hit their district's TV stations at 7 a.m. today – to be repeated at regular intervals through the day and evening. No doubt in her mind that the claims of those so-called former 'college cronies' had been engineered by the top brass of the opposition, determined to save Paul's seat in the House.

With a sudden burst of energy she left her bed and hurried into the bathroom. Shower, dress, be at campaign headquarters in time to hear the first telecast of that ghastly lie. How would it play with prospective voters? How much had they been paid to do the commercial? What favors guaranteed them? Or were they sicko, fanatical conservatives determined to tear her down?

A few minutes before 7 a.m. she was pulling into a parking spot just outside headquarters. Somebody would have to run out every two hours to drop quarters into the meter – but it was important to have the car close at hand.

'Hi!' Larry's voice spun her around. He'd parked just behind her car. Few spots taken this early in the day. 'I figured we'd watch that monstrosity together. And plot our response—'

Fresh rage surged in her. 'I can't believe this is happening! I know,' she rushed ahead, anticipating him, 'I should have been prepared for some horrible lies. That's part of the campaign scene these last few years.' *Thank God, Larry and I can forget that night together. It's as though it never happened. Almost.*

Larry fell into step beside her. 'Those women graduated the same year as you – with just passing grades. They've all four wandered from job to job. They've—'

'But that rotten commercial will be blasted out time after time until people will begin to accept it as truth,' Diane broke in. 'We've seen this happen in recent elections. The question is – what can we do to make voters understand it's a lie?'

'Joan and I are both working on it,' Larry comforted. 'You focus on your public appearances.' He grinned. 'I didn't realize we had a beauty running against Paul. That new hairstyle is great.'

Diane was startled. 'I'm not running in a beauty contest.' But she'd allowed Elaine to supervise her so-called 'makeover.'

'It helps that you're both bright and gorgeous.' *He called me gorgeous again. He's looking at me that way again.* 'And we need all the help we can get.'

Campaign headquarters wore that 'not ready for business yet' aura. Deserted except for Jill – already involved in phone calls – and Joan, fiddling with dials on the TV set. She clucked in impatience as a commercial for a local restaurant boomed its message, lowered the volume.

'My eardrums thank you,' Larry murmured, dropping into a chair before the TV set.

'You're finally here,' Joan drawled. 'I thought I might have to endure the unveiling of the "abortion commercial" alone.'

'We wouldn't dream of missing it,' Diane hissed, pulling up another chair.

'There's coffee and a bag of bagels there—' Joan pointed to a nearby table. 'Let's settle in for the rat race.'

'Hal said it's brutal,' Larry warned and reached for a

container of coffee. 'But we can handle it.' He accepted an onion bagel from Diane.

'I've incorporated the commercial in my talk this morning.' Diane pulled the top from her coffee container, reached for a bagel. 'At the Levy Senior Center. Seniors are great about voting.' Her voice tenderly approving. 'And I'll do the same this evening at the meeting of the Linwood Professional Women's Group.' Her face tightened. 'I'll face a tough audience there. They're sure I'm all for raising taxes.'

Jill came charging to join them. 'It's almost time.'

The four of them sat facing the TV set, waited with grim expressions for the first news items to give way to the commercial they knew would be a vicious attack on Diane. The atmosphere heated as the thirty-second commercial made its debut.

'That is low,' Diane said through clenched teeth. 'The lie of the century!'

'Not quite,' Larry objected. 'That belongs to the present administration.'

The shrill shriek of a phone in the near-empty campaign headquarters was jarring. Jill rushed to pick up.

'Campaign headquarters, good morning,' she chirped and listened for an instant. 'Yes, he's here.' She beckoned to Larry.

He reached for the phone. 'Hi, this is Larry—'

He listened for a moment. His face somber yet impassive. *What's happening now?* 'Hal, we owe you. Thanks again!'

'What now?' Diane demanded as Larry put down the phone. 'That was Hal Watson,' she guessed.

Larry nodded. 'He managed to hear a new TV commercial scheduled to begin running with the six p.m. news tomorrow. Paul is "shaken, shocked by the story of Diane's abortion,"' he quoted. '"He's grieving for the child he's lost."'

'I'll kill him!' Diane raged. 'Just keep him out of my sight!'

'A violin section playing behind him?' Joan exuded contempt. 'A quartet in flowing black robes?'

'Hal was spared – he just "overheard" the commercial. He couldn't see.' Larry stared into space, then turned to Diane. 'You and Paul were married ten years – and you never got pregnant?'

'No,' Diane acknowledged, hesitated a moment. 'And we never took precautions—' In a corner of her mind she knew she'd hoped she'd get pregnant. A baby would fill a void in their marriage, she'd told herself.

All at once Larry's face was strangely alight. 'Wouldn't it be a howl if we could prove Paul can't have kids?'

'It could be me,' Diane said slowly.

'You're out in left field again,' Joan reproached Larry. 'Come back into the real world.'

'We're not desperate yet,' Jill pointed out. 'It's too early to run on hunches.'

'Some of the best reporting I've ever known came out of following a hunch,' Larry said. A glint in his eyes. 'All right,' he conceded, 'this is not our top lead. But I'd like to follow up on it. Just in between our other efforts,' he cajoled. 'I've got these strong vibes—'

'What else have you got?' Diane challenged.

'What can cause infertility in a man?' he pursued, glancing from one to the other of the three women.

'A sexually transmitted disease?' Jill suggested and Diane shuddered.

'No.' Diane was decisive. 'He'd have passed it on to me.'

'A sports injury in the critical area?' Joan offered. 'That can cause traumas that damage the sperm-making equipment.'

Larry turned to Diane. 'Did Paul play football? Or hockey?'

'His major physical activity in college and law school was cutting classes.' But Diane's mind leapt into high gear. Following Larry's lead, 'What about mumps?'

'What about it?' Jill asked.

'Mumps can bring on infertility in some cases. The adolescent boy's nightmare.' Larry flinched. 'The chance of this increases as the boy grows older.'

All at once the atmosphere was electric. 'Did Paul ever have mumps?' Jill asked Diane.

Diane shook her head. 'Not in the years that I knew him. But it could have happened earlier—'

'It won't be easy to track down,' Joan warned. 'And he could have had the mumps with no bad results.'

'But if he did and was one of those whose sperm count went down to nothing,' Larry persisted with a calmness refuted by his eyes, 'then Paul had better start looking for a job as of January, 2007.'

'It's a long shot—' Joan was ambivalent. 'Can we afford

to allot time for something so far out? Election day is breathing down our necks.'

'I'll sandwich in research somehow.' Larry exuded determination. 'We can't afford to ignore a strong hunch. OK,' he acknowledged, 'so it's my hunch.'

'Most likely it's wishful thinking—' Diane was dubious about following this up. 'We can't let ourselves be derailed.'

'We can't overlook any possibility,' Larry insisted.

Jill turned to him. 'I'll work with you. Just tell me how I can help.' She chuckled. 'So for the next ninety days, I'll get by on four hours' sleep a night.'

All at once Diane was decisive. 'We need to hang on to that seat in Congress. Larry's right – we can't afford to ignore any possibility. No matter how slim. Go for it, Larry!'

Thirty

Larry charged into the foyer of his sister's house with an aura of apology. He'd promised Andrea he'd be here for dinner tonight – and no later than seven o'clock. It was already twelve minutes past 7 p.m.

He heard the kids in good-humored argument in the living room. Andrea was humming an aria from *Tosca* in the kitchen at the rear of the house. Jimmy was in a heated phone conversation in the den.

'Hey, did everybody forget I'm due here for dinner tonight?' he called out in mock reproach. These were rare occasions.

'Uncle Larry!' Joey bolted out into the foyer, was followed by an exuberant Claire.

'How're my two favorite kids in all this world?' Larry demanded, wrestling with Joey, managing at the same time to deposit a kiss on Claire's cheek.

'You're late,' Andrea trilled from the kitchen. 'But tonight that's all right. The pork tenderloin needed another few minutes in the oven. I don't want to give us all a case of trichinosis. Go to the dining-room table – food's on the way.'

Jimmy emerged from the den. 'I was on a call with the chairman of our Keep Hall-Stores Out of Linwood committee.' He grunted in frustration. 'Linwood's still split down the middle.'

'I'll help Mommie bring in dinner.' Claire charged towards the kitchen. 'I set the table,' she called over one shoulder.

'I brought in the napkins,' Joey reminded, hanging on to Larry.

Jimmy was grim. 'We saw that lousy TV commercial this morning. It set my teeth on edge.'

'There's another one set to go – with Paul playing a soap-opera husband. But don't mention it around just yet,' Larry exhorted. 'My mole brought us the word. He said it'll debut tomorrow evening on the six p.m. news.'

'All right, everybody sit,' Andrea ordered, balancing a large platter with pork tenderloin and a mountain of garlic-mashed potatoes in one hand and a bowl of broccoli in the other. Claire followed with a huge salad bowl. 'After all,' Andrea joshed, 'it's a major occasion when ex-Lieutenant Larry Grant spends an evening with his family.'

'I'll have to run after dinner,' Larry said with a note of apology. 'Back to the grind. We've got a candidate to promote into office.'

'It's going to be tight.' Jimmy was sympathetic.

'Too close to call,' Larry admitted. 'Low down and dirty on the opposition side.'

Andrea bristled. 'You know the old platitude – "what's sauce for the goose is sauce for the gander" – or whatever.'

'Di won't play dirty.' Larry's smile was wry. 'The party won't play dirty,' he emphasized. 'But we're digging for the real dirt – as opposed to lying dirt – that we can unearth. And you'll be amazed at the response we're getting to Diane's blog.'

'And matching contributions?' Jimmy probed.

'It's good.' Larry was triumphant. 'The Internet is coming through for us. Small checks – but they're beginning to flow in like lottery-ticket purchases when the ante goes high. Not just from this state – from all over the country. Voters in other states realize this election can have nationwide effects. I know,' he silenced Andrea's imminent retort, 'we're dealing with just one vote in the House of Representatives. But that can be the crucial vote.'

'You have all the drama of an ex-wife battling her ex-husband.' A glint of avid curiosity in Andrea's eyes now. *She's developing ideas again about Diane and me.* 'Diane's looking great. She spoke to my Parents' Association meeting last night. But you know that,' Andrea drawled. 'I hear you've become her shadow these days.'

'I don't do just publicity – I'm her co-campaign manager.' Larry tried for a casual rebuke. 'And erase that wise-guy look. We share a professional relationship. Nothing more.' *No room in my life for a full-time personal relationship. No matter how I feel about Di.*

'You're thirty-five years old—' Andrea was about to launch a familiar refrain. 'When are you—?'

'Stop pushing the clock ahead,' Larry broke in. 'I'll be thirty-five next April. And—'

'Knock it off, you two,' Jimmy ordered. 'Eat and enjoy.'

By 8.15 p.m., Larry was searching for a parking space before campaign headquarters. Not one to be had.

'Damn!' he swore and headed for the public parking area three blocks away.

He'd arranged to meet with Jill when she took her dinner break – tonight from 8 p.m. to 9 p.m., though in truth she usually brought a sandwich and coffee back to headquarters. But Jill knew this research on Paul was urgent – in conjunction with his hunch.

He'd talked with Joan earlier in the day – hoping to dredge from her mind some useful information about Paul. But she'd pointed out that she'd moved to Linwood along with Diane and Paul when they'd decided this was the town where Paul's career could best be launched.

'Paul was born in Linwood – Di and I had never been here. His father had been the district's Congressman for eight years. It seemed a natural. Talk to Jill – she's lived here all her life.'

Larry parked, strode back to the restaurant next to campaign headquarters. He spied Jill seated in a booth at the rear. The dinner crowd thinning out already.

'Joan's holding the fort,' Jill greeted him. 'Why so late?' She clucked in reproach.

Larry grinned. 'My sister and brother-in-law – and the kids – expect me for dinner now and then.' He pantomimed to the waitress approaching their table to bring him coffee. To legitimatize his presence here. Now he focused on Jill. 'OK, you've lived here all your life. Were you at school with Paul? A few years behind him, of course—'

'He was in the fourth grade when I was in the first – both of us in the same school. He was an arrogant, snotty kid – sure he could get away with anything because his father was a political big wheel. And I've told you – I remember no mumps outbreak in our school. Maybe an isolated case here and there.' Jill waited for more questions.

'How did he do in school?' Larry was searching his mind for the route to go. *So the odds against my being on the right track are bad. But my vibes order me to dig.*

'The way I heard, he was no bright scholar. But you know

that. For the eight years his father was in Congress, he went to boarding school. The junior-high and high-school years,' Jill pinned down.

'And his father probably bought his way into college and law school,' Larry surmised. 'Let's go back. You said he went to boarding school when the family was living in Washington. Do you know where he went to boarding school?'

Jill's face brightened. 'I don't know about the junior-high years – but my cousin Ralph was in a boarding school for a year, when his mother was having serious health problems. Paul was at the same school. Because they came from the same town, they were assigned as roommates.' She grunted in disgust. 'Ralph hated that.'

Larry felt a surge of adrenaline. 'Where's your cousin now?'

'Here in town. He's a local lawyer. Ralph Andrews.' Jill reached for her purse, pulled out a notebook and pen. 'I'll give you his address and phone number – home and office.'

Larry reached for the slip of paper Jill extended. 'Which is his home number?' *Is it too late to call now?*

'The bottom number is the home phone. Call him now,' she urged, reading his mind. 'Tell him I explained he was at boarding school with Paul. That you need to talk with him.'

The waitress brought Larry's coffee. He took a fast few swigs. 'I'll call from the cell phone in the car. If he's clear, I'll drive right over.'

Thirty-One

In his car Larry brought his cell phone out of the glove compartment, punched in Ralph Andrews' home number. Andrews answered the phone on the second ring, listened to Paul's explanation.

'Come right over,' Ralph told him. His voice saying he'd do anything to help defeat Paul Somers. 'We're at the edge of town. The house is kind of hard to find – let me give you directions.'

Larry swore at his slowness in arriving at his destination. In his rush he missed a couple of turns. *Damn, it's past nine p.m. already.*

At last Larry sat with Ralph in the cozy den of his sprawling ranch house.

'I'm babysitting tonight,' Ralph explained good-humoredly. 'My wife's out campaigning for Diane. But what's this about Paul's boarding-school days?'

'Jill said you were his roommate for a year—'

'Right.' Ralph grimaced in recall.

'You've seen that vicious TV commercial that claims Diane had an abortion while she was in college—' It was a statement – not a question. *Has anybody in this district not seen it by now?*

'Elise – my wife – was livid. As soon as we saw it, she called Jill to ask what was being done to blast it as a lie.'

'We're working on that. Now about Paul at boarding school – was there an outbreak of mumps the year you were there?'

'Yes,' Ralph recalled, puzzled by the question. 'All the guys were scared – they knew how it can cause infertility. And the older you are, the worse the scenario.' He shuddered. 'Anyhow, it never touched Paul or me the year we were roommates. But what's this got to do with the elections?'

Larry ordered himself to be casual. 'Just a way-out possibility we've been trying to follow. Thanks for your cooperation.'
Am I chasing a dead lead? My vibes all wrong?

By the time Larry returned to campaign headquarters – at
close to 10 p.m. – the day's activities were winding down.
Most of the volunteers had left for the evening. He remembered that Diane was speaking to a group in a nearby
community, part of their district. Joan was with her.

Jill was checking the mailing to go out the following
morning. She glanced up as Larry strode into view. 'You talked
with Ralph?' Her eyes hopeful.

Larry nodded. 'We talked.' His face reflected his disappointment. 'There was an outbreak of mumps the one year that
he and Paul were roommates. Neither of them contracted it.'

'What about the other years that Paul was at boarding
school?' Jill was reluctant to abandon this chase.

'We'll have to do more digging,' Larry admitted.

'What about when Paul was in college?' Jill pursued. 'We
ought to follow up there.'

'Do you know where he went to college?' Larry asked.

'No – but Di will know.' All at once Jill tensed in sudden
alertness. 'Wait a moment—' She was squinted in thought. 'I
was a high-school freshman when Paul was a senior. I
remember a guy I had a crush on that year said he was going
to the same college as Paul.'

'Who is this guy? Do you remember his name?'

'It was my first crush – I remember. Hank Roberts. I thought
he was so cute. He's an accountant here in town. He married
a longtime friend of mine.' She sighed. 'He's not so cute now.'

'Is he a registered Democrat?' Larry pushed with fresh
excitement. 'Can you find out?'

'He has to be a Democrat.' Jill was convinced. 'Betty Lynne
would never have married a man who wasn't.'

'Call her,' Larry ordered. 'See if you can set up a meeting
for me with her husband.' He hesitated a moment. 'Maybe
this evening?'

'At this hour?' Jill clucked in reproach. 'Suppose I call first
thing tomorrow morning? With two young kids they're sure
to be up early.'

'Call,' Larry said. 'This could be a real breakthrough.' He

paused. 'You're sure he's a Democrat? We can't afford to spill what we're after.'

'I told you – Betty Lynne would never have married him if he was anything else.' Jill chuckled. 'Her parents would have disowned her.'

'What about Maria Shriver, from a long line of Democrats?' he challenged. 'She married Schwarzenegger.'

'You don't know Betty Lynne. She said she had to change TV remotes three times in the last year. Whenever George II appears on TV, silence reigns in her house. But I can't call until morning,' she reiterated. 'They have a three-year-old and a pair of nine-month-old twins. If I wake them, I'm toast.'

'OK,' Larry agreed reluctantly. 'Call first thing tomorrow morning.'

Am I chasing a dead lead? But we can't afford to overlook even the wildest possibility.

In the morning Larry pulled up into a parking space in front of campaign headquarters as Jill was unlocking the door. She smiled in instant comprehension.

'I'll buzz Betty Lynne in a few minutes,' Jill promised. 'She's sure to be up by now.'

Larry followed Jill inside, stood in tense anticipation as she called Betty Lynne.

'Hi, it's me – Jill,' she said when someone responded at the other end. 'Honey, this is kind of important – though it may sound way-out. Didn't Hank go to college with Paul Somers?' She listened, chuckled. 'No, he'll never win a popularity contest with anybody in their right mind. But we're trying to nail down some weird possibility that'll cut his throat in the coming election. One of our sharp staffers – he's Andrea Martin's brother – needs to talk to Hank about Paul's college years.' She paused, pantomiming approval to Larry.

'When can I talk with the guy?' Larry whispered.

'Yeah, he'd like to talk to him as soon as possible.' Jill's face lighted. 'Great! He'll be there in ten minutes.'

In barely ten minutes Larry was in the Roberts' cozy cottage and explaining to Hank the information he was seeking.

'Paul and I were both there from freshman through senior year. I don't recall any mumps epidemic at the college.' Hank squinted in thought, as though hoping to dredge up some such word. 'No, nothing,' he repeated. 'Wish I could have been helpful.'

'Thanks for seeing me.' Larry concealed his disappointment. 'We just want to be sure we don't overlook any angle.'

'You can be sure we're voting for Diane,' Hank said with conviction. 'We don't vote for turncoats in this family.'

Larry left, drove back to campaign headquarters. So it was time to forget that track, he told himself. Yet in his heart, he knew he wasn't ready to let go. As he'd said so often, the best reporting often evolved from a journalist's hunch.

But how do I get past this dead end?

Thirty-Two

Diane knew the weeks ahead would be frenzied, yet she found it difficult to cope with the relentless repetition of the opposition's lying TV commercials against her. Paul was personally campaigning – like herself – in every square inch of their Congressional district.

Elaine had given a highly successful fund-raising dinner. Small checks were coming in via their Internet fund-raising in gratifying numbers. Yet in no way could they match the opposition's war chest.

By the end of August – hot and steamy in Linwood – Larry was trying to persuade her to take a couple days' respite from campaigning. Wherever air-conditioning prevailed, people were comfortable – but it was painful to walk into the sultry streets for the necessary personal-approach tactics.

Now Diane and Larry sat with Joan in the rear conference room late on this last Thursday evening of the month. This was the day for their usual roundup of the past week's activities. Volunteers gone for the night. Jill about to close up.

'You're looking dead tired,' Larry told Diane solicitously – and Joan nodded in agreement. 'Go away for the Labor Day weekend – just sleep and eat,' he coaxed.

'Are you kidding?' Diane reproached. 'Paul and his entourage will be everywhere. It's prime campaigning time!'

'At least, we'll see less of Paul and his mob after Labor Day,' Joan said with an effort at optimism. 'He'll have to go back to Washington. This is not the time for him to miss out on votes.'

'I worry about Hall-Stores,' Diane admitted. 'So their first offering was rejected by the zoning board. They've just made another offer. They're talking about health care—'

'When they know most employees can't afford to pay their share,' Larry rejected in contempt. 'So health insurance goes out the window.'

'They're making a strong effort to convince the board they're like a Christmas gift to the town.' Diane's voice deepened with sarcasm. 'Bringing their big guns into town, running huge ads about what they'll do for Linwood.'

'And entertaining the board members in the way they best appreciate.' Larry shook his head in distaste. 'Hal keeps me posted.'

'But remember,' Joan pointed out, her smile smug, 'Hall-Stores still has to be approved by the Town Council. We must make sure Council members are bombarded with e-mails and snail-mail – all objecting to Hall-Stores's presence in this town. Maybe even some door-to-door canvassing,' she considered.

'We're already set to go on that if the zoning board approves,' Larry reminded. 'Plan's all worked out.'

'The Town Council makes the final decision. That's when we leap into action,' Diane pinpointed.

'Andrea tells me the "Keep Hall-Stores Out of Linwood" group is expanding by the day.' For the moment Larry seemed complacent. 'But that's just one issue,' he conceded, complacency evaporating. 'We've got to find a way to fight those damn TV commercials. They're becoming a plague.' He slammed on the table with one hand in candid frustration. 'How can prospective voters believe that garbage?'

'Those lying TV commercials are causing damage.' Diane flinched in recall. *The polls are scary – I didn't expect them to be this bad.* 'Some voters see me as a hard, career-driven woman, with no sense of "family values." And that's what we have to beat.' Diane's voice trailed off.

'You told me Elaine offered you the use of her lake cottage,' Joan reminded Diane. 'She left the key with you. She's off to East Hampton for two weeks. Drive out there tonight – don't come back into town until Saturday afternoon. Give yourself a break. The rest of us will carry on.'

'That's ridiculous,' Diane thrust this aside. 'I can't waste a minute away from the campaign trail.'

'Do it,' Larry ordered. 'I'll drive you up tonight—'

'This close to the election?' *I don't want to be alone with Larry – not the way I feel.* 'When every moment counts? I have to be here.'

'You don't have to be here,' Larry mimicked her tenderly.

'I'll drive you out tonight, pick you up at ten a.m. Saturday morning. That'll bring you back into town for the Saturday rally in Somerset Park. You'll come back refreshed. Looking like a candidate ready for action.'

'You need that, Diane.' Joan was forceful. *Oh yes, it sounds wonderful. A chance to refuel. But not driving out with Larry. Alone with him.* 'You can disappear for a day.'

'You have nothing formal scheduled for tomorrow – nothing that Joan or I can't handle,' Larry insisted. 'Come back looking like a fighting candidate.'

'I shouldn't,' Diane hedged – but the prospect was inviting. She felt so drained. So fearful. Elaine's cottage – just an hour's drive from town – sat at the edge of a lake. It would be cool out there – even without the CAC. As with everything Elaine acquired, the cottage was a small masterpiece. Sitting on a two-acre plot, secluded from neighboring cottages by towering trees. 'Maybe I'll drive up in the morning – just for the day.'

'No, I'll drive you up tonight.' Larry was firm. 'No need to put yourself through that long drive. No need to delay.'

'You don't have to take anything with you,' Joan pointed out. 'Elaine keeps a wardrobe there, the kitchen supplied with quick meals. Sleep on the drive out, go to bed as soon as you arrive and sleep till noon tomorrow. Then lie on the deck and gaze at the water. Another good night's sleep before Larry comes out to bring you back into town for the Saturday rally. You'll feel like a new person.'

'I hope I don't regret this,' Diane capitulated. 'But what about my car? It's—'

'It'll be OK in the parking lot,' Joan soothed. 'Just get into Larry's car and let him drive you out there. Now.'

As the air-conditioning drifted into the car, Diane dozed. She awoke when another car sped past with its radio blaring hard rock.

'Stupid kids,' Larry muttered as Diane stirred into wakefulness.

Diane gazed out into the night. The sky a murky dark red that hinted at rain. 'Are we almost there?'

'In about ten minutes.'

'Larry—' She hesitated.

'Yes?'

'Do we have a chance to win this insane campaign?' Doubts had tugged at her for days now. 'Voters have this awful image of me.' *I'm letting the party down. Letting the volunteers down.*

'We're going to change that,' he vowed. One hand left the wheel to reach for hers. 'Don't you dare believe anything else!'

'Are we both terribly naive to think that we can help change the bad things in the world? When my father was angry with me, he said I'd fallen in love with the Sixties stories.'

'The good Sixties,' he stressed. 'When people cared about others, weren't caught up in enormous greed.'

'When I was about seventeen – the summer before I went away to college – I was searching in the attic for something or other – I forget just what. But I found a scrapbook my mother had left up there. Larry, they took part in peace marches, fought for civil rights, were committed to helping make the world a better place for every human being. What happened to them?'

'They grew comfortable in their affluence,' Larry said bluntly. 'They forgot about those commitments.'

'Are those like us the exceptions?' she challenged. 'Are we becoming an endangered species?'

'We're growing in number,' Larry insisted with sudden intensity. 'We'll help make the country what the founding fathers meant it to be. We'll see that happen, Di.'

'I'm so tired,' she whispered. 'And we have so far to go.'

'You'll rest up at the cottage – you'll be in fighting shape again. We're going to win this fight – don't you believe anything else.'

Larry slowed down, watching for the side road that would take them to the cottage.

'This is the road,' Diane told him. Conscious of his closeness here in the darkness of the car. Struggling to ignore the emotions that surged through her.

'We'll be there in a few minutes,' he told her while lightning zigzagged across the sky and thunder roared overhead. Rain began to pound on the roof of the car.

He pulled up before the cottage, reached across her to open the door on her side. 'Run for it, Di!'

Despite the brief distance to the house, they were drenched by the time Diane unlocked the door and they walked inside.

His arms reached for her. Her arms closed about his shoulders.

'I didn't mean for this to happen,' she whispered.

'It had to be,' he told her, his mouth reaching for hers. 'We belong together, Di. For always.'

All at once she stiffened. Mind battling emotions. For an instant mind won.

'Tonight, Larry,' she whispered. 'No commitments. Let's just live for tonight—'

Thirty-Three

Diane lay on one of the chaises on the deck of Elaine's much-glassed cottage this Saturday morning. Waiting for Larry to pick her up for the drive back into town. Trying to convince herself that Larry understood their passionate encounter on Thursday evening didn't signify the beginning of a permanent relationship.

It was something they both had needed at the moment. They were living in chaotic circumstances. For herself it was just that she was on a rebound from the divorce. She couldn't trust what she was feeling for Larry.

Gazing at the shimmering lake, listening to the morning symphony provided by the birds, she wished for the moment that there was no need to rush back into the fury of the campaign. That she could stay in this blessed serenity forever.

She tensed at the sound of a car approaching. Larry would drive her to the parking lot in town. She'd go home and change into fresh clothes, check with Jill at campaign headquarters. Their rally in Somerset Park didn't begin until 1 p.m.

Larry pulled up before the house. Without waiting for him to approach, Diane hurried from the deck to join him in the car. Fighting self-conscious recall of Thursday evening.

'You look rested,' he approved. 'Gorgeous, as always.' But his mood was light, she noted in relief. *It's going to be all right – he's put Thursday evening behind him.*

'I feel better,' she admitted. 'I was just so exhausted.'

'We'll stop for breakfast down the road,' he began. His eyes rested on her for an ardent moment.

Diane tensed. 'OK.' *Can we go back to the professional relationship?*

'I'm famished, boss,' he picked up. 'And we need to go over the format at the rally—'

Now reality intruded. They must fight Hall-Stores's efforts

to open up in Linwood in addition to campaigning. The Town Council had held up considering the zoning board's acceptance of Hall-Stores's new offer until after Labor Day.

Over breakfast at a pleasant roadside diner they discussed the numbing repetition of what they'd labeled 'the abortion commercial.'

'In this supposedly enlightened day – if I'd had an abortion, which I didn't – it shouldn't be earth-shattering,' Diane said with an edge of defiance.

'But in this so-called enlightened era,' Larry reminded, his tone acerbic, 'we're moving back into the Dark Ages. Some of us,' he corrected. 'This sharp turn into ultra-conservatism affects only a segment of the population – but they make a lot of noise.'

'We're getting nowhere in disproving my so-called abortion,' Diane said in fresh frustration. 'What do we have to do to make people realize it never happened?'

'Prove Paul is a liar. Prove that this whole business of his being the injured husband, deprived of family – even of a pup,' he mocked in sardonic amusement, 'is a fantasy. Prove him a liar, and watch the "abortion commercial" lose its zing.'

'We couldn't make it with your hunch about his being sterilized by mumps,' she joshed and grew pensive. 'I know Paul only from the law-school years. Can there be something in his earlier years that we're missing out on?'

Larry sat motionless. Diane knew his mind was charging after answers. 'Maybe we should do more searching in that area,' he agreed. 'And Paul won't be floating around the district so much after this weekend.'

Diane nodded. 'He'll have to head back to Washington. Thank God for that.' She dreaded face-to-face encounters with Paul. She hadn't even suggested debates – though that would attract enormous attention. She knew Paul's high-level team wouldn't allow debates. She switched to the more immediate problem. 'But what do we do about the Hall-Stores situation?'

'The Town Council hasn't scheduled a meeting yet,' Larry pointed out. 'I know – it's imminent.'

'Council members are up for re-election in October. They'll be super-sensitive to the feeling of voters—'

'Let's put the heat on them.' Larry signaled the waitress for more coffee. A sure sign, Diane noted, that he was about to launch a plan of attack.

'We have mailings out – snail-mail and e-mail,' she reminded. 'Crews making phone calls.'

'A petition!' Larry pounced. His eyes locked with Diane's in mutual excitement.

'Let's come up with a petition signed by enough prospective voters to make Town Council members take notice.' Diane glowed with fresh optimism.

'We have to move fast. We don't know when they'll vote on Hall-Stores.' Larry squinted in thought. 'I'll go to Bill with this. The *Enquirer* will plug the need for signatures for our petition.'

'The "Keep Hall-Stores Out of Linwood" group will help us solicit signatures—'

'I'll talk to Andrea about it – she's working like a madwoman with them.' He chuckled. 'She even has Claire and Jimmy helping with their mailings.'

'OK, I've had my time off,' Diane summed up. 'Let's go in for the kill. Both for Hall-Stores and Paul's defeat.'

I won't even look at the polls right now. So they're bad for our side. We'll change that.

Thirty-Four

On an early September Friday morning just past 9 a.m., Diane received a phone call from a local lawyer who introduced himself as representing Paul. A lawyer she knew by reputation – an avowed conservative Republican.

'The final divorce papers have come through,' he reported. 'I'm forwarding copies to you. Also at this time, Paul requests that we make the changeover of ownership on the house here in Linwood and the condo in Washington. I've drawn up the necessary papers and—'

'I'll drop by your office and sign them,' Diane said crisply. 'Would five p.m. this afternoon be convenient?'

'Very good,' he accepted, seeming relieved at not encountering hostility. *Paul probably said I'd give him a hard time.* 'Let me give you my address.'

'Yes, please—' She listened, scribbled down the address.

'Paul was inquiring about one more thing.' He seemed to be searching for the appropriate words. 'Will you be resuming your single name?'

'No, I won't.' Diane was crisp. 'I've had this one for ten years. I'll stay with it.' Paul and his party were hoping she'd disappear into the woodwork under her single name. No deal.

'I'll expect you at five p.m.' The lawyer was terse. 'Goodbye.'

Diane sat back in her chair. Startled to realize her heart was pounding. In her subconscious she'd known this date was approaching. *I'm divorced. A single woman again.*

It was all over – her ten-year marriage with Paul. Not a real marriage, she derided. A partnership. They'd shared a career – little more.

Call Elaine – tell her the divorce is final!

No, not yet, she cautioned herself. Elaine would be fast asleep. She struggled with this decision, discarded it. Elaine would be thrilled to hear the Guam lawyer had come through for her, also. Even at this hour.

I should be thrilled, too. I knew the marriage was dead – I want Paul out of my life. I'm starting a whole new life now. But that's scary.

'Yes?' Elaine's voice slightly querulous when she picked up on the fourth ring – just before the answering machine would intrude.

'Elaine, your Guam lawyer came through! You're talking to a divorced woman.'

'Oh, baby, this calls for a celebration! Dinner tonight at the Colonial Inn. Invite your inner circle to celebrate with us.'

'Elaine, we're working our butts off,' Diane rejected. 'We're eating three meals a day at our desks.'

'Not this evening. Dinner at ten p.m.' Elaine was firm. 'You can take off by then – for one night, at least.'

'The Colonial Inn is closed by ten p.m.,' Diane objected.

'They'll stay open for us,' Elaine purred. 'They'll provide us with a special – though limited – menu. Everything will be perfect. I'll ask for six or eight place settings? Or shall I run up that number?'

'Five will be fine,' Diane capitulated. 'Counting you and me. The Colonial Inn, ten p.m.'

'Great, baby. See you then.'

Diane put down the phone. Her mind darting about on many tracks. As she was debating about calling Elaine again, her private line rang. She picked up.

'Good morning—'

'Word just sneaked through,' Larry reported tersely. 'The Town Council is meeting tonight to discuss the Hall-Stores offer. They're trying to keep it a secret because they don't want demonstrators outside when they meet.'

'So much for our petition—' *Why didn't we realize the value of a petition earlier?*

'Any strings you can pull?' An unfamiliar desperation in Larry's voice. 'You've been around this town a lot of years—'

'A way-out possibility,' she said after a moment. 'Let me call you back. Oh, be open for a small dinner party late this evening. Elaine's treating. My divorce papers just came through.' *Why did I say that? But I had to explain the dinner party tonight.*

'Congratulations.' Larry sounded upbeat. *He's not mis-interpreting this, is he?* 'I'll call Bill – let him spread the word. That'll be a negative blow to your ex.'

'Right.' *Why don't I feel like celebrating?* 'I'll call you later,' she added hastily. 'If you're tied up outside today, remember the dinner party – ten p.m. at the Colonial Inn.'

How is Larry taking the divorce being final? Is he going to feel that it changes our relationship? No – I'm still an ex-wife on the rebound. I can't trust what I feel for him.

Determined to push Larry out of her thoughts, she reached to punch in Elaine's phone number.

'What did you forget to tell Mommie?' Elaine murmured indulgently. 'A night of purple passion?'

Diane ignored this. 'A way-out thought. You must know we're fighting like mad to keep Hall-Stores out of town?'

'The message got through to me,' Elaine admitted. 'What gives?'

'The Town Council is holding a secret meeting this evening to discuss the new Hall-Stores offer. Elaine, we can't let that monster store move into this town! I know this is a way-out possibility – but do you know anybody on the Town Council?'

'Run the names past me,' Elaine ordered.

On the fourth name, Elaine stopped her. 'Ted Hawkins,' she said and chuckled. 'He was almost my second husband. Too conservative for me.' She paused for a moment. 'I can twist his arm.'

'Twist hard!' Diane ordered. 'And fast. They're meeting tonight. Right now, the way we hear it, the Council is split down the middle. It's a tie. This guy could be the swing vote. If he's so conservative, I don't think he's currently concerned about keeping Hall-Stores out.'

'No way,' Elaine confirmed. 'He's all for big business. He'd love to see Rush Limbaugh running for President.'

Diane's heart was pounding. This could be the vote they needed. 'Elaine, use whatever you need to make him vote to keep Hall-Stores out of Linwood!'

'I'll talk to him. I suspect he'll listen.' She chuckled again. 'It's nice to know where the bodies are buried.'

All through the day Diane kept hoping to hear from Elaine. Each time her private line rang, she reached to pick up with soaring excitement. But Elaine didn't call. Was she having a problem reaching Ted Hawkins? Elaine must talk with him before he went to the meeting tonight. Talk and 'twist his arm.'

She remembered the three-times-divorced Hawkins was known as quite a 'ladies' man' – and one of the wealthiest in the state. His money part inherited, part earned on the stock market. She rebelled at the knowledge that the fate of the Hall-Stores campaign to set up shop in Linwood could depend on the vote of one member of the Town Council.

At the break in the campaign-headquarters schedule – the quiet period when daytime volunteers had left and evening volunteers had not yet arrived – Jill brought sandwiches and coffee into the conference room, where Diane and Joan had been consulting for the last hour on their financial situation.

'We'll eat light – with that dinner party just four hours away.' Jill was determinedly cheerful – difficult in the face of the most recent poll in the district. 'We haven't heard from Larry since early in the afternoon – I didn't bring a sandwich for him.'

'He's out there chasing down town-council members,' Joan surmised. 'Fighting for votes.'

'I haven't heard from Elaine,' Diane worried. Both Joan and Jill knew Elaine was on a mission for them. 'I know she has a busy social schedule—' Her voice drifted off.

'We won't know a thing until late tonight – if then. So for now let's anticipate a great dinner party. One where we won't be pushing politics every minute.' Joan reached for her sandwich. 'And we need sustenance for the hours between now and ten p.m.' Her face crinkled in laughter. 'Now how did Elaine persuade the Colonial Inn to serve dinner after normal closing hours?'

'She brings in a lot of business,' Jill guessed. 'They want to keep her happy.'

'Let's hope her friend on the Town Council wants to keep her happy. Let's pray he votes to keep Hall-Stores out.'

'It'll be good for the town.' Diane was somber in reflection. 'But it won't mean we're unseating Paul.'

Thirty-Five

B y 9 p.m., local radio was predicting an imminent summer storm. Murky clouds hung over Linwood. The moon and stars in total eclipse. An occasional rumble of thunder was heard. At 9.30 p.m. Joan was circulating among the volunteers, urged them to head for home before the storm arrived.

Now headquarters was deserted except for Diane, Joan, and Jill – the familiar late-evening scene. Jill was preparing for the following day's deposit of funds that had arrived that day. Joan was repairing her makeup. Diane paced about headquarters. Upset that she'd had no word from Elaine about Ted Hawkins.

The phone rang. Diane rushed to pick up. Hoping the caller was Elaine.

'Hi, I may be a few minutes late for the party.' Larry was apologetic. 'I'm meeting Hal for a quick drink when he goes off duty.'

Diane felt a flurry of alarm. 'Something up?'

'Probably not,' Larry brushed this aside. 'I think he's going to ask me to talk with his mother about the brother who died in Iraq. She lives about a hundred miles away – but she's coming to Linwood with the hope of talking with me. That's going to be rough—'

'But you'll see her?'

'You know I will,' Larry reproached, hesitated a moment. 'You said you had a string to pull. Any results?'

'It's in work – I just haven't heard yet.'

'I shouldn't be more than a few minutes late for dinner,' Larry began, paused for an instant. 'Here's Hal now. See you a bit past ten at the Colonial Inn.'

Larry and Hal sat at a deserted end of the bar, ordered their drinks.

'Mom will be in town next Friday. Can you find time to have dinner with us?' Hal asked, faintly apologetic. 'I know how rushed you are these days—'

'The three of us will have dinner,' Larry promised. 'I'll make time.' His eyes were quizzical. Hal could have discussed this over the phone.

'I heard about a new TV commercial that'll start airing on Monday—' Hal dropped his voice, though it was unlikely any patrons were close enough to eavesdrop.

'Did you see it?' Larry demanded. Tense in anticipation.

'Part of it. Larry, it's a bitch. It brings Paul Somers together with those creepy women who started that abortion deal. They're hot on the "family values" theme. The women claim Diane was always running for some office during the college years, never winning. Paul says Diane chased him from the minute they met in law school – because she saw him as a winning politician. They're building her as a woman who'll do anything to further her career.'

'All lies – and tough to disprove.' Larry fought to conceal his rage. 'Thanks again, Hal. The party owes you.'

'The polls are not good,' Hal said and sighed. 'Women who were all for Diane when Paul Somers jumped the fence are having second thoughts.' He shook his head. 'It's going to take a real turnaround for Diane to win.'

'She'll win,' Larry vowed. 'We'll find a way.'

Expecting a heavy storm to hit at any moment, the three women drove to the Inn in their individual cars – to be able to drive straight home from there. They arrived just as Diane spied Elaine's red Jaguar come to a stop in the parking area. She remembered the battle with Paul when they bought the Lincoln Town Car. He'd sulked at her insistence. He'd wanted a red Jaguar.

'Hi,' Elaine called, emerging from her car. 'Hey, it's raining! Run for the door.'

The four women – dodging what thus far had been a light drizzle – raced to the entrance, hurried inside. As always, the spacious dining room was softly lighted. A huge vase of fragrant summer flowers sat on the table set for the single party to be served.

They settled themselves amid lively, casual conversation.

Joan and Jill both knew Elaine – no need for introductions. Now a courteous waiter provided the special menus provided for their party, then left them to study these.

Churning with anxiety, Diane turned to Elaine. 'What about your friend?' She avoided mentioning his name. 'Were you able to reach him?'

'I spent three long hours with him – from cocktails at five p.m. until I left him at his meeting a little before eight p.m. I didn't call because I had no real word yet. But he swore he'd call me after the meeting and tell me what happened.' Her eyes were solicitous. 'I wasn't thinking straight – I should have let you know we'd talked.' Her smile was dazzling now. 'And, sweetie, I twisted hard.'

Elaine focused on creating a festive atmosphere. She provided a provocative report on her own two divorces.

'Di, this is the day when your new life begins. Sweetie, may it be everything you wish for—' She stopped dead because Diane's gaze was focused on the entrance to the dining room. Larry was arriving – and his expression was grim.

'Well, here I'm the sole male among four beautiful women!' He was striving for lightness as he approached the table, turned to Elaine with an ingratiating smile. 'I'm—'

'Larry Grant.' Elaine's own smile was dazzling. 'I'm Elaine—'

'What did Hal have to tell you?' Diane broke in.

Larry's air of levity evaporated. He sat down – somber now. 'It wasn't good news,' he admitted, and related what Hal had reported at their brief meeting. 'We all know the TV commercial is a rotten lie—'

Diane's face was drained of color. 'I never ran for any office at college!' *Here we go again – another pack of lies!* 'I didn't chase after Paul – he chased after me.'

'Let's demand they prove you ran for office at college,' Joan challenged. 'Let them show us one instance.'

'We'll have to dig into the budget for a new TV commercial,' Jill warned and winced. They were being outspent by four hundred per cent. 'I'll send out an emergency appeal for funds on our website tomorrow morning. Larry, help me with it—'

The five at the table fell silent when the waiter appeared to take their orders. For a few moments they were a festive dinner party. As their waiter left their table, they were startled to hear a cell phone ring.

'Sorry,' Elaine apologized and reached for the cell phone in the pocket of her jacket. 'Hello—' The others on sharp alert as she listened to the caller. 'That's a good boy, Ted,' she purred. 'Thanks for your efforts. Bye now.'

'What happened at the meeting?' Diane asked. All eyes fastened on Elaine.

'Hall-Stores's out,' Elaine reported in triumph. The others broke into a joyous outcry. 'Just as you thought, Di – Ted was the swing vote. He's not happy – but Hall-Stores won't be opening up in Linwood.'

But we still have to face an ugly new TV commercial the first of next week. How do we fight the opposition's storm of lies?

Thirty-Six

The atmosphere at the dinner party was a blend of triumph and disquiet. Triumph that Hall-Stores – again – had been denied official permission to open a store in Linwood. Disquiet in the knowledge that the opposition was about to launch another obscene attack on Diane.

Earlier than Diane had anticipated – with the Colonial Inn's superb Black Forest cake demolished and equally superb coffee consumed – Elaine made a move to disband. Elaine always had that special sense of when to end a festive occasion, Diane thought in gratitude – though tonight's celebratory mood had been tainted.

They emerged from the Colonial Inn to discover the storm was over. The moon slid in and out behind the clouds. A handful of stars flickered in the sky.

Diane was relieved that she'd be driving home alone. She'd been aware of the question in Larry's eyes. He was impatient to talk with her about the new TV commercial – despite the hour. To focus on how to fight it. But she knew how such a meeting would end. And she wasn't sure that was the right way to go.

Drive home. Alone. Go to bed. Try for a solid night's sleep – short though it must be. And prepare for what lies ahead.

'We have to work fast to defuse that new TV commercial—'

Larry lingered at the door of her car before heading for his own. 'The committee will OK the funds for an answering commercial—' His eyes clung to hers.

'The first business tomorrow morning. It can be arranged immediately' she concurred. Her heart pounding. The body could be such a traitor. More than anything else in the world at this moment, she wished she and Larry were making passionate love. But the road she meant to travel offered no such detours.

Am I what their new TV commercial claims? A selfish, self-centered, career-driven woman? Driven, yes – but driven to make good things happen. That's what will give true meaning to my life.

She knew sleep would be elusive tonight. She was too wired for sleep. Her mind assaulted by the recall of what Hal Watson had told Larry. All fabrication – woven together not by Paul but by those manipulating his campaign.

Never in her four years of college had she run for any office! She'd fought alongside the graduate students the year they went on strike. She'd joined the group that made personal calls on the town's poverty-level families to explain that the state was providing health care for all children.

And that lie about her chasing Paul! She churned with fresh rage as she considered this. Paul had made up his mind that she was the one who'd push his career ahead. Only later did she recognize his obsession to outdo his father as a politician.

The only way they'd ever rebut those TV commercials, she told herself with fatalistic calm, was to prove Paul was a liar. *But how are we to accomplish that?*

Larry lay back against a mound of pillows and gazed into the night darkness of his small bedroom. This might be noon instead of past two a.m., he taunted himself. Why was Diane fighting him this way? Why this 'no commitment' routine? She was divorced now. Free. She had a right to a life of her own.

Yet in a corner of his mind he understood her ambivalence. Hadn't he told himself – over and over again – it was not a bright move to become involved in a relationship at this stage in his life? Deep inside he knew he wanted more than a relationship with Diane. He wanted the whole deal – Diane as his wife, the two of them with a pair of kids.

Maybe she was right. Each of them destined to travel their road alone. Barriers to be overcome. Important things to be accomplished. Something to give life a real meaning.

Now his mind turned again to the new TV commercial the opposition would launch the first of next week. His throat tightening as he visualized its affect. Time was running too fast – election day moving alarmingly close. Paul's manipulators were sharp. Lying – but sharp. Face it, he ordered himself – this election would be won on the candidate's 'family values.'

They must prove to prospective voters that Paul lied. They'd explored his earlier hunch that Paul was sterile. They'd explored that possibility – which would make it glaringly clear that Paul was a liar – but came up with nothing.

What in Paul's life had escaped them? Something that would be his downfall—

In the weeks ahead Diane put up a passionate defense, declaring Paul was incapable of telling the truth. Their team plus dedicated volunteers battled against this latest attack. Now the polls indicated some ambivalence. One week Diane was ahead, the next Paul pushed past her by five or six points.

On a late October evening – with election day devastatingly close – Diane and her inner circle settled down in campaign headquarters to discuss a new strategy. Volunteers had departed for the night – their mood varying from despair to defiance. Election day was just eight days away – and Paul was pulling too far ahead for comfort.

'We've got to turn this thing around in the next few days,' Diane said with uncharacteristic bluntness. *What are our chances of doing this?* 'We're being outspent like crazy. Bombarded with lying TV commercials and newspaper ads. We need to prove that Paul and his team are malicious liars.' She glanced about at the other three. 'How do we do that?'

'We must nail Paul to some rotten act. Did he ever drive through a red light and kill or maim somebody?' Joan challenged. 'Does he have a secret criminal record?'

'If he'd done either,' Jill drawled, 'Daddy dear would have bailed him out.'

'What about it, Di?' Larry prodded. 'Search your mind. Do you have any knowledge of something we can exploit?' His voice gentle now. 'This has become a dirty campaign – ethics out the window.' He allowed himself an ironic smile. 'In a campaign supposedly focused on "family values."'

'I know nothing about Paul's life before law school.' Diane gestured the futility of pursuing this path. But she squinted in concentration. 'Except that he went to boarding school before college. Briefly he went to school here in Linwood. Public school,' she emphasized, 'because Daddy considered that a political necessity, no doubt.'

'All right, we start exploring.' Larry seemed all at once

energized. 'I know – it's rough to take time away from the other work on hand, but we can't afford to overlook any angle.'

'Jill, you have to stay with running the day-by-day operations,' Diane pinpointed and turned to Joan. 'You're on a fifteen-hour day already—' Diane took a deep breath. 'Larry, you and I research. Every minute we can spare—'

'Not in stolen moments,' Larry objected. 'We have to do this right. We know where Paul went to college.' *In a town barely two hours' drive from here – in the state's other Congressional district.* 'It'll be rough, but we take a day off, drive there. Cover the four years he was a student at State—'

'We can ask Hank Bernstein to check into the local school years.' Diane's mind was a fast track now. The elderly Bernstein was an avid volunteer – and bright. 'He's a retired elementary-school teacher – he'll have access to all information. If there's anything we should know about Paul's activities in those years he attended Linwood schools, Hank will find out.'

'Di, you have only one daytime appearance tomorrow—' Joan was scanning the following day's program. 'I can reschedule that. Search into the college years.' She giggled. 'Yeah, I have a hunch, too. Or maybe it's wishful thinking.'

'OK.' Diane turned to Larry. 'Pick me up at seven a.m. tomorrow morning. We'll drive to Spencerville.' The home of the college Paul attended. 'We'll explore newspaper files of every day of those four years Paul was at State.'

'We'll grab breakfast in the town,' Larry plotted, paused for a moment. 'I know Spencerville isn't part of our Congressional district – but there's a possibility you'll be recognized. It won't be wise for you to show up at the newspapers – we might be tipping our hand—'

'I'll go to the public library.' Diane seized on this. 'All the local newspapers will be on microfilm. I'll read there.' *So much to read. Can we do it in one day?* 'And if Paul was involved in any indiscretion during his college years, we'll find it—'

'Like Larry says—' Joan glowed. 'The best reporting in this world is often born of a hunch.'

Thirty-Seven

Minutes before 7 a.m., Diane was waiting on the small, white-columned porch for Larry to arrive. She knew he wouldn't be a moment late. Like herself he was obsessive about being on time.

The houses around her in this exclusive suburb were early morning quiet. The sun already on brilliant display. A good omen for the day, she told herself. What they might discover today could decide the coming election. Her entire future. *But don't wallow in hope. This is a long shot.*

Larry drove into view, pulled up before the house. She hurried to the car. The weather was steamy, but it would be comfortable in the air-conditioned library.

'I'm starving,' he announced, reaching to open the door for her. 'What do you say we stop at a diner a little out of town?'

'I'm for that.' Diane settled herself beside him. Conscious of a glint of approval as his eyes swept over her sunlit yellow slacks and matching top. Larry, too, was dressed casually – a sports shirt, chinos, sneakers.

While they drove, they dissected the task ahead. Both conscious of what was at stake.

'I went online,' Diane reported. 'Spencerville has two daily newspapers – the *News* and the *Ledger* – plus a freebie. The weekly freebie was just established nine years ago – we don't need to track that down. There's one library in town – quite a big deal for a small town, I gather.'

'So you'll follow through on the *News*. I'll take the *Ledger*. OK?'

'OK.' She'd have no problem at the library. No curious reporters to question her presence. An Iraq vet with a press card from the Linwood *Enquirer*, Larry would have instant access to the *Ledger*'s back-issue files.

The diner's parking area held only a sprinkling of cars.

Employees mostly, Diane assumed. She and Larry walked into the comfortable air-conditioning of the diner. A pair of truckers – the sole patrons but obviously regulars – were exchanging good-humored insults with the counterman.

Diane and Larry settled themselves in a booth near the entrance. A friendly waitress came over to take their orders. The glint in her eyes said she recognized them. *Does she see something romantic in this early breakfast?*

'Order hearty,' Larry advised Diane as they focused on the menu. 'Lunch may be late. Very late.'

'Right,' Diane agreed. She'd be holed up in the library – Larry in the morgue of the *Ledger* – for hours, Diane surmised. They'd have their cell phones for contact.

They ate quickly, headed back for the car. The offices of the *Ledger* would be open by the time they arrived in Spencerville. The library, Diane reminded herself again, wouldn't open until 10 a.m. So she'd go into a coffee shop to kill time. Call headquarters on her cell phone, see what was happening there.

While they drove, Larry talked about his sister Andrea, the efforts she and her husband Jimmy had put into the anti-Hall-Stores drive. Now he reported that he was buying a car for himself. He'd hoped for a hybrid, but there was a waiting list.

'Andrea and Jimmy insist I can use her car, but it's not fair. I figured it was time to dip into my cash reserve.' He chuckled. 'Jimmy accuses me of being a penny-pincher – but I like to feel I have a healthy reserve.' His eyes left the road for a moment to dwell on Diane. 'Besides, once we're in Washington, I'll have to acquire a car.'

'Larry, we're not in Washington yet.' Her heart was pounding. *Will we be there? Larry means to be with me. With us – he's part of the team.*

'We'll be in Washington,' he insisted. And now she felt unspoken questions in him. *Can there be a future for us? Is what I feel for Larry now – at this moment – real?*

'The next turn takes us into town,' she pointed out. Anxious to derail her thoughts. 'It's a minute past nine – you can head straight for the newspaper. I'll have to find a coffee shop where I can waste time till the library opens—' She'd check with headquarters, talk with Joan.

Spencerville was a pleasant little college town, she thought.

The business section modern, well kept, active at this hour. Larry cruised while Diane consulted the town map she'd printed out from the town's website. They quickly located the municipal parking area, then the three-story red-brick building that housed the *Ledger*.

'The library is just three blocks away,' Diane noted on the map across her lap. 'Now let's find a nearby coffee shop.'

She'd have a cup of coffee, then head for the library. They would have old newspapers on file. Most small-town libraries kept these on microfilm or microfiche.

'Right there—' Larry pointed to a pleasant-appearing corner coffee shop. 'I'll drop you off, head back to the municipal parking lot, then tackle the *Ledger*.'

As Larry had anticipated, he had no difficulty acquiring access to old editions of the *Ledger*. Now he was seated at a table and gearing himself to read through an awesome number of microfilm reels. Start with Paul's senior year, he told himself – work backwards.

The *Ledger* featured a weekly column dealing with current Spencerville College activities. But glance through the general daily news as well, Larry exhorted himself. The sort of news he sought might be too big a deal for the college column – or be brushed aside out of respect for the college's reputation.

He viewed the first reel of the six months' editions he'd requested – conscious of the short period of time a reel covered – removed it from the microfilm projector and inserted the next reel. This was going to be a long, odious process. But Diane's future – their future – depended upon what they could dredge up about Paul Somers that would destroy his campaign for re-election.

Diane sat in the sparsely occupied reference room at the Spencerville Library and fed another reel of the microfilm containing editions of the *Spencerville News* into the projector. Her back ached from tension. Her eyes tingled from the endless reading, but she was determined to make it through the full four years of newspapers that covered Paul's attendance at the college.

She'd sensed curiosity in the librarian who was providing her with the reels of films. But the librarian couldn't possibly know what she hoped to find. With the new reel in place, she paused to glance at her watch. She'd been sitting here – staring at the film on display – for almost four hours. She was conscious of an insistent hunger.

How was Larry doing? Had he come up with anything yet? Of course not, she ridiculed her questioning this. He would have called her on his cell phone if he'd discovered anything useful.

Are we just wasting valuable time chasing after this? So much to do – so little time in which to do it!

Larry suppressed a series of yawns as he read. Blinked at intervals – his eyes in rebellion. Conscious of a faint, reproachful rumbling in his stomach. Lunch would have to wait, he rejected this summons with grim determination. So far he'd come up with nothing. Twice a mention of Paul in the weekly college column – in conjunction with some endowment by his father. To cover an infraction of rules by Paul?

He changed reels yet again. 'Damn,' he swore under his breath. He'd picked at random from the year's line-up of tapes beside the projector. He should have started with September of Paul's sophomore year. Here he was reading in April of that school year. But what was the difference, he jeered at himself – he had four years to cover.

Now he was fighting drowsiness along with hunger. *Be alert – you can't afford to miss any lead, no matter how small.* But all at once he was wide awake. His eyes glued to a segment of the weekly college column:

> A sophomore at the college was unfairly attacked with a paternity suit by a freshman co-ed. DNA tests cleared the sophomore. The co-ed has been asked to leave school.

This needs exploring! All right, it could have been any member of the sophomore class – but follow it up. Just in case.

Larry read the next four college columns with infinite care. No further mention of the paternity suit. So the college preferred to play it down – what about the news section of the *Ledger*?

Feeling himself on the brink of a breakthrough – though his mind warned that there was little reason for this – Larry geared himself to backtrack. Search each page of the *Ledger* for follow-up on the paternity suit mentioned in the college column.

But what could he expect to discover that would be of value to Di? Suppose the suit was against Paul? The student involved had been exonerated. *This is a waste of precious time. Leading us nowhere.*

All at once his eyes were riveted to a small article on a back page – a follow-up on the college-column report.

> Spencerville sophomore Paul Somers has been cleared in a paternity suit filed by freshman co-ed Leona Nichols. Somers was quite cocky in his reaction: 'She was sleeping with half the guys on campus. DNA testing proved I couldn't be the father. I told them it couldn't be me – I had a bad case of the mumps two summers ago. I can't have kids – I'm sterile.'

Thirty-Eight

Diane was startled by the musical tinkle of her cell phone. She glanced about in apology as she reached to pull it from her purse. Neither of the other two occupants of the research room seemed disturbed.

'Hello,' she whispered.

'Di, meet me at that coffee shop where I left you this morning.' His voice urgent. 'It looks as though we've hit a gold mine.'

'I'll be right there—' She understood. Whatever Larry had dug up should not be discussed over a phone line. Particularly over a cell phone – where the curious could eavesdrop if they wished.

Rushing into action, she rewound the reel in the projector, returned it to its box, gathered the cluster of boxes together, and returned them to the librarian. Her heart pounding in anticipation of what Larry would tell her. She hurried from the library, strode in the direction of the coffee shop. Hardly a five-minute walk, but now it seemed a mile away.

Was this a breakthrough – or in his anxiety had Larry latched on to something that would fizzle into nothing? They were both so tired, so tense, so wired.

She charged into the coffee shop – the lunch crowd gone now – and gazed about for Larry. He sat in a booth at the rear, lifted a hand at her appearance.

'You won't believe this,' he said as she slid across from him in the booth. 'I printed this out from the microfilm—' He extended a sheet of paper.

She read the brief article Larry had printed out. Excitement spiraling in her. 'We didn't check the summer months – when he was away from school,' she realized.

'This will kill Paul's chances of re-election.' Larry's face reflected a blend of relief and triumph. 'This shows him for the blatant liar he is! So much for his charade about ethics and "family values." He'd forgot he'd ever said that.'

Unexpectedly Diane chuckled. 'The idiot,' she whispered while the waitress headed towards their table. 'Paul never knew when to shut up. It was enough to say that DNA testing cleared him. He didn't have to tell the world he was sterile.'

Diane and Larry ordered a substantial lunch. Both admitted to being famished.

'We should be lunching in some fabulous place to celebrate this moment,' Larry said when the waitress had left them.

'No time,' Diane murmured. Heady with the knowledge there was a strong chance that in January she'd be replacing Paul in Congress. He had cut his throat with those few words: *'I told them it couldn't be me. I had a bad case of the mumps two summers ago. I can't have kids – I'm sterile.'* After the continuous soap opera about how he'd longed for family, but she'd denied him this. 'Somebody upstairs was on our side.'

'We've got a lot of work to do,' Larry warned, 'to spread the word around between now and election day.'

'I know.' And already doubts were infiltrating her confidence. *Are we jumping too fast? Will the opposition come up with some insane counter-attack?*

'Right now call headquarters,' Larry told Diane. 'Let Joan and Jill know we're off the hook.'

Diane's regular crew plus volunteers poured their energy into spreading the word. Bill and the *Enquirer* gave them lavish space each day. Diane's blog reached out to the Internet watchers. E-mail and snail-mail went out to cover the Congressional district. Larry and Joan contrived for last-minute national coverage on radio, TV, and the news magazines.

The opposition fought back, used the old tactics of repetition. The Diane Somers campaign was lying, they shrieked. But Paul's words to the reporter at the Spencerville *Ledger* were repeated everywhere – and backed up by the reporter himself.

The whole scene had changed. Independents were coming out strong for Diane. Voters who'd been undecided now indicated they were behind her. Forty-eight hours before election day, polls were predicting a landslide for Diane.

Election day arrived. Flanked by Larry and Joan, Diane

voted at minutes past 7 a.m. Today there would be no encounter with Paul as at the Special Primary, Diane surmised. But already voters were streaming into view. Oh yes, there would be a heavy turnout.

'I keep expecting the opposition to pull some unspeakable trick at the last moment,' Diane murmured to Larry and Joan when she emerged from the voting booth. Refusing to allow herself to accept victory at this point. 'Face it – we won't know the real results until every vote is counted. Forget the polls.'

'You can be sure of one thing—' Joan was smug. 'Paul must be cursing himself for jumping the fence.'

'Thank God, he did.' Larry's eyes rested on Diane with disconcerting intensity. 'It's changed our lives.'

The atmosphere in the ballroom at the Palace Hotel was one of shocked depression. Volunteers milled about in anticipation of a lavish midnight supper, but they knew this would not be a victory celebration. The party elite – and their candidate – huddled before the huge TV screen installed for the occasion. Dazed yet defiant, Paul reached for Ronnie's hand.

'Both the *Enquirer* and the *Evening News* declare victory for Diane Somers,' a commentator was announcing. 'It appears to be a landslide!'

Now the TV cameras switched to the joyous crowd at Diane Somers' campaign headquarters, lingered for a close-up on the new Congresswoman-elect – in a passionate embrace with the handsome young man the Congressional district had learned was an Iraq combat veteran and a major player in her campaign.

'You asshole,' Carl Somers hissed at his son. 'You even screwed up this!'

'You told me I couldn't lose,' Paul began but his father was already striding away from him. 'Ronnie?' He was startled that she was pulling her hand from his. 'Let's go somewhere for a drink. I need it—'

'I don't think so, Paul—' Her eyes opaque as they met his. 'I'm flying back to Washington with Dad.'

He gaped in disbelief as he hovered alone while those about him were heading towards the caterer's tables being set up. He might have been some stranger who'd wandered in from nowhere. Struggling to comprehend what was happening to him, he reached for his cell phone, punched in his mother's personal number.

'Hello—' His mother voice revealed her agitation. She'd heard the TV news.

'It's all over,' Paul told her aggrievedly. 'The rotten party let me down.'

'Darling, I've always told you. You're too sensitive for the insane political world. Come home. I'm arranging a small dinner for a few close friends on Friday evening. And I want you to meet the prettiest girl. Her father's very important—'

Walking about hand in hand with Larry to thank their exuberant volunteers, Diane suspected the victory party here at campaign headquarters would go on forever. Everyone exhilarated by the outcome of the campaign. Everyone convinced, she thought tenderly, that their victory was the turning point in the direction the country was taking.

Joan's mother – who'd been here since 5 p.m. – was introducing Joan to the attorney son of 'one of my dearest friends.' From what Diane overheard, the attorney was planning to return to Linwood – 'away from the crazy pressures of my New York law firm.'

'I'll be heading for Washington soon,' Joan told him exuberantly. 'We'll be searching for living accommodations there now that Diane's been elected.'

'Should I be looking for an apartment in Washington?' Larry asked softly. His eyes searching Diane's.

She froze. 'You're coming with me – with us,' she amended. 'You – you said you would if I was elected.'

'I'm debating about it.' He was pensive. 'Half a loaf isn't enough, Di. It's painful.'

'Larry, please.' Her eyes clung to his. 'I want more than the career,' she whispered. 'I need you.'

'I don't think it would look right – in your position – to have a live-in boyfriend—' His eyes asking questions.

'I don't hear you suggesting anything else,' she reproached. But her smile was dazzling.

'Would you marry the guy, if he asked nicely?'

'Oh, yes,' she said with conviction. *This isn't rebound. This is the real thing!* 'How could I refuse?'

* * *

On the Sunday after Thanksgiving – in the living room of Andrea and Jimmy's house – Diane and Larry were married. Though just family and closest friends were in attendance, a wedding reception – to which the entire volunteer crew was invited – was to follow in the Palace Hotel ballroom.

Diane and Larry left the reception early on and headed for a five-day honeymoon in Bermuda.

'We can't stay any longer than five days,' Diane warned Larry as they boarded their flight to New York, where they'd pick up their Bermuda flight. 'We have to find a place to live in Washington.'

'Not a fancy condo in Georgetown,' he said with mock horror. 'We need to save for the future. First a dog—' His smile was rhapsodic. 'Maybe a Bernese mountain dog or a Labrador—'

'We'll go to the animal shelter,' Diane said firmly. 'And see who most wants to adopt us.'

'A dog that's good with kids,' Larry stipulated. 'We'll give ourselves time to settle in to Congress – but that dog will need a little boy or little girl in his life.'

'It took us a long time to find each other—' Diane's eyes were luminous, 'but we've made it, Larry. And this time it's the real thing.'